BURNT SIENA

A FLORA GARIBALDI ART HISTORY
MYSTERY

BURNT SIENA

SARAH WISSEMAN

FIVE STAR
A part of Gale, Cengage Learning

GALE
CENGAGE Learning·

Farmington Hills, Mich • San Francisco • New York • Waterville, Maine
Meriden, Conn • Mason, Ohio • Chicago

GALE
CENGAGE Learning

LIBRARY OF CONGRESS CATALOGING-IN-PUBLICATION DATA

Wisseman, Sarah Underhill.
    Burnt Siena : a Flora Garibaldi art history mystery / Sarah Wisseman. — First edition.
        pages cm.
    ISBN 978-1-4328-3068-7 (hardcover) — ISBN 1-4328-3068-6 (hardcover) — ISBN 978-1-4328-3059-5 (ebook) — ISBN 1-4328-3059-7 (ebook)
    1. Women artists—Fiction. 2. Art restorers—Fiction. 3. Murder—Investigation—Fiction. 4. Arts—Forgeries—Fiction. 5. Art thefts—Fiction. 6. Siena (Italy)—Fiction. I. Title. II. Title: Flora Garibaldi art history mystery.
PS3623.I8475B87 2015
813'.6—dc23   2014047855

First Edition. First Printing: June 2015
Find us on Facebook– https://www.facebook.com/FiveStarCengage
Visit our website– http://www.gale.cengage.com/fivestar/
Contact Five Star™ Publishing at FiveStar@cengage.com

Printed in the United States of America
1 2 3 4 5 6 7 19 18 17 16 15

For Charlie, who makes it all possible

ACKNOWLEDGMENTS

This book could not have been written without the helpful readings and suggestions of many people. I thank especially my critique partners Molly MacRae, David Ingram, and the members of the Writer's Café at our local Osher Lifelong Learning Institution; also Brunilde S. Ridgway of Bryn Mawr College, Kathe Brinkmann, Jim May, Kathy Hubenet, and Kristy Blank Makansi of Treehouse Publishing and Blank Slate Press. For information on the Italian police system, I thank Sarah Zama, Graziano Bernini, Eric de Sena, and Sharon Michalove. Kudos to Dianna Graveman of Treehouse Publishing Group for her excellent proofreading. As always, I thank my beloved husband Charlie for putting up with my distracted self and burnt suppers when I am writing.

The looting of antiquities from Italy (and other countries) is still a huge problem despite massive efforts by the Italian Carabinieri's Art Squad and other bodies. Forging antiquities, less well documented since so many successful forgeries still lurk in our museums and in private collections, is also very much a problem. Several books and articles were helpful to me in crafting this book. I recommend:

Jason Felch and Ralph Frammolino, *Chasing Aphrodite: The Hunt for Looted Antiquities at the World's Richest Museum* (2011)

Peter Watson and Cecilia Todeschini, *The Medici Conspiracy: The Illicit Journey of Looted Antiquities—From Italy's Tomb Raiders to the World's Greatest Museums* (2007)

Eric Hebborn, *The Art Forger's Handbook* (1997)

Roger Atwood, *Stealing History: Tomb Raiders, Smugglers, and the Looting of the Ancient World* (2004)

Mark Jones (Ed.), *Fake?: The Art of Deception* (1990)

Sheridan Bowman (Ed.), *Science and the Past* (1991)

Robert K. Wittman, *Priceless: How I went Undercover to Rescue the World's Stolen Treasures* (2011)

Thomas Hoving, *Making the Mummies Dance* (1993)

CHAPTER ONE

Hunger fought with worry in the pit of her stomach as she ran down the stone steps bowed in the middle by thousands of feet. The massive front door of the Archives clanged shut behind her. Flora crossed the courtyard and stepped into Banchi di Sotto Street, dodging a garbage truck as she turned north. She had no intention of returning to work on this warm Saturday afternoon. Her plans included lunch at the apartment, followed by an espresso and a gelato—hazelnut and chocolate—at her favorite café. And she was dying to talk with Ernst and discover what had spooked him. Flora hurried toward the Piazza del Campo. Crooked pavers pressed on her thin soles while petunias and marguerites nodded at eye level from every window box. She ignored the pigeons fluttering in the eaves and brightly colored laundry drooping on lines strung between windows above her head.

What had Ernst said?

They'd been talking about their employers. She and Ernst worked as painting conservators at the Restauro Lorenzetti, but he'd joined the company a month before she had.

"Was Pietro such a jerk when you started last March?" Flora had asked.

"Naw. Then, his behavior was almost normal. He made me switch projects halfway through a painting only once a week or so. Now he does this almost daily. Drives me crazy."

"He's doing it to me. I can't finish any restoration project on schedule." She admired the way his brown curls flopped over his forehead.

Ernst sipped his wine and leaned closer across the kitchen table of their shared apartment. "It's almost like Pietro has another agenda . . . as if he wants to keep me off balance."

"That doesn't make any sense, Ernst. What other agenda could he have?"

"I don't know. But the Lorenzettis have their fingers in a lot more besides painting jobs. Why, the other day I saw—"

The slam of the front door announcing their roommate Linda's arrival had put an end to Ernst's confidences.

Distracted by her memories, Flora collided with one of the flag tossers practicing for the Palio horse race. He wore a gorgeous costume of blue and yellow with a mushroom-shaped hat and yellow tights.

"Scusi, scusi!" she said as she backed away.

The handsome flag tosser smiled at her. *"No importa,"* he grinned and handed Flora her bag, which had fallen on the ancient paving stones.

Siena's signature event was scheduled for later this week. She remembered the vivid contrasts the Palio presented, from the magnificent pageantry of the parades before the race to the wild behavior of the losing *contrade* after the winning jockey was announced. Flora and Ernst planned to get ringside seats on the second-story porch of some friends who lived on the curved side of the piazza. There they'd be able to see as well as cheer for their favorite horses without getting too close to throngs of grown men crying, screaming, and fighting.

Almost home. She hoped their roommate was out so she could speak with Ernst in private. Ernst kept quiet around Linda because her vivacity and flirtatious manner overwhelmed him. Dodging tourists and pigeons in the center of the piazza, Flora rushed to the apartment on the north side of the Campo. Their building squatted on a corner across from a tavern.

A finger of unease touched Flora when she found the door of their fourth-floor walkup slightly ajar. This was hardly unusual, she told herself. Ernst hardly ever locked the front door. He'd gone out for cigarettes and not even bothered to close it. Ernst would be back soon and they could share the leftover garlic noodles.

"Ernst?" Flora called as she pushed the door open and dropped her bag on a chair. "Are you home?"

Their domain looked scruffy at best, festooned with the discarded clothing, shoes, and used glasses and ashtrays of three expat twenty-somethings who weren't quite domesticated yet.

She passed the tiny bathroom (single sink and claw-legged bathtub with rubber showerhead, the kind you had to sit to use) and pulled pasta, salad fixings, and the dregs of a quart of milk out of their pint-sized fridge. The shutters were still closed over the unscreened window (what, no mosquitoes in Italy?). Flora pushed them open to let in a little daylight.

Holding her breath as she lit the antique gas stove, she braced herself for the expected whoosh of flame and slapped a secondhand aluminum pot over the burner.

Garlic pasta, fresh tomatoes, and fresh basil . . . yum. Flora crossed into Ernst's room to get the basil. He'd scored the only balcony, but they all shared it when he wasn't sleeping, and it made a dandy place for a small box garden overlooking the alley.

She reached out to grab the freshest leaves of the green herb outside the railing, her gaze taking in the neighbor's matching balcony and the quiet alley below.

Quiet, but not empty.

The bile rose in her throat and her knees buckled.

A body lay face down on the paving stones. Brown curly hair, long legs clad in shorts, and Birkenstock sandals. A sinister pool of dark liquid near the head.

Her roommate and secret crush, Ernst Mann.

CHAPTER TWO

All Flora remembered later was grabbing the railing to keep from falling and vomiting the remains of her breakfast over the hapless basil plant.

Her phone call to 113, the numerals painted on Siena's blue-and-white police cars, produced a surprising number of police. Flora saw men in two types of uniforms, blue jackets with gray pants and also black uniforms with red stripes. The cars were mostly *pantere*, panthers or, rather, Alfa Romeos. Her mind refused to make sense of this; how did one phone call reach both State Police and the army-based Carabinieri? Their speed in arriving on the scene was negated by their arguing about who was in charge as soon as the two units—or was it three?—met. Confusion reigned over the next half hour while an ambulance showed up and the apartment was searched. Crime scene technicians took over, and Flora found herself outside being questioned by a squat, dapper man about twice her age. His nametag informed her that he was Captain P. Rizzo, Carabinieri. So the other guys—the ones in the light blue uniforms—were probably the Polizia di Stato.

"Sit down here across the street, Signorina. You don't look well."

Flora's legs trembled, but she managed to sit on the step leading up to a neighboring apartment building. Now they faced the entrance of her own apartment building, cluttered with crime scene officers going in and out on their grim business of sudden death.

Ernst . . . Ernst . . . how could you be . . . dead? She shuddered.

"Name and age? Citizenship?" Rizzo barked. He motioned to a younger cop, a tall skinny man with hazel eyes, to take notes. "Signorina?"

Flora glanced at the assistant's nametag and saw that he was "V. Bernini, *Sottotenente.*" Second lieutenant, or something like that. Her eyes refocused on the stocky man in front of her. "I'm Flora. Uh, Flora Garibaldi McDougal. I go by Garibaldi while I'm in Italy."

"Your names are Italian and what, Scots or Irish?"

"That's right." She explained that her father was American but with Scottish ancestors, and her mother was a native of Siena. "I'm twenty-eight."

"Can you identify the dead man?"

Flora gulped. "Yes. He is Ernst Mann. He's German."

"How well did you know him?"

"Reasonably well. He's my roommate, along with Linda Maguire. We three shared the apartment."

Captain Rizzo's brown eyes flickered over her petite figure with a lightning down-and-up glance. "Signorina, where were you today?"

"I was catching up at work. Most of us work on Saturday mornings."

"What time did you leave your workplace?"

"About twelve o'clock. I was hungry."

"Tell me exactly what you saw after you entered the apartment."

Flora hugged herself and stammered. "I, um, went to the fridge and got out some leftover pasta and salad stuff. I mean, lettuce and basil . . . except the basil was in Ernst's room . . . oh, God . . . I don't believe this!"

"Take your time, Signorina."

The covered body lay on a stretcher near them, but she could still remember the blood and nameless bits of tissue in the alley below the balcony. She gulped and faced the other way, leaning against the marble doorjamb of the entrance.

"I thought Ernst had gone out for cigarettes. That he would be back for lunch . . ." She cupped her hand over her mouth as the tears started.

"Signorina, there are signs of a scuffle on that balcony that indicate your roommate may have been pushed over the railing—"

"Pushed? I don't believe you!" Flora's stomach lurched, and she thought she might throw up again on his shiny black shoes. *Murder?* If Ernst had been murdered, then this cop must consider Flora a prime suspect! She swallowed bile and forced herself to meet his watchful eyes. "What signs?"

Captain Rizzo stared at her face as if debating how much to say to a half-American, half-Italian civilian. "A fresh cigarette on the floor, as if it had dropped from his hand. A scrap of fabric on the wire grid behind your basil plants. Also, one flower pot is knocked over."

Flora winced. Then her mind jittered as she realized the obvious: *Someone had been in their apartment!* And it wasn't their other roommate Linda, because she was out of town!

"What was your relationship with Ernst Mann?" asked the younger policeman.

Who was it? Who had come into the apartment and pushed Ernst over the railing?

"Signorina?"

"Uh . . . as I told you already, he was my housemate. He is . . . was . . . also a colleague at work. And my . . . friend."

Officer Bernini's steady gaze revealed that he wondered if Flora and Ernst had been more than friends. Flora turned her tear-stained face away from him and focused on Rizzo.

Rizzo continued the questioning. "And where do you work?"

"I work as a painting conservator at Restauro Lorenzetti, in the State Archives building complex."

The two officers looked at each other.

"The conservation facility run by Beppe Lorenzetti in the old Palazzo Picolomini?" asked Rizzo.

"Yes, the fifteenth-century palace on Banchi di Sotto. The Lorenzettis have two locations for their business, one at the State Archives and one behind the family home."

"Did Signor Mann have any enemies, any difficulties at work?"

"Enemies?" Flora squeaked. No enemies, just a boss who was hardly ever there and a supervisor who seemed to dislike all his employees. No difficulties, just a hypervigilance by the Lorenzettis about what each employee was allowed to do and when. She could hardly tell the Carabinieri that their workplace felt more like a sweatshop and less like a cozy family business; it was only a feeling, not fact. "No, not that I know of. Ernst Mann joined the Restauro Lorenzetti in early March, about a month before I did."

"Who had keys to your apartment, besides yourself and Ernst Mann? Any friends or neighbors who could come and go?"

"Linda Maguire, our roommate. Our only other roommate. No neighbors had keys because our boss, Beppe Lorenzetti, is also our landlord."

The eyebrows of the captain flew up, almost touching his hairline.

Flora knew he wouldn't like the next part. "The Lorenzettis managed and rented several apartments. They kept extra keys inside their office somewhere, the inner accounting office, that is, where only senior members of the family worked."

Rizzo grunted. "An odd arrangement." His associate scribbled in his notebook.

"It worked well. Visitors to the lab couldn't get at those keys, or at least not easily. And most of the employees are related in one way or another to the family. And—"

Rizzo barked at his subordinate. "Bernini, we need a list of all the employees. Yes, Signorina?"

"Ernst wasn't good at locking up. He often left the front door open when he nipped out to buy cigarettes. That's what I thought had happened when I found the door open today."

Sottotenente Bernini groaned.

"Tell me more about the laboratory arrangement. You said there are two workplaces, at the State Archives building on Banchi di Sotto Street and the other in the Lorenzetti family compound a kilometer from here?"

"Yes, that's correct. The employees hardly ever visit the family labs. We spend nearly all our time here, behind the *biccherne* room . . . the room with the thirteenth- and fourteenth-century miniature paintings and book covers."

Both men nodded as if they knew the collection. Captain Rizzo coaxed her through the rest of her statement while his young assistant watched her carefully and took notes. "Wait here," Rizzo said. "Since you worked closely with the dead man, I want you to come to the State Archives lab with me and show me exactly where Signor Mann worked."

Flora nodded and leaned her elbows on the step behind her while Rizzo and Bernini interviewed the neighbors. She didn't trust herself to stand up yet. And despite her love for Siena and all things Italian, she wished she were somewhere else. Like Chicago, with her parents.

Mamma Garibaldi's nagging voice echoed in Flora's head. *I told you this job was a bad idea. You think a good Italian girl would take a job with a family she didn't know? Remember I said you would surely get into trouble?*

Yeah, yeah. But no one could have anticipated murder.

Flora's other roommate, Linda Maguire, wouldn't be home until later; she was visiting a friend in Florence for the weekend. Flora dreaded telling her that Ernst was dead. Linda had an obvious and vocal crush on Ernst and his soulful brown eyes. Flora's feelings were more complicated. At first, Ernst had seemed like the brother she'd never had, someone who would alternately chastise her, tease her, and comfort her, depending on the situation. A rare person, someone she could lean on . . . but lately, she'd begun to think of him as more than a friend. Her eyes brimmed over again.

The captain spoke to her. "Signorina, a change of plans. We will go first to see the Lorenzetti family at their home, and afterward you will show me where Signor Mann worked at the State Archives."

CHAPTER THREE

Flora stood and brushed off her khaki pants. She was surprised to find her legs steady. She accompanied Captain Rizzo and Lieutenant Bernini down the street and across the Piazza del Campo.

This was a little odd, wasn't it? Why didn't the captain finish interviewing Flora first and then go to the family's house? No doubt the Italian police had different procedures than Chicago cops. Flora shrugged and kept walking.

At her favorite hole-in-the-wall pizzeria, they turned right and followed a twisty little street to the Lorenzetti compound. The family owned three houses around a miniature piazza. Marco, the middle Lorenzetti son, had told Flora about the setup. Beppe and Gia occupied the big house, while the other two houses were occupied by the married son, Pietro, Pietro's wife and children, and a widowed aunt. Marco said Mamma Lorenzetti put out bread crumbs every morning on the pavement for the pigeons and leftover pasta underneath the cars for the feral cats.

Now, the pigeons pecked crumbs until the feet of the humans scattered them, but the only cat in view gave them a surly look and returned to its meal. Flora still wasn't used to the Italian habit of keeping cats outside, at risk from automobiles, small stone-throwing boys, and other animals. Most of them were mangy, lop-eared tough guys, as unlike her pampered, indoor cats in Chicago as she could imagine.

Captain Rizzo raised the lion-headed knocker and rapped several times while Second Lieutenant Bernini vanished around the side of the house. Flora wondered what he would find back there. Or maybe he would enter the house from the rear, chat with people in the kitchen, and then listen in on the interviews.

Through the open windows, laughter and the clink of glasses sounded. Saturday lunch was still in progress. No doubt the three sons, the daughter-in-law, and the grandkids were there. Flora smelled garlic and roast meat and tomato sauce and parmesan . . . her mouth watered as her stomach recalled it had never had any lunch—or time to digest breakfast before she'd upchucked on the balcony. Would she be invited to lunch?

Heartless hussy. How can you be hungry at a time like this? Her mother's voice whispered in her head.

Food is for courage, Mamma. And to keep up my strength for further interrogation.

You always were a glutton!

Gianetta Lorenzetti answered the door. "Why, Paolo! What is the problem?" She was a big woman, solid without being fat, with long hair tied back in a neat bun.

Oh, so that was it . . . the captain was a friend of the family. It would be interesting to see how he mixed policing with friendship. How *did* one go about interviewing good friends who were possible murder suspects?

Rizzo explained. "Gia, I am so sorry to disturb your meal. I have sad news. Your employee, Ernst Mann, has met an unfortunate death. I must talk with all your family."

"Oh, no!" she cried. "We *can't* have a death in the business . . ."

Flora's eyebrows arched. What an odd reaction to tragedy!

"This is terrible! It is not good for Siena's premier painting family. We must preserve our reputation! In our entire history, we Lorenzettis never had any encounter with the police . . ."

Her bizarre monologue faded as she bustled ahead of them into the house. "Beppe, you must come! *Immediatamente!*"

Beppe (Giuseppe to strangers) appeared at his wife's shoulder. As the head of the family and owner of Restauro Lorenzetti, he radiated authority tempered with warmth. "Ernst is *dead?* How terrible! Terrible. Come in, come in, Paolo. Have some lunch with us and tell us what happened. How we can help." Beppe's paunch preceded him into the house. His manner at the moment was genial, as it usually was when outsiders visited, but Flora recalled several shouting matches between Beppe and his sons. It happened often enough that Flora figured shouting at the tops of their voices was the family's normal mode of communication.

The captain, obviously as hungry as she was, led the way to the dining room. The charming room had wide shutters open to the breeze. Flora, who had never seen the interior of the family home, drank in all the details of potted flowering plants in the corners, the white tablecloth, the table set with cutlery and wine glasses. A roast of veal waited on a large platter, surrounded with piles of potatoes and green beans swimming in olive oil. Beppe pulled out a chair for Flora and someone filled her class with a rich red Chianti.

"Cara Flora, benvenuta!" said a low voice in her right ear. She turned to face Marco Lorenzetti's wicked brown eyes and devastating smile. Tall and muscular, he had tight little curls on the back of his neck and powerful shoulders. His voice oozed Italian phrases like a chocolate fountain, and his shapely hands created dreams in the air when he described his latest sculpture. Flora appreciated the purely physical effect Marco had on her, but she preferred a man like Ernst Mann who had brain to accompany his brawn.

"Grazie mille, Marco," Flora said. "I just wish it was a happier occasion."

"What do you mean? What happened?"

"Ernst Mann is dead. He fell off our balcony." Her voice choked up.

Marco's breath hissed in his throat. "What a calamity! How is this possible?"

"He . . ."

Flora caught Captain Rizzo's glare. He drew his finger across his mouth in a zipping motion and waved to everyone to sit down. She noticed he accepted food but took no wine.

"*Shhh.* The captain will tell you everything," she whispered to Marco. "Let me eat a little before I keel over."

As she turned away from Marco, she caught Pietro watching her with a sour expression on his face. Bernini entered the dining room and took the empty chair on Rizzo's right.

Rizzo, his mind clearly intent on sustenance before inquisition, dove into roast veal with the potatoes and green beans as if he hadn't seen food in a week. Flora had the feeling he caught most of his meals on the fly.

She could only manage a few mouthfuls before the mental image of Ernst lying bloody and still on the pavement stole her appetite. Her wine glass clutched in one hand for courage, she surveyed the Lorenzetti family. Pietro ate quickly, casting suspicious glances at the police captain and Flora. His wife Maria ignored everyone except her baby son, who was at the dropping-food-on-the-floor-to-make-mommy-mad stage.

Filippo Jr., Beppe and Gia's middle son, sat on his father's left and talked rapidly about a painting exhibition he'd seen in Florence, apparently oblivious to the fact that a senior officer of the Carabinieri had joined the family table. Filippo was Flora's favorite of the three boys; he always had time to flirt with her and pass the time of day until his father shouted at him to get back to work. Next to him, a young, svelte woman with long dark hair and a cat-with-cream smile ate daintily.

Flora leaned over and whispered to Marco. "What's Costanza doing here?"

Marco grinned. "She's my mother's niece, didn't you know? And a special friend of our Filippo. They've been dating a few weeks now."

And she's an employee at the lab, thought Flora. Interesting. She couldn't warm up to Costanza; Costanza asked way too many personal questions, especially of Flora.

Costanza caught her gaze and smiled. A smug smile that conveyed she was completely sure of her place at the family table, but what the heck was Flora doing there?

The widowed aunt, Matilde, pretended to listen to the conversation while drinking too much wine. She was one of those older Italian women who didn't hesitate to dress in a sexy fashion. Matilde wore a low-cut, flowered blouse, chunky amber jewelry, and discreet makeup. Her gaze lingered on Rizzo's face a couple of times.

Flora saw the two policemen glance at each other. Bernini pulled out his notebook.

Captain Rizzo folded his napkin and quietly started his inquisition. He never raised his voice, but everyone except Maria stopped talking and listened.

"Young Mann was pushed over the balcony, which means I have to question everyone who knew him, everyone who worked with him. We will start here, at the table, and then I want those who worked most closely with Mann to make statements. Then we will tour your laboratories . . ."

Flora felt a wave of heat in her face and neck. Oh, no—she'd consumed most of her wine on a nearly empty stomach. She set the glass down and forced herself to concentrate on the expressions of the various Lorenzettis. Beppe looked solemn, the picture of shock and concern, but Pietro's face looked shuttered as he studied his plate. Marco stared at a family portrait across the room and clenched and unclenched his right hand.

She knew that pose, that vacant glare and the moving fist.

He wasn't shocked or even surprised.

Marco was angry. Why?

Chapter Four

Captain Rizzo sipped his water, waiting until the right moment to begin his questioning of the family.

He was in an awkward position. His old friends the Lorenzettis were implicated in this murder investigation because of their double connection to Ernst Mann: they employed him, and they rented an apartment to him and his roommates. Unless Rizzo and Bernini found a friend or neighbor with a motive to kill the young foreigner, the Lorenzetti family would move to the top of his list of suspects. But why would Beppe, or any of his family, go so far as to push a young German off the balcony of one of their own rental apartments? What possible motive could they have?

Rizzo watched Flora Garibaldi responding to Marco Lorenzetti's flirtations. Attractive young woman, he thought. A bit too skinny for his tastes, though. He preferred more robust women, like his own wife Emilia. No one would ever call her fragile.

The American woman was definitely in a state of shock. She didn't look capable of pushing anyone off a balcony, but he would reserve judgment until he knew a great deal more about her.

Rizzo smiled at Matilde Lorenzetti, the luscious and available widow who made eyes at him from across the table. It wasn't that Rizzo didn't love his wife Emilia; she was a good wife and an admirable mother. But Matilde gave him something that was rare in a family dominated by three active children: companionship and conversation about things other than the children's schooling and activities. And Matilde loved to gossip about the old families of Siena, especially the Lorenzettis. Rizzo watched her across the table, admiring how her low-cut blouse and amber necklace showed off her perfect skin. He pretended they were talking together, just the two of them.

"Paulo, see that Marco? What a flirt! Too bad he isn't interested in his Italian fiancée. He is wasting his time on that American." Matilde loved people watching.

"He will learn. He is an excellent sculptor. So dedicated," Rizzo said.

"Yes, but—oh, look at that! Now Costanza is going to work on Filippo! She wants to be the next Lorenzetti daughter-in-law. That one wants a cushy situation: I bet she won't work a day outside the home after she gets married."

"She will have several jobs at once if Gia has anything to say about it," Rizzo said with a chuckle. "She is Gia's current favorite, but no young lady will lead a life of leisure in this family. She'll cook, clean, chase children, learn accounting . . ."

Matilde's greatest contribution to the current investigation would be her extensive knowledge of the Lorenzetti family and all the details about the daily lives of its members. Most interesting to Rizzo was the information about just how many pies his dear friend Beppe stuck his fingers into: restoration of paintings, copying of paintings, and perhaps even trafficking in illegally excavated antiquities.

Rizzo hoped very much that Beppe was not involved in trafficking because then he, Rizzo, would have to get off his behind and do something about it. Identifying and prosecuting antiquities smugglers were the highest priorities of the Rome-based division of the Carabinieri for the Protection of Cultural Heritage. Rizzo should know; he used to work for the Florence office of that division until he got demoted to territorial work.

But his former boss, Major Esposito, would still expect co-operation and hard work to prove what he suspected. He'd have to convince the odious prosecutor that he, Rizzo, had enough evidence to organize a search, then obtain a warrant to search the extensive Lorenzetti properties. And for what gain? Remnants of packing cases that could be used either for the legitimate transfer of goods or illegal transportation of antiquities? Lists of names and phone numbers that turned out to belong to only lawful customers? No. Finding what the Americans loved to call a "smoking gun" would require catching the Lorenzettis red-handed in the middle of a smuggling operation. For that he needed specific information about a shipment coming in or going out, and perfect timing—two things that were very difficult to achieve given the multiple branches of the Italian police that didn't play well together and the hideously complicated paperwork required to make any move . . .

Rizzo snapped back to the present. The family had split into multiple two-person conversations, and everyone sipped refilled wine glasses. Time to take the reins.

He nodded to Bernini, who slid out his notebook. Rizzo struck his fork against his empty wine glass, and the satisfying "clink" made everyone turn toward him. "My friends, I am sorry to disturb you, but you must pay attention. This is now a murder investigation. Young Mann was pushed over the balcony, which means I have to question everyone who knew him, everyone who worked with him. We will start here, at the table . . ."

Costanza Brunetti ate her lunch daintily, letting her gaze drift around the table so she could observe all the Lorenzettis. Since she intended to marry Filippo, it behooved her to learn as much about her new family as possible. Of course, Filippo had no idea he was going to marry her—yet. But Aunt Gia already approved. Costanza was the daughter of Gia's brother Guido and his second wife.

She crossed her slender legs, letting her short skirt ride up. Filippo smiled and dropped a hand on her knee. Costanza acted like the hand wasn't there, but she felt a pleasant glow as her target massaged her thigh. The Lorenzetti men all had roving eyes—except maybe Beppe. He was totally cowed by Mamma Gia. And he had no clue that his sister Matilde was the mistress of his good friend Paolo Rizzo.

Before the luncheon, Costanza had soaked up tidbits of family conversation in the kitchen as she helped prepare the meal. The Lorenzettis were already so used to her presence that they forgot to guard their tongues. Good. Costanza had a brain like a filing system. Every scrap of information, good and bad, about the people around her was tucked away in case she needed it. That was how she'd gotten close to Gianetta Lorenzetti. Once she figured out that Gia valued tradition and women who accepted long-expected roles within the family, Costanza knew just how to behave. Convince Gia that Costanza's biggest ambition in life was to get married and have babies—with maybe an accounting job on the side. In other words, butter up the parents while she seduced the son.

The interaction between Captain Rizzo and the family played out like a ping-pong game. Back and forth, with occasional zinger balls as someone grew uncomfortable. Costanza knew how to keep a poker face, but Pietro certainly didn't. His negative emotions passed over his face in succession: outrage, anger, and sullen acceptance.

When Rizzo rose to continue his investigation in the family laboratory, Costanza cleared the table while Gia and Maria, Pietro's wife, put away the leftovers.

"Costanza, what do you think of the American woman?" Gia asked as she covered the leftover meat with plastic wrap.

"Flora Garibaldi? She's all right. Good worker, but a little nosy. Always wandering around the lab and talking to Ernst. Well, not anymore . . ."

"Does she seem unduly interested in how we run the business?"

Costanza stuffed the forks into the dishwasher while she pondered. "Not really. But lately she spends more time talking to Marco—and avoiding Pietro."

"Avoiding Pietro? Why?"

"Pietro's her supervisor, and Pietro can be a little brusque. He doesn't sugarcoat anything; he lets you know exactly what he wants done and how quickly." Costanza didn't add that Pietro always wanted everything done yesterday. He had no patience at all and grumbled continually about the number of orders the Restauro had to fill.

Gia Lorenzetti's eyes glittered as she zeroed in on Costanza, forcing her to pay attention. "I want you to keep an eye on that girl. Who she talks to, when she leaves work, when she arrives. Everything. Start a little notebook."

Costanza frowned. "You really think an American like her is a threat to the family? I mean, beyond her flirtations with Marco?"

"I am not sure. That is why I want your help."

"Want me to follow her when she leaves work?"

"Only if you can do it without her noticing."

Costanza smiled. "I can manage that."

CHAPTER FIVE

"Signorina Garibaldi, I'd like you to go along with Lieutenant Bernini now to the main laboratory at the State Archives while I visit the laboratories behind the house," said Rizzo.

"All right," Flora agreed.

The captain gave rapid-fire instructions to Bernini. "Take her to the lab; get her to show you where Mann worked and give you a tour of the place. I will catch up with you there."

Sottotenente Vittorio Bernini was happy to oblige because it would give him time with the lovely young American. In the course of his daily work, he met many attractive women, but this one was something special. She was slender, graceful, and very sexy in her black leggings and loose top. More intriguing than her looks, though, was the sadness in her large brown eyes and her visible efforts to hold herself upright. Bernini suspected that visiting her work environment would show another side of her personality, the competent professional woman in her own territory, and he was looking forward to seeing it.

They crossed the Campo, now filled with late-afternoon shoppers and people meeting their friends for drinks in the cafés around the edges. The slanting light brought out the creamy whites and tawny golds of the rectangular pavers and the herringbone pattern of the bricks. The pavers, nine of them, symbolized the government of the nine who ruled over the city of Siena during the thirteenth and fourteenth century.

As they passed clusters of tourists with maps and cameras,

Bernini reflected on his boss's heavy-handed, aggressive approach to questioning suspects. Rizzo preferred shock-and-awe tactics, saying that people revealed more when they were scared. Bernini believed gentle and nonthreatening questions, delivered in an even, sympathetic voice, produced better results. And when the suspect was as pretty and fragile-looking as this one— well, best to keep things friendly, but professional. He touched Flora's arm. "So, Signor Mann was a friend as well as a colleague?"

"Yes," she said. "He was a roommate too. Nice guy, very easy to live with." Flora led the way into the courtyard off Banchi di Sotto Street.

The State Archives were housed in the Piccolomini Palace, built in the late 1400s. The former palace also sheltered the Biccherne Museum. To the southwest was a newer building, built during the 1950s, that now housed the Restauro Lorenzetti. When the new construction had blocked the original separate entrance to the conservation laboratory, the family had petitioned the State Archives for an extra door to be cut through the common wall. The builders had created a hallway that led to a back stair for after-hours access, when a metal grate protected the museum. During the workday, anyone could pass through the museum if the guards were present.

As they mounted the outside stairs, Bernini asked, "Did Ernst Mann have any conflicts with people at work?"

"Your boss already asked that. No more than I did. The family isn't very keen on our wandering around. We are expected to stick to our stations and keep our noses out of the family's private business." She unlocked the main door of the State Archives and they crossed the biccherne room.

Bernini had seen the museum before and didn't give the exquisite little paintings a glance. Like a bloodhound, he focused on the task at hand, notebook open and ready for her responses.

Flora unlocked the inner door that led to the laboratory and they stepped inside.

Dio mio, what a rabbit warren! thought Bernini.

The lab's large, high-ceilinged rooms stretched out like a train car from the front to the back of the building. Crumbling plaster showed in the upper corners of each room, and archaic light fixtures fought with modern desk lamps. The first room gave the impression of clutter barely tamed. Big tables littered with bottles and paint brushes sat next to rubbish barrels and containers of acetone; storage cabinets and racks marched down the middle of the room, subdividing the space into seven smaller areas. Painting stations hugged the oversized windows, where natural light made the work easier. On the biggest surface lay paintings—a Martini, a Caravaggio, and one of the ancient Lorenzettis from the Palazzo Pubblico—at different stages of restoration.

"This is where I work," Flora said, showing Bernini her worktable and materials storage cabinet. Her table displayed the picture frame she was repairing with gesso and gold leaf. She opened the drawer that contained the little Madonna painting and told Bernini how she meant to impress her boss with this example of her abilities very soon.

Bernini was certainly now seeing Flora's professional side— and her ambitious nature. He stared at the pictures of her family that Flora had taped to the side of the cabinet.

"Your parents?"

"Yes. My Italian mamma and my Scottish father. They live in Chicago."

He leaned closer and smiled at her. "You are quite a mixture."

"You can say that again. Most people don't know what to make of my background. But at least it explains the red in my hair and my blue eyes."

"A very striking combination, if I may say so." His smile widened.

"Don't get any ideas."

"I never mix business with pleasure," Bernini said, a bit put off by her brusqueness. That was a lie, of course, but he wasn't going to reveal that fact right away. He wondered if he could find ways to see the signorina outside of work while pursuing the investigation. She wore no wedding band; that was a start.

Flora eyed him. "I don't think I believe you."

"You don't have to believe me," he said, his good humor gone. Signorina Garibaldi was no young innocent. Her keen gaze told him she was accustomed to every kind of flirtation and didn't think much of his efforts. "But you do have to answer my questions to the best of your ability."

Now Flora looked slightly disappointed. Had he given way too quickly?

She moved briskly to the southern end of the laboratory, pointing out the fume hoods for venting solvents and the shop area for separating paintings from their frames and building shipping crates.

"Ernst sat here." She stopped at another table, flanked by tall bookcases.

Bernini noticed that the murdered German, hemmed in on three sides by conservation journals, painting supplies, and other paraphernalia, had rated a more private alcove than Flora did. Flora's very public domain stood right in the main traffic flow.

Flora said, "He did some really fine touch-up work. Adding details back to the paintings after the preliminary cleaning, matching colors, that sort of thing."

"What was his training?"

"A degree in art history, like most of us, then he added specialized training in art conservation. Ernst had more chemistry background than I do. He worked in a commercial chemistry firm for a while."

"Do you need chemistry for conservation?" He already knew the answer, but he wanted to draw her out.

"Yes—the more, the better. You need to be able to analyze the composition of older materials and test new ones. To have some knowledge of the instruments used to do the analyses. And you can make much more informed decisions about which materials to use on a restoration project."

"Give me an example."

She lifted her charming eyebrows. "Well, to clean a painting, I need to know what surface treatment was used originally so I can choose the best solvent to remove it. Then, to do the in-painting, I want to determine what kind of paint the artist used so I can match it as closely as possible, both the color and the composition."

"But most of what you work on here is oil paintings with a varnish finish, correct?"

"Yes, but sometimes conservators take on other projects, such as modern paintings created with acrylics or watercolors. Or we work on other materials such as ceramics."

"What happens there?"

Flora's face was animated now that she discussed her work. "A friend of mine had to restore a Peruvian ceramic bowl. Some early restorer back in the 1940s had covered it with plaster and paint so he could recreate the original design of birds."

"So what would you do now?"

"Strip off the spurious layers, test the materials used by the restorer, and then use modern, reversible materials to mend the ceramic in such a way that the viewer can clearly see the restored part.

"And no embellishing with decoration that's no longer there."

"Correct. I remember studying some Greek vases where

someone had continued decoration around the rim. The shapes of the leaves were totally imaginary, not based on what the original artist had painted. That would not happen in a modern conservation lab."

They eyed each other in mutual appreciation. Bernini's spirits lifted as he noticed how engaged Flora appeared, and her smile bathed him with warmth. He hated to go back to questioning her. "I'm sorry, but I still have a few more questions."

"Fire away," she said.

"Who were Signor Mann's friends?"

"His friends were mostly people who worked here: Graziano and Costanza in particular. Their desks are over here." She pointed. "And Linda and I, we were all friends as well as housemates. We ate together most evenings." Her hands clenched.

"Linda Maguire, right?" Bernini noted the hands and the change in her voice as she spoke about the dead man. Did that mean she had feelings for him? A little surge of jealousy heated his insides. "Did he have a girlfriend?"

"Not that I know of."

Too bad. It would be much better if Ernst Mann had had a lover—that is, anyone except Flora. He made sure his own voice betrayed no emotion. "What about family? Do you know where they live?"

"Munich. From what Ernst said, I had the impression he was an only child. This will be so hard on his parents. But I have no idea of their address or phone number."

Bernini surveyed the large room. He didn't see enough desks to accommodate all the members of the conservation firm. "Where do members of the Lorenzetti family work?"

"Through there." Flora pointed to the doorway past Ernst's desk. "The large room you see just on the other side of that door is where a couple of Lorenzetti cousins and nephews work as framers and carpenters. They dismantle old frames and build new only, so it's basically a woodshop. The room beyond that is Packing and Shipping. Boxes are assembled, filled, and padded. Then someone else seals the boxes and prepares shipping labels." They stepped into the packing room.

"And there is the inner door that leads to the family offices. Pietro, Marco, Filippo, and Beppe have individual offices. Marco's not here much because he likes to work at home. Pietro is in and out since he is in charge of orders and deliveries. Then there's one big room. That's where the women take care of accounts and filing—in shifts, since they all have duties at home as well."

"Which women?"

"Well, Gia, of course, her daughter-in-law Maria, and I think sometimes the aunt comes in to help with paperwork."

"Hmm." Bernini took a couple more notes. "What's the aunt's name?"

Flora thought a moment. "Matilde. Matilde Brunetti. She's from Gia's side of the family."

"How many employees work here, altogether?"

"I'm not sure. Costanza, Carlo, and Lisa work full time. Graziano and Stefano come in two days a week. And then there's Diana, she's also part time. Maybe ten total?"

"Do you know their surnames?"

"Sorry, no. I'm sure there's a list somewhere. Ask Gia Lorenzetti."

"How many of them are family members?"

Flora frowned. "Um, Marco told me the other day that Costanza is Signora Lorenzetti's niece on the Brunetti side. Graziano is a nephew or a cousin, but I don't know which side of the family he's from. The others, I don't know about."

"Have you seen the second laboratory, the one behind the family home in the Giraffa Contrada part of the city?"

"No. But I hear things about it. Marco says they built it

themselves over a few weeks. It sounds jerry-rigged: several sheds composed of miscellaneous bits of plywood and plastic. All the men take work home with them. Marco told me . . ." She bit her lip.

Bernini gave Flora a severe look. "This is a murder investigation. You mustn't hold anything back." He might be gentle in his interrogation techniques, but he was tenacious. This young woman wouldn't be able to hold out, he was sure of it.

She gulped and avoided his gaze. "Okay. Marco told me the family does special commissions at home as well as the regular work of the Restauro Lorenzetti business."

"What kind of commissions?"

"I think it's making copies of paintings for tourists, but you'd have to ask Beppe. I mean, Signor Lorenzetti. All I know is the regular business: the restoration of Sienese paintings, including the biccherne, and other old masters from museums and private collections all over Italy. Oh, I think they have a branch in Chiusi too."

"And what is your relationship with Marco Lorenzetti?"

She stared at him. "Is that relevant to your investigation?"

"Yes," he lied.

"Okay, he's a friend, but he wants to be my boyfriend. I like him as a person, but not as a potential boyfriend."

"At lunch, he was quite a flirt," suggested Bernini.

Flora rolled her eyes. "That's his normal behavior with any young female. It doesn't mean anything." Her eyes shone with another message: *And what's it to you, Lieutenant?*

The slamming of the massive door at the north end of the lab made both of them jump.

Rizzo's penetrating voice rang out. "Bernini! Bring Signorina Garibaldi back here and we will let the head of Restauro Lorenzetti show us around."

"*Si, immediatamente.*"

They joined Beppe, Pietro, and Captain Rizzo near Flora's desk.

Just two of the three sons, noted Bernini. Where was Marco, the amorous sculptor? He eyed Pietro's thunderous face, wondering what was eating him. Pietro didn't seem to care whether the police found him cooperative or pleasant. Beppe, on the other hand, appeared calm and completely in control of himself. Beppe flashed Signorina Garibaldi a confident smile. "Flora, you have been showing them around?"

"Only the front rooms, where Ernst and I worked. We haven't been in the back, in the accounting department."

"Fine, fine." Beppe took the lead, spouting the history of the family business, which went back fifteen generations. He pointed to photos on the wall of famous paintings undergoing treatment and some framed letters from satisfied customers. He gestured, pirouetted, and declaimed the virtues of his business and his ancient family connections from Rome to Venice.

When the performance ended, Bernini saw from the blandness of Captain Rizzo's face that he was not taken in. His expression said, "Okay, my fine friend, I hear your PR speech, but you are not telling me anything I cannot read on your website." Rizzo waited until Beppe ran out of breath and asked a few pointed questions about Ernst Mann's work and his recent assignments.

"What kind of work does your family do besides restoring museum paintings?"

"We create museum-quality copies of paintings for the tourist trade and sell them to galleries all over Tuscany."

"Did Signor Mann help you with these 'special commissions'?"

"No," said Beppe shortly.

Rizzo nodded and pointed at Ernst's desk. "Signorina Garibaldi, please open these drawers and tell me if you find anything unusual."

Bernini saw that the captain was paying close attention to how Flora's hands shook as she touched the dead man's possessions. Rizzo had often commented about how much he could learn about a person by watching his or her hands. Bernini kept his face expressionless; he hoped his boss had not picked up on his fascination with the lovely American.

Flora did as she was told. Top drawer: pencils and pens, paper clips, a stray paintbrush or two. Right side drawer: a few files with conservation articles. Lower left drawer: a stack of printed articles on Greek sculpture. On top was a copy of a *Burlington Magazine* article called "Blinded by Science," opened to the picture of the J. Paul Getty Museum's *kouros*. She picked it up.

"What's this?" Rizzo asked.

"I know this article—I read it for a class once. It's an article about a famous marble statue in California. A young Greek man. It's controversial because people are still split down the middle on whether it is authentic or a howling fake."

Bernini was familiar with the article. He recalled the harshness of the author's assessment of the scientific method. That writer, an art historian, claimed that scientists could never diagnose forgery as accurately as a true connoisseur could. A connoisseur, he wrote, had the advantage of detailed, hands-on knowledge of works of art that trumped any scientific tests. Bernini disagreed. He thought science and art could—and should—work together to determine the authenticity of major paintings and sculpture. "Why does a painter have such a thing in his desk?" he asked, curious how Flora would respond.

"I don't know," Flora said, sliding the article back in the drawer. "He was an art history student, same as me. Such things are of interest to anyone in the art field."

"This article is of interest to you," Rizzo said, his black eyes fixed on her face.

"Well, yes. The Getty Museum paid eight or nine million dollars for it. If it's authentic, it's one of the few statues of that size in American museums—"

"And if it's a forgery, it's one of the best ever produced," added Bernini, interrupting her.

Flora's expression grew animated as she turned to Bernini. "You've read the article too?" she asked.

"I was an art history major before I joined the police," Bernini said with a lilt in his voice. Now he had a real connection with the beautiful Signorina Garibaldi. All he had to figure out was how to build on it.

Captain Rizzo forced them to pay attention to him again. "So, the presence of this article is not unusual, that is what you are saying, Signorina?"

"No. Ernst had broad interests and read a lot on his own time. We all read what we could on controversies in the field and how experts study artifacts." Flora glanced at Beppe Lorenzetti.

Bernini looked at him too. Beppe's poker face showed nothing at all. And his son, Pietro? That surly, closed expression again. That was just as good as a bland expression for hiding what he was really thinking. Bernini would love to apply some pressure to Pietro to make him cough up what he knew.

Captain Rizzo sauntered over to the table holding the Martini. "Very fine painting. Didn't I see one just like it in your home laboratory?"

Beppe opened his mouth and shut it again.

Pietro jumped in. "Oh, that one is part of the same series, from the Palazzo Pubblico. Of course, they were painted during the same year and so they look very similar. I took it home to apply a new coat of varnish. We will return both paintings to the museum this week."

Really? thought Bernini. Pietro is talking too much.

40

What did those overly bland, expressionless faces mean?

Time to figure out the best way to pump each of the Lorenzettis, and of course Flora Garibaldi, for more information.

CHAPTER SIX

Rizzo and Bernini, representing the Carabinieri for the Territory of Siena, met with their colleagues Commissioner Mancini and Inspector Querini from the Polizia di Stato in the cramped Questura office north of the Campo. Besides the four senior men, an assortment of junior officers from the two branches of police jammed the room to listen to the initial briefing. Also present was Rizzo's former boss, Major Esposito from the Florence office of the Carabinieri for the Protection of Cultural Heritage.

Captain Rizzo was sleepy. He'd eaten too much lunch at the Lorenzettis' and all he wanted right now was a nap. Nor did he want to discuss the possibility that his oldest friend might be involved in murder. But he'd better take command of this meeting or Commissioner Mancini would have the upper hand. And Rizzo's old boss Esposito was watching him closely. "All right, folks," said Rizzo. "I'll summarize what we know so far . . ." He gave a quick report, adding, "Comments? Questions?"

The background noise of a loud conversation taking place next door and a motorcycle revving outside the window forced Querini to raise his voice. "Looks like a murder connected to an old Siena family. Everyone knows the Lorenzettis are from a long line of respected painters going all the way back to the fourteenth century, when Ambrogio Lorenzetti painted those fine pieces now hung in the Palazzo Pubblico."

"Skip the art history lesson, Querini; we all know about our

famous Sienese painting families." Mancini glanced at Rizzo
with a sly smile. "Another way to put it is the crime's the murder
of a young foreigner in an apartment rented out by Rizzo's
good friend Beppe."

Rizzo sighed. "Yes, Beppe Lorenzetti was the victim's
landlord." He steepled his hands and leaned back precariously
in his wooden chair so that his weight rested on only two legs.
"But that family connection may have nothing to do with Ernst
Mann's death. We may find a motive in Signor Mann's private
life for his murder." He hoped that was the case. Steering the
investigation toward Ernst Mann might produce some new
suspects, or at least delay focusing on the Lorenzettis. Beppe
was a slippery character, but that didn't make him a criminal.
He and Rizzo had known each other since primary school.

"Signor Mann was a conservator from Munich," Bernini
contributed. "He's only been in town since March and doesn't
have that many contacts in Italy—"

"We've gotten nothing useful from the neighbors?" Rizzo cut
in.

"No, sir. Only one woman saw Miss Garibaldi leave the apartment midmorning, on her way to work. The same person saw
Ernst Mann on his balcony after she left. The other neighbors
had nothing to contribute. It doesn't seem like the roommates
had much contact with the people in their neighborhood. They
all worked or studied full time, and they socialized elsewhere."

"Did you draw a plan of the neighborhood?"

"Yes, sir. Right here."

Bernini produced his map, and the five senior men leaned
over the crude drawing that showed the intersection of the main
streets with the alley running along the back of the apartment
building. Mann's body had been found under the balcony in
the alley, out of sight of the corner of the building where the
two streets met.

"So, there is no ghost of a motive for pushing Ernst Mann off that balcony?" asked Major Esposito.

Bernini replied, "Not yet. But the Lorenzettis were Ernst Mann's employers, not just his landlords. There may be a connection there."

Captain Rizzo snorted. "Bernini, you have a talent for speaking the obvious. You think I do not know this?"

"Of course you know it, but our colleagues in the Questura might not. Besides, you've hinted before that the Lorenzetti family isn't above dabbling in a little trafficking or other illegal pursuits. If that's true, it could provide a motive for the murder."

Now the fat was in the fire. Rizzo's stomach clenched as Mancini waded in with glee. "Yes, the Lorenzettis along with half the families in this city! It's true that Beppe and his sons have been sliding on rigatoni with the law for years now. They run their Restauro quite efficiently, but the sideline businesses of the Lorenzetti nephews and cousins spread out like a big spider's web."

And Beppe cheats on his taxes, thought Rizzo. He wasn't about to tell his colleagues this. The finance police would figure it out soon enough. And when they stuck their sticky fingers in, the investigation would slow down without Rizzo having to do a thing.

Major Esposito shifted his modest bulk in his chair and fixed his sharp gaze on Mancini. "Any proof of 'trafficking or illegal pursuits' as our sottotenente suggested?"

"No proof," said Mancini, sipping his coffee. "Yet." Again he glanced at Rizzo as if to say, "There's proof to be had, but I'll find it before you do. Hang on a second." He gave his junior colleagues assignments and the room cleared out, leaving only the five senior men.

Cocky bastard, thought Rizzo as he watched Mancini being efficient. He lit a cigarette, ignoring the "no smoking" signs prominently posted on the walls. "The Lorenzettis are like so many families in Tuscany. They've lost their historic income and do all kinds of business to make ends meet and provide a living for their children and grandchildren . . ."

"We know all this," cut in Esposito. "I want to hear about the setup. The family has two different centers of operation, yes? Bernini, you tell us."

Rizzo listened sourly as his second-in-command gave a succinct summary of the two laboratories at the State Archives and the family compound. Trust Esposito to sideline him again, just like he'd done when Rizzo worked in Florence. Maybe if Esposito had been a less dictatorial boss, Rizzo would have performed better and not been demoted to this territorial post five years ago.

"What happened when you visited the family's home laboratory?" Esposito asked.

Rizzo sat up in his chair. "Bernini wasn't with me then. Lorenzetti gave me the grand tour, as if they had nothing to conceal. The building is a giant shed, hastily constructed. I saw the studios of Beppe and all three of his sons. There were at least two empty storerooms with bits of packing material strewn all over the floor."

"Huh," Bernini said. "Packing material could mean either supplies received or shipments going out. Do they ship finished art works from the family lab, or only from the lab connected to the State Archives?"

Esposito's eyebrows shot up. "Good question, Bernini. Find out." He rose and motioned for Bernini to join him in the hallway.

Mancini's ferret-like face bore a smug expression. "Good officer you have there, Rizzo. So he does all the hard work, eh?"

"The fetching and carrying, certainly. That doesn't mean he does all the brainwork," growled Rizzo.

Bernini returned to the table. "The major has to get back to Florence. He wants us to report to him on a daily basis."

"Yeah, sure," said Rizzo. "We'll do that. But how are we going to help out the Cultural Heritage division *and* solve the murder? You're shorthanded, Mancini, aren't you?"

"Yes indeed. Half my men are on duty around the Campo, what with all these tourists descending on the city for the Palio." Mancini stood up and began writing on the whiteboard they used to gather evidence. "Let's see what we have so far. If Mann's roommates didn't commit the murder, then one of his acquaintances might have. The Lorenzettis don't come into the picture unless we can show that one of them was near the apartment at the crucial time. And that time is . . ." He paused expectantly.

Bernini produced. "The window for the killing is quite broad, between the time Flora Garibaldi left for work—about nine— and when she arrived home for lunch. Two and a half hours, approximately."

"The other young woman—what is her name?"

Bernini pulled out his notebook. "Linda Maguire, sir. An American postgraduate student in art history at the University for Foreigners."

"She was out of town, correct? So she can't be a suspect," Mancini said.

"That's right, sir. She is due back in town Sunday—tomorrow—evening. She'll be useful for background information, though. About Signor Mann's friends and extracurricular activities."

Rizzo watched Mancini and Bernini with growing exasperation. Mancini was taking over, all right, and Bernini was behaving like his pet dog.

"So, does Miss Garibaldi have any reason to push her housemate over the railing?" asked Mancini.

"You mean, a love triangle with Maguire or something? The signorina was very upset talking about him." Bernini looked down at his hands.

Aha! thought Rizzo. Bernini's trying to hide his attraction to the lovely signorina from America! Rizzo could make use of that . . .

The discussion continued.

"Another item: you said there are all those keys floating around. Do you know if the Lorenzettis all used one key for the rental apartment, or did some of them have individual copies?" Mancini sat down and waved to Querini to take over at the whiteboard.

"Signorina Garibaldi thought there was only one. But it would be so easy to copy it. I'll check on that, sir. But someone who didn't want us to know he had a key would lie about it." Bernini put his pen down. "Maybe Mann knew something about antiquities smuggling or some other illegal sideline—"

Mancini slapped the table, making his junior officer jump. "Excellent! Now we're getting somewhere. If Mann saw something he shouldn't have, that could be the motive for someone to take him out. And it needn't be a member of the Lorenzetti family. It could be one of their employees."

"But most of the employees *are* family!" argued Bernini. "Besides, it's so much more likely that one of the Lorenzettis is involved. They have the most to lose. My money's on Pietro, the sulky son, or maybe the crazy sculptor—Marco. Of course, they both work for their father."

Rizzo shot him a sharp glance. "You are overeager to focus on the Lorenzetti men, aren't you? What about a woman? Don't you fancy that Costanza Brunetti as a murderess? Or maybe Signorina Garibaldi?"

"Maybe Costanza, if we could find a motive for her. I don't think Flora Garibaldi is our killer," said Bernini. "Especially since the neighbors confirm that she was nowhere near the apartment when Mann was killed.

"Naturally not." Rizzo smiled. "You fancy her in other ways."

Bernini focused on his shoes.

Rizzo chuckled. "Don't worry. We'll make use of your interest somehow. Let me think on it."

Querini was eager to shine. "Since Bernini didn't turn up much from the neighbors, we'll delegate someone to dig up Mann's background in Munich. Search further for his friends and contacts. See if anyone besides the roommates might have had a motive to kill him."

"And don't forget to contact the family," said Mancini. "That should be done first, in case the parents want to travel to Siena to pick up Mann's belongings."

"I can do that, sir," Querini said.

"I'll interview the employees at the State Archives lab," Bernini offered. "And interview the American girl when she's less upset. She may remember more than she did right after the murder."

Rizzo slipped in another little dig at Bernini. "Naturally you want to interview the signorina—she's attractive, isn't she?"

Bernini flushed.

A uniformed officer stuck his head in the room and spoke to Mancini. "We've got a crisis in the Campo, sir. A gypsy family of pickpockets is robbing tourists, and we need extra men to nab them."

"All right," groaned Mancini. "Go ahead and stay longer if you want to, Rizzo. I'm sure you have things to say to your *junior officer.*" He grinned, and he and Querini left.

Rizzo gazed at the peeling paint on the ceiling, waiting for Bernini to finish taking notes. This double investigation would tax all of them. He was so damn tired of it all. Perhaps it had been for the best, his demotion. He didn't miss the frenetic pace of the Florence division.

Rizzo fixed Bernini with a sardonic gaze. "So, Bernini, you like working with that imbecile Mancini?"

"He's okay, I guess." Bernini changed the subject. "What else can you tell me about the Lorenzetti family? You know them well."

Bernini's tone was properly deferential. Rizzo relaxed, putting his hands behind his head and leaning back. "When you've lived in Siena for as long as I have, you can't help but know the major families. I've been in and out of their house and many others countless times. Beppe is an old friend, a good friend, but a very slippery character. He will talk for hours about the aesthetics of painting or the life he wants for his grandchildren, but not about the business. He is very selective about what he tells me about his work."

"His family has always been in the business of painting and restoration, right?"

"The Lorenzettis have always been painters, but it was only in the nineteenth century that they established Restauro Lorenzetti. That was a financial decision, I think, when commissions for creating original frescoes on building interiors began to dry up. They had to find another way to support the family. Using their painting skills to restore historic paintings to their former glory was the answer."

"So Beppe inherited the business, roped his sons into it, and presumably has connections throughout Tuscany?"

"Not just Tuscany. Umbria and Latium as well. Beppe's brother is based in Rome. He's an antiquities dealer."

"Hmm," said Bernini with a grin.

"Hmm, indeed," Rizzo agreed. "It would be useful to check on that brother's situation. What kind of antiquities, precisely? Are there any rumors about illegal transportation of statues or Greek vases from southern Italy or Sicily? That sort of thing."

He didn't give a fig for Beppe's brother, and this would be a good way to deflect Bernini's attention away from the family in Siena.

Bernini reached into his briefcase and pulled out his laptop. "I'm on it, sir. Do you know the brother's first name?"

"Filippo, I think." Rizzo rubbed his chin, which needed a shave. "No, that's not right—I was thinking of the son. Fabio Alberto Lorenzetti, that's his name. His shop is near the Spanish Steps."

The tapping of computer keys filled the office.

"Bernini, wait, there's something else."

"Yes, Boss?"

"I've thought of how we can use Miss Flora Garibaldi. Given her obvious fondness for the dead man—"

Bernini dropped his pencil onto the floor.

"—I agree she is an unlikely killer. But she is ideally placed to observe the family members and perhaps overhear their conversations. Did you notice what a rabbit warren that laboratory at the State Archives is? And how the family offices back up against Flora's space?"

"I did."

"Make friends with her. Milk her for information. See if you can get her to report on a regular basis to you."

Bernini grimaced.

Rizzo gave him a knowing smile. "Cheer up, Bernini. It might even be fun."

CHAPTER SEVEN

Linda Maguire returned close to midnight from the train station. She climbed the stairs, inserted her key in the door, and dumped all her luggage in the hallway before closing the door.

"Hey!" she said to Flora, who was sitting up in the kitchen waiting for her. "How was your weekend? I had a great time." Linda flopped down in one of the other chairs and reached for the open wine bottle.

Flora waited until Linda had taken her first sip out of a full glass. "Awful. I have something to tell you, Linda. Brace yourself."

Linda's blue eyes widened. "You don't look well at all, Flora. What is it? What happened?"

Flora took a deep breath and told her story. "So I came home for lunch, hoping to chat with Ernst some more about the odd comments he'd made the night before about the Lorenzettis. I went into his room to get some basil to mix with the leftover pasta . . . and found him lying in the street."

"Dead?" asked Linda in a horrified voice.

"Yes, dead. And worse still, the police think he was pushed off of our balcony."

The color drained from Linda's face. "So they think it's murder? That *is* awful! Do they suspect you? Who could it have been? Tell me every single thing."

Flora smiled slightly at the characteristic flood of questions from Linda and did her best to answer them.

51

As Linda listened, her eyes filled with tears, echoing the ones running down Flora's cheeks. When Flora finished her tale, they were both silent for several moments.

"I just can't take it in," said Linda finally. "Ernst seemed so indestructible. And he was such a sweetheart. We couldn't have had a nicer roommate."

"I agree. He was a special person." Flora pulled a tissue out of her pocket and wiped her face.

Linda gazed at her with concern. "I could tell he was more than a casual friend to you, Flora. I think you were starting to fall in love with him a little."

"Maybe. I really did like him. And he was a good ally at work. I wish I had been able to find out what was bothering him."

"Do you think whatever it was is the reason he was killed?"

"I don't know." Flora shuddered as her mind raced over the possibilities: an acquaintance of Ernst's? A neighbor? No—it had to be someone who had a key! Their landlords, a past tenant who hadn't returned a key, or maybe a repairman the Lorenzettis had loaned a key? But none of these people could have had a motive for killing Ernst.

Then she remembered what she must tell Linda. "The police want to interview you. Not because you're a suspect; you were out of town. But to question you about keys, neighbors, friends of Ernst's, that sort of thing. Tomorrow, first thing, at the Questura."

Linda took a big gulp of white wine. "Okay, I will do that. I'm willing to help in any way I can—I just can't imagine I know anything useful. But you're going back to work, to that den of weirdo Lorenzettis and all the people they employ. Maybe you can find out something the police cannot."

"That's my plan. To work hard, watch, and listen. Maybe I'll find an opportunity to snoop around a bit."

"Good luck, Flora. Let me know if I can do anything." Linda looked at her cell phone time. "It's late. I'm going to crash. You should try to sleep too."

The next morning, Flora dosed herself with caffeine and warm pastries and decided that what she really needed was a quiet morning outdoors, away from the apartment and anything to do with painting. She grabbed sunglasses, her phone, and a paperback book and made her way to the Campo. The weather was perfect, clear and hot. She walked slowly, deliberately looking at her favorite features of Sienese architecture: the heavy double wooden doors, exquisite iron fences, arched doorways with views into private courtyards. Shutters in different colors framed every window, and flowers filled every window box.

Soon Flora lay on her back in the city's central square, the Piazza del Campo, surrounded by pigeons and lovers. The warm paving stones cradled her shoulders as she soaked up the sun and tried to blot out job, roommates, and murder.

The families of Siena were out in force. Eddies of people reveled in the summer weather and the ambiance of the Campo. It opened in front of her, a huge scallop shell with sloping sides, studded with cafés and restaurants around the edges. Such a magnificent place, especially because the Sienese had the good sense to block vehicle traffic from the encircling street. That was now reserved for strolling shoppers, couples, and families, except during the twice-yearly parades and suicidal horse races of the Palio.

Flora loved the subtle colors of the medieval palazzos flanking the square: cream, rose, and deep gold. Normally, knowing that the best coffee in the world was a few steps in one direction, or a plate of decadent *tortellini alla panna con funghi* (with a perfectly chilled glass of Pinot Grigio) could be found in another would make her tingle with anticipation. Today both the colors and her appetite seemed flat.

She closed her eyes and let her spine settle into the herringbone pattern of bricks underneath her back while her
thoughts revolved like hamsters on a wheel. How lucky to end
up in Siena after finishing her conservation course in Florence.
She'd enjoyed staying with her aunt Antonia while apartment
hunting, but then a tip from a student led her to Linda and
Ernst, who already rented a place and wanted a third roommate
to share expenses. Linda, that odd combination of flirtatious
female and lucid scholar. Ernst, the nice guy who'd threatened
someone so much that he or she had pushed him off a balcony
. . . no, don't think about Ernst.

Flora's mind returned to the first time she'd met the Lorenzettis last March and her work interview with Beppe.

Beppe Lorenzetti had impressed her favorably. Not tall, but
solid and respectable-looking, with a twinkle in his eye. "We are
a family business," he'd said. "And if you come to work for us,
you will be part of our family and all we do here." He gave her
a tour of the laboratory in the State Archives compound and
explained the organization of the business. Then they sat in his
office and sipped coffee while he interviewed her. "Tell me
about your background and training for this position. You are
half Italian, correct?"

"Yes, that's right." Flora explained about her mixed parent-
age, her upbringing in Chicago, and her many trips to Italy to
visit her mother's family. "They live just outside Florence, so
I've been in Siena before."

"And your Italian is quite good. An obvious result of all those
trips."

"Mamma speaks some Italian at home too."

Beppe called in two of his three sons and introduced them.

First Marco, the youngest Lorenzetti brother. A hunk of a
guy with charming manners and come-hither eyes.

"Piacere," she said, as Marco took her hand and gazed into her eyes.

"We will make you very welcome, Signorina. You must accept the job."

Flora laughed. "Your father has not offered it to me yet!" She wondered if the handsome Marco had brains and passion under his gorgeous exterior. Or was he just a playboy?

"Of course you have the job, Signorina Garibaldi," Beppe assured her. "You have the requirements we are looking for. And this is Pietro." Pietro, the sulky older brother, barely glanced at her face as he shook her hand. Maybe he was too busy being his father's right hand in the business. According to what Beppe had told her during the lab tour, Pietro organized all the painting restoration commissions for the firm and assigned tasks to employees during his father's frequent trips to Rome and Chiusi.

And so Flora had moved to Siena. But the job hadn't turned out to be what she'd expected after finishing an advanced course in painting restoration. Gesso preparation and gold leaf application on picture frames were tasks any undergraduate student could handle. As she lay on the warm bricks, she wondered when—if ever—Beppe and Pietro would allow her to do real restoration: removing old varnish, mixing precise colors, and in-filling worn areas with new paint. Her fingers itched to wield a brush as she was trained to do.

Flora opened her eyes on the bluest of blue skies that mocked her mood. To her left, she heard the lilting Italian of a young couple lying near her, billing and cooing like the pigeons that strutted around them. No problems in their charmed lives! Off to her right, a small crowd gesticulated and bellowed from a miniature grandstand, egged on by a film director wearing a green kerchief around his neck. Marco'd told her the Campo was the setting for the latest James Bond film, and that she'd no doubt see tourists being recruited to play extras in a scene from the Palio horse race. Although the real Palio was days away, she saw the brightly colored medieval costumes of a group practicing flag tossing. The yellow and red with blue bands on their costumes and flags marked them as members of the *Chiocciola* ("Snail") *Contrada*.

Tiring of the hard bricks and pavers digging into her arms and shoulder blades, Flora hoisted herself to her feet and dragged herself in the direction of an inviting café-restaurant with umbrellas on the north side of the piazza. It boasted a superb view of the curved side of the piazza and the Palazzo Pubblico with its picturesque Torre del Mangia tower. She nabbed a round table as soon as it was vacated by two scruffy tourists and eased into a chair, plunking her purse on the ground while keeping the long strap safely looped over one knee. This wasn't the train station in Rome, but there were still pickpockets waiting for opportunities.

Flora glanced at her watch. Almost two p.m. She wasn't ravenous, but she'd hardly had any breakfast. She ordered a glass of white wine and the plate of luscious tortellini that usually awakened her appetite and natural greed.

Off to her right, a little man in a battered cap and red shoes, bearing two bulging shopping bags, appeared. He winked at Flora as he deposited his bags under another table and extracted a plastic bottle and a cane from his gear. She sipped a little more wine, wondering what he was up to. A street player, perhaps?

Yup. The man adjusted his striped cap (pink and purple stripes that clashed with the screaming orange of his shirt and sneakers) and chose his first target: a slender young woman with a knapsack, an umbrella stashed in its side pocket. Moving silently behind her as she crossed in front of Flora's table, the little man stalked her. Then he raised his plastic bottle and squirted water above the young woman's head while he matched her steps from about three feet behind. The young woman never looked behind her. When the tourist noticed water drops falling on her head, she whipped out her umbrella, raised it, and kept walking. Flora chuckled.

The street performer smiled gently and imitated the comical, loping stride of a tall young man moving in the other direction. He reached out the cane and hooked the man's satchel, yanking him to a stop. The gathering crowd in the café tittered in appreciation. Not quite finished, the little man cast around for one more victim and found two: student lovers oblivious to their surroundings, arms wrapped around each other's waists. He looped colored yarn around them as they passed, tying a bow that went unnoticed until the young woman tried to reach for her purse and discovered she was tied to her boyfriend. After the couple disentangled and laughingly waved away the performer, the player doffed his shabby cap and wandered among the watchers, collecting money. Flora handed him a couple of small coins as a thank you for the distraction from thoughts of murder and received another wink.

A shadow loomed over her café table. "Why if it isn't our little American. Enjoying your day off?"

Flora squinted into the sun and recognized Pietro Lorenzetti. She'd just been thinking about her employers, and lo and behold, here was one of them.

Uneasy without knowing why, Flora took a moment to reply. "Yes, very much. Would you like to sit down?"

Pietro yanked a chair away from the table, turned it around, and sat on it with his arms draped over the back. He gave her a slow smile. "You are settling into the job, yes? I think you like restoring paintings."

Surprised at his unusual politeness, Flora replied, "I do like the job, yes. And I'm delighted to be in Siena." This was already the longest conversation she'd had with Pietro since her arrival at the beginning of April.

Pietro reached for an uneaten piece of her bread and took a big bite. "Ah, yes, our city is the best place to live. And you picked my favorite place for lunch!" He narrowed his raisin-colored eyes as he focused on her face. "So, what is your ambition? Do you want to restore paintings for a living, or are you just trying it out?"

Stung at his assumption that she might be less than a professional, Flora said, "I'm as ambitious as any other freshly trained conservator! I certainly want to continue the work—whether I can make a living at it remains to be seen." Pietro knew darn well that internship salaries were ridiculously low.

His dark eyebrows lifted. "You are trained? Where?"

So Pietro had never seen her resumé? How peculiar! But it was his father Beppe who'd hired her, after all.

"I have a master's degree from New York University. Before that, I majored in art history and chemistry as an undergraduate. And, as your father should have told you, I just finished a special course in Florence, at the Uffizi Gallery. Although I'd done some painting restoration in college, this course taught me new methods, and we used the newest solvents and high-grade oil paints in our work."

Pietro chewed more bread with his thick lips and watched her.

Flora decided to needle him a little. "I've spoken to your father about doing more skilled work, the way Ernst did. Making gesso and applying gold leaf is hardly what I trained for."

Pietro frowned. "Do not bother my father about such things. I am your immediate supervisor. And Ernst is gone now."

His callous dismissal of Ernst angered her. "It's your father who hired me! And he has directed my work."

"All of our employees start with the basics and then move up as they prove themselves. In America, you say 'learn from the ground up,' yes?"

"But—"

He pushed back his chair. "*Basta!* Enough. I must go. We will talk again in a few weeks, after I have seen how you work."

"Pietro, I was just trying to—"

"And another thing, Signorina Garibaldi—stay away from my brother Marco. He finds you distracting."

"Marco? What does he have to do with anything? We are friends, nothing more!"

Pietro glared down at her. "My little brother is always behind in his work. And you are too pretty for your own good." He strode away.

Flora stared after him. What a jerk! The tortellini, drenched in cream and decorated with fresh, chopped porcini mushrooms, appeared in front of her. The young waiter flashed her a charming smile as she inhaled deeply, savoring the hunger that anger had revived. Flora reached for the pepper and dusted the pasta. It tasted divine.

She ate slowly, refusing to let her memory of Pietro's bad behavior spoil the pleasure of a solitary meal. She focused instead on the peculiar T-shirts and baggy pants of passing tourists and the contrast they presented to well-dressed Sienese families strolling in groups. An exquisitely shaped young woman, arm in arm with a brother or cousin, drew the gaze of every man within view. Her expressive dark eyes evaded eye contact with anyone, watching her delicate sandals while listening to her escort. No freedom from the family watchdogs for this young lady—not until she left home to go to college or get a job. That lush female form spelled trouble. And she couldn't be more than fifteen.

The tortellini disappeared and Flora wished she could pick up her plate and lick it, like a child.

But you are no longer a child and must behave like a young lady. How will you ever find a husband with your indifferent table manners and your impulsive habits? Not to mention your temper!

Her Italian mother was never far away in spirit, though her body lived in Chicago, Illinois.

Hush, Mamma. I am doing just fine here in Siena, and I don't need a character assessment right now.

Flora carried on frequent conversations in her head with Fabiana Garibaldi, but it was her half-Scottish, half-American dad she telephoned when she wanted to talk. William McDougal allowed his only daughter a very long leash, and he was the most tolerant person Flora knew.

Dad approved of her sojourn in Italy and had no worries about Flora's ability to handle herself abroad. Mamma, though, carped on Flora's tendency to speak first and think later and bemoaned her lousy taste in men. Surely Flora would end up in some disastrous situation without her parents there to bail her out! And now she had.

She sipped her wine and conceded that Mamma was right about her boyfriends—at least some of them. Flora's bones usually knew which guys might be good for her, but she couldn't help flirting with the handsome losers, the boys-masquerading-as-men who only wanted fun without responsibility. Artists were the worst, in Flora's opinion. They were so caught up in the creative journey that they had little time for practical matters or serious relationships. A girl for a night, or as an antidote to creative stagnation—that's what most of them wanted.

Ernst had been an exception to the rule. The week before he'd been pushed off the balcony, she'd had a long philosophical conversation with him over wine. Flora had sensed that their friendship had moved to a new level, a new depth. She'd looked forward to more conversations, cooking meals together, long walks—all the things that good friends did together as they got to know one another. Flora remembered only one or two "best friends" from her past—they were few and far between. Ernst had been the next, and one of the best because they shared professional interests as well as personal ones. She preferred not to dwell on her more recent feelings, such as how aware she'd become of Ernst's physical presence, his face, his voice, his laugh . . .

A tear rolled down her cheek and she wiped it away with one hand. Now that Ernst was gone, she was surrounded by men who expected things from her she could not give: impossible work demands from Pietro and impossible advances from Marco—

A second Lorenzetti brother descended upon her.

CHAPTER EIGHT

"There you are, *cara* Flora." Marco pulled out the chair next to her and draped his tall form over it.

For a split second, Flora's mind had room for nothing but annoyance. So much for privacy. Then she realized she could turn this chance encounter to her advantage. "Hi, Marco. I thought I'd escaped from everyone who knows me. How did you find me?"

"I have Flora detectors on," he said modestly. "You've had lunch already?"

"Yes." She smiled and added wickedly, "It was delicious." She watched his face carefully, wondering what made him tick. She decided to find out by spending as much of the afternoon with him as she could.

"Mind if I join you? I'm starving." Marco widened his eyes like Oliver Twist asking for more gruel, but the effect was spoiled by his well-developed shoulder muscles straining through his shirt. He might be hungry, but he sure wasn't starving.

Another healthy appetite despite sudden death, thought Flora. Maybe she wasn't abnormal after all. Just hungry like any healthy twenty-something.

"Go right ahead." She flinched as his arm brushed hers.

Marco ordered a plate of *spaghetti alla carbonara,* followed by roast chicken and potatoes. Flora added a salad and another glass of Pinot Grigio to the order. Might as well keep him company while he ate.

Marco picked up his fork and spun it on its tines. "So, have you spoken with the Carabinieri?"

"Yesterday, before I had lunch with you and your family."

"My father says you were the one who found Ernst Mann."

"That's right. I was the last to see Ernst before he left for work. Then I found his body when I returned to our apartment."

"That must have been very hard for you." Marco overdid the sympathy, but he did it very well with those melting brown eyes and sweet smile. Flora had always admired good acting.

Other than that, Mrs. Lincoln, how was the play? Flora figured Marco wouldn't recognize the allusion, so instead she said, "Yes, it certainly was. I've never seen a dead body before. And Ernst was a good friend as well as my housemate."

"Death is never easy. I saw my grandfather die, but at least he was in his own home in his own bed." He sighed and fixed his gaze on her face. "The cops questioned me too, and all our family, about the working arrangements. Where we go, who we work with, everything."

And did your family answer all those questions completely and truthfully? Flora wondered.

The spaghetti and salad arrived. She took a mouthful of arugula and tomatoes, dressed with just a little olive oil, vinegar, salt, and pepper. *Yum.* "You do most of your work at home, right, Marco? I hardly ever see you at the State Archives."

Marco smiled. "Yes. But I come more often now to run errands for my father. And, of course, to see you."

A blush warmed Flora's cheeks as her mother spoke in her mind.

Remember, darling Flora, all men are after just One Thing. But if you actually want their attention, all you have to do is get them to talk about themselves.

Thanks, Mamma. I think I get it. Stay out of my head, Mamma, she added to her mother's omnipotent spirit.

Flora smiled at Marco and leaned forward. "Tell me about yourself. When did you become a sculptor?"

Marco tilted back, balancing precariously on two chair legs as so many men (or, at least, all Flora's male relatives) did. "I trained first in painting restoration here in Siena because that is what Papa wanted. But I did not like it; I itched to try something new, something more . . . energetic. Then, I spent a summer in Bologna as an apprentice to a marble carver and fell in love with sculpting. Since then, all I want to do is work with a chisel. Preferably outdoors."

"Why didn't you like painting restoration?"

"Too finicky, too delicate. And too much sitting down." He rubbed his neck and resumed eating.

"I have a friend who makes pottery. She says she loves the tactile quality of the wet clay and how powerful throwing it makes her feel."

"That's part of it," said Marco. "What grabs me is the challenge of having a block of stone, just a hunk of raw material, staring at you. Then you start chipping away to reveal the figure hidden within. There is nothing more satisfying." He smiled broadly and moved his hands as if he felt marble beneath them.

Flora recognized the single-minded devotion of a dedicated artist. Marco's passion for sculpting was what made him tick. She sensed that didn't sit so well with the rest of his family.

"Marco, how did your father react to your change in career?"

Marco groaned and stabbed a piece of pasta with his fork. "As you might expect. He was not happy; nor was my mother. My parents want their three boys to put all their energies into the Restauro, into the paintings that are our livelihood now and for generations of Lorenzettis before us. But now—" he raised his head. "Now, I am beginning to develop a name among sculptors, to attract my own business." His face shone.

Flora felt his pride. "And you like it."

"Si, Signorina. I like it very much. Sometimes, I daydream about setting up my own sculpture studio, my own business. But first the Restauro needs to be on a surer footing . . ." Marco brooded, ignoring his food and looking out over the Campo where families gathered and tourists lingered.

So he does have ambition, thought Flora. Just not in the direction his family wishes for him—or for themselves. She found herself liking Marco better as a person, but she still had no desire to date him.

She definitely wanted to see his sculpture—not to mention the other family studios that were off limits to lowly employees like her. She tried to think of a clever way to gain access to the family laboratory. Should she be devious or direct? Flirtatious or careful?

Flora wasn't known for her patience.

She said boldly, "I'd love to see your work. Will you show me? Today?"

Marco's eyebrows shot up to his wavy hairline. He stared at her, then shifted his weight in his chair. "Show you? Well, Papa doesn't usually like us to take people around the family studios, but you are an employee . . . and a family friend." He gave Flora something between a smile and a leer. "And, he is visiting relatives in Firenze today. Want to go now?"

CHAPTER NINE

Vittorio Bernini felt unclean. At the Questura the day before, he'd bounced back and forth between two senior officers, trying to please both, and come away with the feeling that policing in Italy was too damned complicated. The several different forces of the Italian police operated independently, collaborating only when forced to, and then reluctantly. Rather like single children forced by their mothers to play nicely together, they went through the motions, but you knew as soon as a parent wasn't looking on, they'd return to running their own fiefdoms. And sharing new toys? Forget it. Maybe he should transfer to another country for a year or two, see how things were done elsewhere. He decided on a brisk walk to deal with his frustration.

He left the office and took the first right, north of the Campo and toward the neighborhoods he liked best near the Porta Orville. Actually, this was the very area the Lorenzettis lived in, a part of the city with less traffic and some green spaces. It was early evening, the best time of day in Bernini's opinion. Families and friends gathered for drinks and chitchat, the cafés filled up, the city settled into conviviality. The number of tourists dropped the farther he moved away from the Campo, and he found himself among apartment buildings and family-owned shops. Here you could find an uncrowded café, or just wander away from people and actually think about things.

This appointment in Siena was going to drive him mad, he was sure. Rizzo's attitude puzzled him. His calculated slow pace spoke of someone who didn't care as much as he used to about the job. Maybe Rizzo had never been that fired up about his work—or he had been a fireball in his youth. Bernini doubted it. Rizzo came across as too easygoing, too inclined to take shortcuts to get a result.

He walked on, stopping to pat a friendly striped cat that was looking for a handout. "Sorry, old fellow, I don't have a thing for you."

Maybe Rizzo was looking forward a little too much to retirement. What was he, sixty-two? Old enough to retire, but not old enough to avoid entanglements with women besides his wife. Rizzo thought Bernini didn't know about the affair with Matilde Lorenzetti, but it was too obvious to everyone in the office. Rizzo spent too much time talking softly on his cell phone, turned away from his colleagues. A dead giveaway. And Bernini had seen the couple together once, locked in an embrace in a cul-de-sac near the office.

On the other hand, Rizzo's relationship with Matilde gave him an inside track to the Lorenzetti family. Could they use that? But Rizzo's loyalty to Beppe stood in the way of using any information they obtained from Matilde. Bernini meditated on how to get around that. Maybe telephone Matilde and pretend to be asking questions that Rizzo had authorized? Bad idea—she would surely tell Rizzo the next time they spoke together.

Bernini's feet ached. He'd covered at least three miles, just walking and thinking. He looked around and discovered he was near a bar he'd never visited before, perched in a tiny piazza—the Piazza B. Tolomei—surrounded by potted plants. He sank into a chair gratefully and ordered a beer and a plate of pasta with a spicy tomato sauce and little bits of bacon.

CHAPTER TEN

Flora gathered up her purse while Marco gallantly paid the bill. Yep, this guy was interested in her. Now to keep him fascinated without giving too much of herself away—or landing herself into a situation she couldn't get out of easily.

Marco led the way back across the Campo to the side street that would take them to the family compound. As the street narrowed, he took her arm. Flora felt tingling all the way down to her toes and told herself grimly to squash the hormones and pump her companion for all the information she could.

He's attractive, but you don't actually want to take this relationship beyond friendship. Concentrate on helping the police and keep yourself out of trouble!

That was not Flora's mamma speaking in her brain; it was her own inner voice advising her.

As they walked, Marco boasted about the marble he was using. "It's a pale gray rock, with tiny gold flecks in it. It's Italian marble, of course—that is much cheaper than Pentelic marble from Athens—and it carves like a dream. My cousin in Chiusi gets it wholesale, and then I bring it a couple of pieces at a time to Siena."

"Cousin?" she asked. "Is this the guy who works in the back in your shipping area?"

"No, no, you're thinking of Marillo Ricci. He's from Roma. I mean my cousin Raffaelo Lorenzetti who lives in Chiusi. He has his own studio there—the one he took over from Carlo."

"What happened to Carlo?" Flora asked, as she made a mental note that Marillo was the employee she'd forgotten to mention to Bernini back at the State Archives.

"Killed in a motorcycle accident. Carlo liked big human figures, like me, but Raffaelo specializes in benches and garden pillars and the like. Not what I call real sculpture. Ah, here we are."

He dropped her arm and led the way around the Lorenzetti house by a paved path flanked with orange marigolds. The path opened into a large courtyard, surrounded by a high brick wall. In the section closest to the house, the family had created an outdoor sitting area with a few scruffy olive trees, potted petunias, and a painted metal table with chairs. Backing this area was a low, rectangular building cobbled together out of fiberglass and wood, with ivy crawling up the exterior walls. Flora saw skylights, but few windows.

Marco pulled out a set of keys and fumbled with the padlock to the door between two small bushes.

"So this is your studio. Where do your father and brother work?"

"My father's studio and Pietro's are behind mine. There is another room at the back of Pietro's workshop where Filippo works."

The padlock snapped open and Marco pushed the door ajar. "Come in, come in."

Marco turned to face her with his arms outstretched and a goofy grin of welcome.

"Wow," she said inanely, pretending she hadn't noticed his inviting pose.

A packed workshop smelling of mildew met her interested gaze. Blocks of crudely cut marble lurked on one side of the long room while a table full of chisels, hammers, and other paraphernalia hugged the opposite wall. At the rear were floor-to-ceiling shelves, stuffed with finished busts and small sculptures of deer, horses, and some kind of large bird. On one shelf, Flora saw a jumble of half-carved column capitals and practice blocks for floral decoration: scrolls, palmettes, and acanthus leaves. A large fan stood near the back door, which Marco now opened to provide a cross draft. He flipped the fan on and immediately the mustiness receded.

In the center of the room, in a welter of marble chips and dust, a half-finished statue stood. It was a kouros, a Greek-style statue of a young man, with hauntingly familiar features. Long, ringleted hair. An idealized, Archaic face. Torso muscles carved in a classic rippled manner. Bulging thighs and well-defined calves. Marco had roughed out three-quarters of the statue, but the arms and feet were still incomplete.

The statue looked like others from the Archaic Period that Flora had seen in museum catalogues and textbooks, but she couldn't remember enough from her college sculpture class to identify the model. Of course, the artist could have worked from more than one model—or memories of sculptures he'd seen and sketched—and combined features into a new kouros . . . Noticing a pile of printouts on Marco's worktable, she moved closer to examine them. Just as she picked up the top two photos of *kouroi* in the Athens museum, Marco took the papers out of her hands.

"But Marco, I'm interested in sculpture. Can you tell me—"

Instead of letting Flora finish her sentence, Marco took her by the shoulders and kissed her. As a way of shutting her up, it was very effective. Unfortunately, despite the physical attraction she felt for him, she did not enjoy the kiss. His lips fastened onto her like a leech attaching itself to Katherine Hepburn's arm in *The African Queen*. Wet, sticky, and surprisingly cool. *Ee-euw!* And his strong fingers gripped her arms with unnecessary vigor, no doubt leaving dents in her tender flesh.

Pushing hard at his chest, Flora broke away. "Marco! I, um, don't think I'm quite ready for this . . ."

His mouth twisted. "Obviously not. We will take it a bit slower, yes?" Marco looked both puzzled and disappointed.

"Yes. I mean, maybe," stammered Flora. "Marco, I am still getting over my last boyfriend so I am nervous. You understand? It is not you at all. It's just me."

"Huh." He turned his head away and stuffed his hands in his pockets.

She could see hurt in his eyes and felt ridiculously guilty even though she'd told him only part of the truth. Never mind that her relationship with Richard had ended nine months ago and that poor, dead Ernst had been much closer to winning her heart than Marco would ever be.

She touched his arm. "Show me the rest of the lab, Marco, and then I'd better head back."

Marco relocked the front door to his studio and turned off the fan. As they moved into the other part of the building, he pointed out the storage rooms on one side of the hallway, his father's and brothers' spaces, and the door leading to the alley at the back. "That's how we get shipments in and out," he said, leading the way out the back door.

"Thanks for showing me, Marco. It's very interesting to see where you work."

He smiled slightly. "It's just a studio. I spend more time here than anyone else. My father is always on the road, Pietro is at the State Archives compound, and Filippo shuttles back and forth between the two labs. Without our cell phones, we'd never keep track of each other."

"What is Filippo's job?"

"Oh, he does painting restoration half-time and shipping arrangements the rest."

They stood eyeing each other in the alley. Flora felt the

awkwardness between them, but couldn't figure out how to change it.

Marco said, "Well, let me walk you home, then."

"Okay."

They had little to say to each other on the way back to the Campo area.

Just as they passed the pizzeria near the Lorenzetti home, Flora noticed Marco's brother Pietro returning in the family car. She almost lifted her hand to wave at him, but then she remembered he'd told her to keep away from Marco. Pietro braked the car and looked up. Flora noted his sour expression and figured she'd blown it—again.

Marco apparently hadn't seen him, so Flora said nothing.

CHAPTER ELEVEN

Flora was back at work on the little Madonna, this time on her lunch break. Her desk was strewn with sandwich wrappers, a coffee cup, her palette, a can of brushes, and all the impedimenta of a busy painter. She made sure her turpentine was closer to the paint than her coffee cup. Turp-flavored coffee was terrible, and she should know—she'd dipped her paint-and-turpentine-covered brush in coffee or water or juice too many times to count.

She had the little triptych with the Madonna on a small desk easel, with a separate canvas next to it so she could go back and forth with her paint. Flora loved sketching with a paint brush. She'd completed a sepia and turpentine outline on the second canvas of the Madonna's face and costume as close as possible to the proportions of the original. Now she worked on the blue of the Madonna's head covering, trying to get an exact match with the greenish tint that turned sky blue to almost aqua.

The part of Flora's mind that wasn't occupied with painting was mulling over Marco's behavior at his studio yesterday. She had the strange but distinct feeling that he'd kissed her in part because he wanted to stop her from looking at those photographs . . .

The outside door slammed and Beppe Lorenzetti appeared. Obviously surprised to see her painting instead of mixing gesso or gold leafing a picture frame, he lumbered over to peer over her shoulder. Flora, resisting the temptation to sweep her desk clean of her furtive restoration effort, waited for his reaction.

A long silence ensued as her boss absorbed what she'd been doing on her own time. "Not bad, not bad at all. You've a very good eye for color and your drawing is excellent." Flora let out the breath she hadn't known she'd been holding. "This is what I learned in the course in Florence, Beppe. We did quite a few restorations in the six months I was there."

"Yes, yes, I can see that." He stroked his chin. "But you have considerable skill as a copyist as well, don't you?"

A little trickle of unease crept down Flora's neck. "Well, I've always been good at copying paintings. Before I had any formal art classes, I used to go to the Art Institute in Chicago and sketch, then paint, in the open galleries. My parents complained that I neglected my schoolwork—"

Beppe interrupted her. "I'd like to see you make a complete copy of this Madonna. Make it as accurate as you can. An exact replica of subject matter, brushstrokes, color choices, everything. Start now. You are excused from your regular work; I will let Pietro know." He left her side abruptly, moving down the long room to check on the work of the other apprentices.

Flora stared after him, her mind spinning like a clothes dryer. A new assignment, much more to her taste than repairing picture frames and mixing gesso. A chance to advance in her job from doing scut work to advanced restoration. So why wasn't she happy?

She rose and took her now cold coffee over to the sink and dumped the muddy liquid down the drain. As she refilled her mug with fresh coffee and cream from the half-sized fridge, she debated with herself.

Copying paintings was completely legitimate, if the finished products were sold as copies and not as originals. When a painter completed a commission for an art replica company or a museum shop, a label was affixed on the back saying it was a copy, "based upon an original by (name of original artist)." It was then sold for a fraction of the price of the original painting. Or at least that was how it was supposed to work. Flora knew that plenty of forgeries existed on both sides of the Atlantic—and that many forgeries hung in museums because "experts" had passed them as "authentic." Copy work was legitimate employment for the many graduates who discovered that a degree in art history or painting hardly ever resulted in a single job that could pay for groceries and rent. Nearly everyone she'd known in school worked two or three part-time jobs; it was rare to hear of someone landing a tenure-track job at the university level.

She'd known the Lorenzetti family dealt in copies, but had believed until the day of Ernst's murder that copying paintings was performed in their home studio. Restoration was centered in the main laboratory. Until now, the assignments that Ernst and other apprentices worked on at the State Archives were original paintings housed in state or private museums that needed cleaning and in-painting to restore them to their former glory.

It was Pietro's reaction to Captain Rizzo's comment on the two Martinis that had caught her attention. If the family was dabbling in copying paintings to sell as reproductions, why hadn't Pietro just said that? She hadn't believed his quick assurance that the painting in question was part of a set of similar paintings from the Palazzo Pubblico.

Rizzo hadn't believed it, either.

Flora wandered over to the window that looked down on the busy street below. She had a nasty feeling that her new assignment would lead to a "damned if you do, damned if you don't" situation. The head of the firm wanted her to make a copy, an exact replica. Very well, she could do that, but the ten-thousand-euro question was, what did he plan to do with it if she did a good job? To sell as a replica, her work would have to be better than good. It must be perfect.

On the other hand, if she elected to make a copy that was competent but not outstanding—say with a couple of minor flaws—and didn't sign her work, it would be very interesting to see what Beppe's reaction was. Would he ask her to try again, or demote her back to gesso and gold leaf work?

She finished her sandwich and rearranged her tools, adding a full set of paints from her drawer. She took the canvas that she'd been sketching and trying out colors on and filled in the background to imitate the original Madonna. That background should have more ochre in it, she thought, and I need more green in the right-hand corner . . .

Flora became so absorbed in her work that she didn't notice that someone had crept up to her cubicle.

"Just what do you think you're doing?" asked Pietro.

She looked up into his scowling face, noting that his lower lip seemed thicker—and sulkier—than ever. "Didn't your father tell you? Just a little while ago, he asked me to make a replica of this little painting to test my skills. I was using the canvas to match colors for the in-painting I was doing—"

"No, he didn't tell me!" Pietro said with a growl. "My father is terrible about passing on information." Pietro cursed under his breath, an Italian phrase Flora did not recognize. "And he pays no attention to how many commissions we have to complete this month. That's my job. I don't think I can spare you for this labor, but let's see what you have so far."

Flora turned the canvases around so he could compare the original with the copy. "I only just started on the background. I sketched the Madonna the other day so I'd have a human face for the flesh tints."

"Hmm." Pietro was silent for a few moments. "I don't think you have the talent for this, Signorina Garibaldi, but you may

continue if my father says so. I just wish Beppe would not commit us to so many projects at once!" He spun on his heel and
was out the front door before Flora could think of an appropriate response.

Pietro's comment about his father was illuminating. Maybe
Pietro's bad attitude could be explained by Beppe's overenthu-
siasm for adding to the workloads of everyone at the Restauro.

But it was Pietro's comment directed at her that really caught
her attention. So he thought she wasn't talented enough, did
he?

We'll see about that, Signor Pietro.

Flora remembered a museum she'd visited in Illinois that
had a so-called Rembrandt in their collection. It held a place of
pride in the Old Masters gallery until a team of Rembrandt
specialists showed up, subjected the painting to every micro-
scopic and stylistic analysis they could think of, and pronounced
it a "not-Rembrandt," a painting not by the master himself, but
by one of his students. Sort of like saying, "Workshop of Ex-
ekias" in the field of Greek vase painting when you couldn't tell
if the master had done it or not. But in the art museum's view,
deciding an Old Master painting was not actually by an Old
Master was damning; it decreased both the monetary value and
the aesthetic appeal. Patrons did not like to be duped, and
everyone liked to think they were looking at the "real thing."
Too often in the art museum world a demoted painting would
be whisked out of the gallery and hidden in basement storage.

In Flora's view, if a student's painting was so good that
experts mistook it for one by the master, then it was an
outstanding painting. It was just a short step from there to a
forgery worth millions on the black market. Her lip curled in a
stubborn line her father would have recognized.

Pietro had challenged Flora to a duel. Could she make a
Martini so good that no one could tell the difference between

her work and the original? Damn right she could. And she was so fired up by the idea that she'd take it home and work on it around the clock. She had a complete set of painting gear at the apartment, now occupying Ernst Mann's old room until she and Linda found a new roommate.

What then? What would Pietro and Beppe do with her masterpiece? She wouldn't sign it "Flora Garibaldi McDougal," but she could put a little symbol inside the folds of the Madonna's cloak in a place and color only she could recognize. Then she'd sit back and wait to see where the painting ended up . . .

Chapter Twelve

Beppe hurried home for lunch. He used his favorite shortcut, from north of the Campo along Via Calzolerria through Piazza Tolomei and then Via del Giglio. He picked up a loaf of Tuscan bread for Gia at his favorite bakery; she liked really fresh bread.

It was an excellent thing that the little American was a talented painter. He could use her on several different projects now—not just restoring picture frames. As he strode along, Beppe made a mental list of clients who were looking for good copyists . . . and the more sidelines he had going, the better the chances of the main business, the Restauro, surviving tax increases and shipping costs.

His wife and oldest son were sticklers for starting new employees very slowly, no matter what their training, but he couldn't afford to wait. Too much work, too many clients. And Beppe prided himself on the power of his intuition, his ability to make a snap judgment about someone. Smart, talented employees should not be overlooked; they should be promoted and given more responsibility so they could make maximum contributions.

I am the big-picture man. Pietro is my lieutenant, the detail guy and general manager.

He stopped in the little piazza close to home and fished some leftover bread from his pocket. Carefully, he crumbled it into little pieces and spread them out under a parked car for the cats. So many mangy, hungry cats without homes! Where did they all come from? Beppe had a soft spot for cats, especially the street warrior tough guys, the ones with lopped-off ears and kinked tails. They looked so wretched, so beaten down. He would ask his wife for leftover pasta after lunch.

Emptying his pocket of crumbs in the potted plant by the side door (it wouldn't do for Gia to find food in his clothes again), he headed for the kitchen. Wonderful smells of chicken roasting and garlic-tossed pasta greeted him. "Gia, where are you?"

"I am right here, you silly man." She gave him a peck on the cheek as she came out of the pantry bearing a salad for the table. "How are things at the lab?"

"Better," he said with a sigh as he deposited the bread on the kitchen table and poured himself a glass of Chianti. Beppe admired his wife's sturdy figure as she moved around the kitchen. "I have some good news. That American girl we hired can paint. I still don't know how good a conservator she is, but she can paint exquisitely."

Gia raised her eyebrows. "Really? She's so petite and self-effacing; I didn't think she had it in her. These pretty, fluffy girls usually aren't good for much—except distracting our boys from their proper work."

He twinkled at her. "When I met you, *you* were a little slip of a thing."

She laughed and slapped his shoulder softly. They both knew this was a joke. "I was never a little slip of anything, and you know it!"

"True. And you used to be quite a good painter. Why don't you go back to it? Join our restoration team?"

"Good heavens! And when would I have time for that?" Gia opened the silverware drawer and collected forks and knives. "It would be nice to take up painting again, if I didn't have the accounting in addition to housework." She turned and studied

Beppe's smiling face. "Maybe I could teach basic painting to our grandchildren!"

"Of course you could. Emilia and Paolo would enjoy playing with paints and water, and then their proud grandmamma could display their artworks on our kitchen walls." Beppe watched her fondly. A wife in a million, he thought. A full partner in the business, with a mind like a computer, and such a good mother and grandmother. Almost too much of a family advocate, but you couldn't have everything. He could not imagine managing Restauro Lorenzetti without his Gia.

Marco strode into the house, slamming the back door. "Mamma! What's for lunch?"

She sighed at the marble dust all over his torso and hands. And the footprints all over the floor. "Roast chicken and garlic pasta. Your favorites. Do wash up, you look like a farmhand."

"Just like my grandfather Brunetti!" said Marco cheerfully. "I am like him; you should be pleased at how hard I work, how much I produce!"

"Oh, yes! You make naked young men and animals in marble. How lovely, how useful! My father made the best cheese in all of Umbria. How can you compare statues to that?"

"I will make more money, you will see. When Papa sells my kouros, we will be rich."

"Not so fast, Marco." Beppe joined him at the sink to wash his hands. "First we have to find a buyer, you know."

"You and Pietro are good at that, Papà. I know you'll find someone." Marco carried the big blue pasta bowl into the dining room and took his place.

Head in the clouds, that's our Marco, thought Beppe. Lives for his art and for chasing girls, but not a practical bone in his body. Pietro is my right hand. I could not run this business without him.

Beppe knew that Marco couldn't care less about the buyer.

All he wanted to do—all he had ever wanted to do—was create sculpture. What his family chose to do with his finished works was not his problem. By the time one statue was moved out of his studio, he was already deep into dreaming about the next one, the exciting process of making sketches from several different angles and choosing just the right piece of marble . . .

Marco said, "How about I invite Flora for Sunday lunch next week?"

His father reflected that the part of Marco's mind not fixed on sculpture was occupied by girls. And that girl fixation had nothing to do with brain power.

Gia whirled around. "What, are you crazy? Family lunch is for family, not outsiders like that little foreigner!"

"Mamma! She is half Italian, a good employee, and a friend of mine. We used to have friends over when we were growing up. Why should this be any different?"

"You know perfectly well why it is not the same!" Gia said, slapping her hand on the table near Marco's place. "You are to marry Catarina next summer, and it is high time you got to know her better! Instead, you sniff around the skirts of someone who will never be part of this family."

"What if I don't want to marry my cousin-by-marriage? Catarina is a cow-faced plod, and she doesn't stir my blood one little bit!" cried Marco.

"Your duty to your family is to marry the woman your parents choose."

"Son, let's try to talk about this rationally." Beppe tried to lower the temperature in the room just as Pietro slammed the back door and strode to the sink. Pietro, who had acutely tuned sensitivities to family drama, immediately picked up on the issue under discussion.

"Marco, we've talked about the signorina before. She is not good for you; she distracts you from your work," Pietro chimed in. "And she was brought up American; she will never fit into a true Sienese family."

Marco lost it. He jumped out of his chair, which fell over backward with a crash. "Basta! Will this family never leave me alone? This is not the thirteenth century! I will date, I will marry, whom I please, whom I choose! And you can all go straight to hell!" He ran out of the room. They all heard his bedroom door slam.

Beppe sighed. "I will speak with him. He will see reason, I promise you." This last was directed at Gia, whose eyes were blazing with anger and unshed tears. He knew, better than anyone, how difficult life could get if his Gia was not happy. He would not allow any of the children to upset her for long.

"See that you do bring him around, Beppe," she said, relaxing her clenched hands. "I will get the table ready. Pietro, go call your brother Filippo and Costanza and your own family. We will eat in ten minutes."

CHAPTER THIRTEEN

After clearing his desk of paperwork that couldn't wait, Bernini glanced at his cell phone and decided this was a good time to visit the Restauro laboratory. He needed to follow up on interviews with the employees who hadn't been available over the weekend.

He walked briskly along the cobbled streets from the Carabinieri office to the State Archives. The heat of the day was so intense that Bernini shed his suit jacket and draped it over one shoulder. Passing behind the Campo on Banchi di Sopra street, he nodded at a couple of tourists who stood in front of a florist's, looking lost.

"May I help you?"

"Where are the Cathedral and the Ospedale?"

"You are heading the right direction. Cross the Campo just here and you will be there." He showed them on their map.

The young couple thanked him, and Bernini continued on his way. He was thrilled to be outside, away from paperwork, so he didn't care how hot it became.

At the Restauro, he said hello to Flora and told her he wanted to speak with her in about half an hour. Then he started at the back of the laboratory and worked his way forward.

Most of the young people working in packing and shipping had little to contribute to his investigation, but Costanza Brunetti was another story.

Bernini eyed her blatantly provocative clothes—tight, short

skirt and low-cut blouse—and the smug expression that reminded him of a cat who's just had cream. Something about Costanza rubbed him the wrong way. Was she too sure of herself? The way she slanted her face, looking sideways out of those perfectly made-up eyes, said she knew perfectly well that she was attractive and not above using her looks to get exactly what she wanted. Yes, a small, dainty cat was a perfect metaphor for Costanza Brunetti.

"So, Signorina, how well do you know the Lorenzetti family?" Bernini suspected very well indeed, since he'd observed how Costanza seemed perfectly at home at Sunday lunch.

"Well enough. I am dating Filippo, so I am often at the family home." Costanza gave him a sweet, satisfied little smile. She shifted in her chair so that Bernini could see down her blouse if he cared to.

He glanced at what was on offer and then asked, "What can you tell me about the family dynamics? Does everyone get along?"

Costanza laughed. "Better than my family, that's for sure! There's a little friction because Marco is more fixated on sculpture than restoring paintings. He doesn't seem as vested in the family business as the rest of them. And Pietro is always difficult. Filippo is the nicest of the sons. Or at least, I think so." She batted her eyelashes at him.

"How long have you worked here?"

"Since last September. I came here straight out of university. I trained in art conservation in Bologna."

"And how well did you know Ernst Mann?"

"Not well enough," Costanza said with a little moue of disappointment. "He was an attractive man, but he cared more about his painting than the people around him."

From her attitude, Bernini figured Costanza had tried to entice Ernst, but he hadn't responded as she'd hoped. This young woman was the sort who would try her wiles on any eligible male almost automatically.

He thanked Costanza and moved on with relief. Now he could talk with Signorina Garibaldi again, as he'd wanted to all along.

Bernini approached Flora's work area. He moved quietly in his soft-soled shoes so she wouldn't immediately notice his presence. Her dark head bent over a picture frame, she reminded him of his mother sewing after supper. The same fierce concentration. But Flora was a lot prettier than Signora Bernini.

"*Buon giorno,*" he said, perching on the corner of her table.

"Oh!" she said, dropping her paintbrush. "I didn't hear you coming. I thought you were still interviewing Costanza."

"I was. Now I want to interview you."

"Again? Haven't you got enough information from me already?" Her eyes widened like a cat mesmerized by headlights at night.

Bernini smiled to put her at ease and pulled out his notebook. "When I spoke with you the other day, you were in shock. Police officers are trained to question people several times after a traumatic event, because most people remember more when they've had time to calm down and think about it."

Flora eyed him dubiously. "Well, you're right. I was in shock Saturday morning. I've never seen anyone killed before, let alone a friend."

"Ah. So Ernst was really a friend, not just a roommate?"

"I thought I explained that. He may have been from Germany, and we hadn't known each other very long, but we had a lot in common. Similar training, similar interests in painting conservation and art history, same attitude about our supervisor . . ." She paused.

"What attitude?" Bernini encouraged her.

Flora fidgeted, clearly regretting her momentary frankness. "Both Ernst and I found Pietro impossible. He expected us all to work hard, but he kept changing his mind about which tasks he wanted completed first. It was confusing—and it made us all very inefficient."

Bernini heard her hesitation and wondered what she was leaving out of her account. "Anything else?"

"Um, well, we both agreed that sometimes Pietro seems to have other things on his mind. His orders to his employees are a bit random, as if he had another agenda."

That was interesting. He changed tack.

"Back to Ernst Mann. Did you spend time with him outside of work?"

"I wasn't dating him, if that's what you mean."

"No, no. I just want to hear how well you knew him, what you might know about him or his background that would help us find his killer."

Flora thought about it. "We chatted at work quite a bit, over coffee and such. And at the apartment, Ernst and I often got home about the same time since we work in the same place. We'd shop for food together on the way home and start preparing dinner because Linda stayed at the library late. She preferred not to return to the University for Foreigners after dark."

"And that gave you and Ernst plenty of time to talk, to get to know each other."

"Yes," said Flora. She pulled a tissue out of her pocket to dab at her eyes. "He was an only child, he told me. His parents were academics. Ernst had wanted to live in Italy since he was a teenager; this job seemed the perfect opportunity."

"And you liked him?" Bernini asked gently, noticing her tears and the way her long eyelashes fanned out over her cheeks.

"I did. He was a really nice guy. Excuse me." She blew her nose.

He asked a few more questions and then closed his notebook. "Thank you, Signorina. That was most helpful."

"Anytime," she said, with the ghost of a smile.

He'd take her up on that, whenever he could. Bernini went away well satisfied.

CHAPTER FOURTEEN

Palio day dawned clear and full of the promise of intense heat. Perfect for a horse race and the sweaty, overexcited throngs that would fill the Piazza del Campo in a few hours.

Flora opened the shutters to fresh, cool air. A sudden rain shower in the middle of the night had forced her to close the shutters, which she hated to do because the apartment became stuffy. She'd moved clothes from her rigged-up clothesline in front of the window and placed a bucket under the ceiling leak. The rain kept her awake for at least an hour, gushing and pouring over the eaves and dripping into the bucket.

Stumbling into the tiny kitchen, she lit the gas and put the coffee pot on. Her grogginess this morning would require at least two cups of coffee before she was functional. Where would she go to watch the Palio now that Ernst Mann was gone? Well, the only thing that made sense was to call Marco Lorenzetti and beg for a place sitting with his family or friends. It might just mollify him after their abortive love scene three days ago.

The time on her cell phone indicated it was too early to call. Marco had told her how he liked to sleep in, when his father didn't roust him out of bed.

Coffee ready, Flora added hot milk and grabbed a pastry. Unable to face the tiny porch from which Ernst had fallen—or been pushed—to his death, she padded downstairs in robe and nightie to their tiny piazza in back of the apartment building. For some reason, hardly anyone else in the building used this spot. Flora found it charming. Brick pavers covered a small, nine-by-twelve-ish surface surrounded by elderly bushes and creeping ivy.

She perched on an ancient, metal chair whose edge bit into her uncushioned behind, inhaled the espresso and milk, and tried to kick her brain into some semblance of wakefulness. What to do first? Biting into the pastry (with yummy toasted almonds and a creamy filling), Flora decided to go first to the lab and pick up the *Burlington Magazine* article in Ernst's desk. Although she remembered the gist of it, she wanted to check a few things. Then, from there, she'd call Marco and beg to be invited to whatever balcony the Lorenzetti family had secured for Palio watching.

Coffee finished, Flora returned to her room and dressed very, very slowly, while her thoughts chased each other around in her head.

Here I am in Siena, Mamma. City of my dreams, except my roommate got pushed off our balcony. Oh, and I am now a suspect in a murder case . . .

Come home this instant! What are you thinking, staying in a job that puts you in danger? Sometimes I think you have no common sense, no sense at all! Get on the next plane out of there! I'll send your father to meet you.

Flora frowned as she pulled on her underwear. No, flying home was the easy way out, running away with nothing solved. Ernst had been a nice guy, a special person in Flora's life. He didn't deserve to get squashed like a bug on a windowsill. She wanted to stay in Siena until she'd found out who pushed him over the balcony—and why.

Could she do that without getting taken out herself?

With that uncomfortable question reverberating in her brain, Flora chose an Indian skirt, cotton gauze and light as a breeze, and a sleeveless white top. Sandals, waist pouch—no purse dangling invitingly from her shoulder today for pickpockets to snatch. Watch, sunglasses, water bottle.

Ready.

Cell phone. She called Marco.

"Hi, Marco . . . yes, I'd like to see you today. You are right, I wasn't myself the other day. Still in shock, I think, from Ernst's death. Hey, do you have a place to watch the Palio from? You do? Can I join you?"

Marco's plan was to visit family friends whose apartment had front-row seats: a balcony right above the Campo. They arranged to meet at nine thirty outside the main lab on Banchi di Sotto Street.

Flora walked briskly around the ring road behind the Campo, Via di Città. She loved Siena at this early-morning hour. Louvered doors ground upward as shopkeepers opened up and laid out their wares. Pastries, tomatoes, daisies, and oleander. Cats slunk around parked cars, foraging for breakfast, and the divine smell of espresso filled the air. And the tourists were gathering, clutching knapsacks and drinks, wearing or waving the colorful scarves of their favorite contrade.

She turned into the courtyard of the State Archives and ran up the stairs. Moments later, she reached into Ernst's desk drawer. Flora rummaged through his pile of articles, looking for the *Burlington Magazine* piece on the Getty kouros.

It wasn't there.

Huh. Had she given it to Captain Rizzo? She squeezed her eyes shut and concentrated. No, she'd put it back in the drawer. Flora looked again. No article. So either the Carabinieri had returned to the lab and taken it—unlikely—or one of the family had removed it.

Beppe or Pietro, she guessed. But why? There was a pile of printouts there, so what made that one special? She couldn't remember. Was there something in there about how false patinas were applied to marble statues? Acid baths . . . Flora needed to look at the article again. She could probably find the article in the library at the University for Foreigners—with a little help from her roommate Linda. Tomorrow, after the Palio madness was over.

Flora glanced at her watch. Time to meet Marco.

She closed up the lab and stepped outside. There he was, at the foot of the stairs, looking up at her with a hopeful expression.

Joining him, she slipped her hand in his. That was the right thing to do; his expression altered to a delighted grin.

"*Cara* Flora, have you had breakfast?"

"A little one. But I am hungry again."

He laughed. "You are always hungry! We will go to the balcony of my friends, the Leones, and they will have a wonderful spread. A brunch, is that what you call it? Pastries, coffee, egg and tomato pie, everything. Sound okay?"

"Lead the way!" said Flora.

The main entrance to the Campo was open, but the piazza was transformed. The center was reserved for standing spectators while the outer rim, with two sharp corners, was set off for the horses. Barriers stood ready to keep people off the sand-covered racetrack at the crucial time. Above the track, people gathered on decorated balconies, arranging chairs and snacks for the lucky few who would be able to sit down during the parade and race.

Flora and Marco stopped to watch the beginning of the parade. All of Siena's contrade—the Snail, the Sea Shell, the Wolf, and all the others—threw their flags and strutted, dressed in medieval finery. The men wore short pants, capes, and tunics, and some wore hats that looked like curled sausages or pancakes. The costumes sported two or three brilliant colors, matched by the performers' tights and flags. Each group competed in pageantry and flag tossing, creating a sea of moving, brilliant color. Flora noticed that some of the male faces—especially those framed with long hair—looked exactly like the men in early paintings in the Palazzo Pubblico museum.

Flora shivered. This was her favorite part. The race itself scared her—it was so brief and so violent. Someone always got hurt, and the crowd behaved like a large, out-of-control animal, hungry for blood.

Marco pulled her along the south side of the Campo and then up a flight of stairs into one of the apartments above the restaurant where they had dined on Sunday. Introductions were made, and Flora was invited to a ringside seat on the balcony and handed a large coffee with milk.

"Marco, *caro*, where are your brothers? Are they joining us?"

"In a little while, they will be along." The family and friends clustered together, standing closer to each other than Americans would. Native Italians had a different idea of what constituted personal space than Americans did; Flora often found herself stepping back.

"Look! The parade is ending. They are getting ready for the main event."

The Leone family crowded out on the balcony, carrying Flora along with them. Marco touched her arm.

"See, Flora? There is our contrada: Giraffa." He took the opportunity to drape an arm around Flora's shoulder.

Flora let the arm stay put—there was scarcely room to move, let alone shove Marco away. "Do you mean the guys with the white tights and red tunics? And the flag that looks like red flames on a white background?"

"Yes. That's the one. It is the traditional painters' contrada, from long ago."

"I didn't know that! So your family, the Lorenzettis, have always been part of Giraffa?"

"Always. You know the story of the miracle of the Virgin?" Marco asked.

"No, tell me." She edged a little away from him, trying to reclaim a body's width between them.

"In the 1500s, the image of the *Madonna di Provenzano* was found in a house in the Contrada della Giraffa part of the city, and that is where their church is built. I will take you to see it, after the race."

"That would be lovely—"

Pietro Lorenzetti's harsh voice interrupted her. "Marco, there you are. Come inside, we need to talk." Pietro acted as if Flora were not there at all.

"Oh, Pietro, can't it wait? We are just watching the parade; the race is about to start."

"There's fifteen minutes yet, you fool. There is always a delay. No, it must be now."

Marco followed Pietro just inside the shutters, while Flora watched the crowd. She heard Pietro's voice rising and falling.

". . . you are such a bone-headed idiot!"

"I am not! I have done nothing wrong!"

"You take unnecessary chances! You shouldn't have brought her . . ."

Pietro was giving his younger brother a hard time, and it sounded like the subject of the disagreement included Flora. Why? So far what she and Marco had was a flirtation, nothing more. Did Pietro find her threatening for some reason? Flora stood up and let Signora Leone take her chair so she could take a new position closer to the two men. She slipped into the narrow space between the balcony railing and the open shutter.

"You can tell me what to do at work—sometimes. But stay out of my private life, Pietro!"

"You watch yourself, little brother! And don't lose your head over an employee—a half-foreign one at that. She is too curious, that one, and her Italian is too good . . ."

"Flora is okay, she won't be a problem . . ."

"She already is a problem!"

So they *were* arguing about her! Too bad she had not been able to hide her nosiness from Pietro. She'd have to be more careful if she wanted to infiltrate the family.

The flag tossers, drummers, and trumpeters exited the piazza. The Palio officials took their places and the crowd pressed up against the barriers, jostling for the best view. Flora saw minor fistfights breaking out and was glad she was safely up above. Every banner-draped balcony around the famous piazza was jammed full of people.

The horses, some dancing sideways, entered the arena. The jockeys, all looking tiny from above, rode proudly up to the starting line. Flora wondered if any of the animals or jockeys took performance-enhancing drugs. She wouldn't be surprised.

Heat rose around her, whether from the actual warmth of the day or the rising adrenaline of the crowd, she wasn't sure. She felt a quiver of anticipation along her spine, and her breath snagged in her throat.

The rope dropped, the horses surged forward, and the crowd responded with yells and shoving. Flora pitied the people standing against the restraining wall; they were surely getting squashed from behind. The horses raced in clumps, crowding the track around the Campo. She held her breath as they approached the first tight corner, which someone had padded with mattresses.

Two horses collided and one jockey flew into the air. He landed in a cloud of dust while his horse galloped merrily on without him. Immediately, two little men with a stretcher whisked across the track to pick up the injured man. He wasn't moving. Knocked out cold, probably. Oh no, wasn't that blood running down the front of his tunic?

Around her, Marco's friends yelled and gesticulated, their attention entirely focused on the two lead horses.

"It's Nico! It's Nico!" shouted the daughter, a dark beauty of nineteen or so. She pointed at the horse wearing the red and white colors.

Marco tightened his grip on Flora's arm. "Giraffa! Giraffa!"

The Giraffa horse was neck and neck with the Lupa—Contrada of the She-Wolf—contender. Captured by the intense emotions around her, Flora stood up and yelled with everyone else.

Then, at the last corner, the Lupa jockey did something that caused the Giraffa horse to jerk. Treachery! The crowd roared as the Lupa horse took the lead over the finish line. From where they stood, it looked like the Lupa horse won by less than a horse's length.

Shouts of outrage drowned the loudspeaker's announcement of the Lupa victory. "Those filthy *Lupaioli*! They won't get away with this!" Marco yelled. He grabbed Flora's hand and pulled her toward the door into the apartment.

"Giraffa! Giraffa!" cried the Leones and their guests as they all rushed down the stairs and outside into the piazza.

Instantly, the heaving and shouting crowd broke Marco's hold on her wrist. Flora found herself alone in a scrum that surged back and forth as the furious Giraffini laid into the Lupaioli. Grown men wailed and wept, and girls grabbed onto their boyfriends and brothers, trying to restrain them. One strapping young woman joined the fistfight, throwing punches right and left.

Someone mashed Flora up against a doorjamb and knocked the wind out of her.

As soon as she could breathe again, Flora ducked into a narrow alley and ran. Fear gave her a speed no high school track coach had ever seen. Marco had failed to keep her safe, and she sure didn't want to meet the rest of his contrada while their blood lust was raging.

She took shelter in the entrance of a small church, gasping and shivering as reaction set in. Flora really hated crowds. She'd thought European soccer fans were the worst, but the rage and grief of the losing contrada exceeded anything she'd seen before.

The hem of Flora's skirt was torn and a graze on her elbow dripped blood. The smell of her own acrid sweat filled her nostrils. But she was intact, which was better than that poor jockey who'd been thrown at the first corner. Was he even still alive? She really didn't want to know.

Then shouts and cheers filled the air as the victorious Lupa contrada and their supporters came into the tiny piazza where Flora rested. To her astonishment, the crowd came straight toward her, and she realized she was in the heart of Lupa territory. The chapel behind her opened, and happy men, women, and children bore the winning jockey inside for a blessing. The horse came in for a blessing too, and no one thought there was anything odd about seeing a horse in front of the altar.

Flora stayed outside, waiting for her chest to stop heaving and her legs to cease quivering.

Suddenly someone grabbed her left arm.

"Flora Garibaldi! Why are you always where you shouldn't be?" Pietro glared at her and tightened his grip on her arm.

"Let go of me, you big bully!" She was getting awfully tired of having her arm grabbed by Lorenzetti men. "I have a perfect right to be anywhere in the city I wish to be. And your precious brother and family did nothing back there to protect me from that murderous crowd. I came here to get out of the way."

"A likely story. Maybe you have another boyfriend, a Lupa? Just to shame us!"

"Don't be ridiculous!" Flora succeeded in detaching her arm and shoved her face close to his. "Stop trying to boss me around! I am an employee of your father's, not your personal property!"

Pietro snarled. "You are a nosy little foreigner, a lousy American, with designs on my brother!"

Flora lost her temper. "Pietro, you don't know what you're talking about! For the record, I am half Italian, and I have relatives in Firenze. Secondly, Marco has designs on me, not the other way around. Mind your own business!" She stalked out of his reach and took a side street away from the celebrations.

The heck with the Lorenzetti family. Flora was going home.

CHAPTER FIFTEEN

Flora asked Linda the next morning about access to the art history library at the Università per Stranieri. Linda spent many hours there as an art history exchange student. Flora understood completely; she had majored in art history as an undergraduate before she got her conservation training. She knew just how much time staring at objects and images and learning languages was required to succeed in the field.

"Sure," Linda said. "Do you want to come with me now? And can we stop by your lab since it's right on the way? I've always wanted to see that setup." Her expression changed. "And I really want to see where Ernst worked."

Flora agreed somewhat reluctantly. Hiding her own feelings about Ernst was hard enough without Linda's probing into his life and work. The very mention of Ernst caused an ache below her sternum.

They left the apartment about nine thirty and clattered down the stairs. Sunshine and the garlicky aroma of *pizza bianca* greeted them as they passed the corner pizzeria. Flora waved at the young woman laying out the day's *panino* offerings in the window.

"I'm hungry," complained Linda.

"You should eat breakfast."

"Can't, I'm dieting." Linda patted her nonexistent tummy.

"Don't you know that skipping breakfast just makes you eat more later in the day?"

Linda tossed her hair. "Says who?"

"My mother."

Ironic you giving diet advice! You eat like a starving puppy! Flora's mother spoke in her head.

They entered the courtyard in front of the State Archives.

Linda chattered away as Flora wrestled with the heavy door at the top of the stairs. "Wow! This is massive! Could be the door to a prison or something."

"The building was a palace, once. I forget how old it is."

"You work here? Oh, my!" Linda spoke as she caught her first glimpse of the stacks of moldering manuscripts in the front room. "This is either an incredible treasure-trove or a pile of junk!"

"Probably both. I don't think anyone's sorted it in at least fifty years. And if you did try, you'd die coughing."

Linda emitted ooohs and ahs as she reached the miniature biccherne. "Flora, I didn't know these were here! Why, we had some of these book covers in a lecture only last month. These are astounding."

Flora watched in some amusement as Linda morphed from her occasionally ditzy persona to focused scholar. Linda might act like a Southern belle when men clustered around her, but she was no dummy when it came to things that really interested her.

They paused in front of a 1471 miniature painting of *La Sapienza Emanata da Dia.*

"Female wisdom coming from God," translated Linda in a matter-of-fact voice. "Look at that exquisite painting . . . and the colors!" She spread her arms. "I'd like to take the entire collection home with me!"

Flora laughed. "You know I can't let you do that!"

Linda moved on to another painting of a king seated with several women, called *Il Buon Governo.*

" 'The Good Government,' right, Flora?"

"Yes, that's it." Flora pointed at the label. "Look: that painter, Ambrogio Lorenzetti, was the one who used to be head of the Lorenzetti clan. The entire family belongs to the Giraffa contrada of painters." She stared at the amazingly detailed garments of the Sienese counselors below the king.

"I could spend hours in here, but I'd really like to see the lab. Lead on!" said Linda.

Flora hesitated. "I shouldn't even bring you in here when the guards are off duty. And I can't show you where Ernst worked unless the Lorenzettis are out."

Linda turned and stared at Flora. "Why ever not? That sounds odd. After all, you are a trusted employee—and this is your workplace. I suppose it's because you're restoring valuable paintings?"

"Partly that. Look, let me check and see who's here. I'd like your impressions of the place." Flora left Linda mesmerized by a miniature painting of St. Michael and a very peculiar-looking dragon.

She unlocked the inner door and walked the length of the lab. Near the inner door, she listened and heard nothing. Sure enough, no Lorenzettis had arrived. Too early for them; they preferred to start work late and linger into the evening.

Flora returned to the biccherne room to fetch Linda. "Coast is clear, come on."

Linda enjoyed the tour, even if she did get teary-eyed and sentimental when they reached Ernst's desk. "Oh, I am so sad that he's gone! I sure hope the police around here are competent; I want to see whoever killed Ernst locked up forever."

Oh, they're competent all right. And they might end up arresting one of us or the family.

By the time they'd reached the shipping room, Linda had pulled herself together.

"Flora, you said the atmosphere in this lab was 'weird.' Want to elaborate?"

Flora leaned against a storage cabinet and crossed her arms. "Most of the time, it's okay. Then it gets tense, for no particular reason. And the Lorenzettis keep such odd hours . . . you can't help wondering where they go and what they do when they're not here. I don't know anything specific. I just have the feeling that I'm not really accepted or trusted, like they have an unwritten policy of keeping employees ignorant and separate from the heart of the business."

"Well, you've only been there a few weeks."

"Yes, but . . . I expected to be more a part of things because of my credentials. You know, if I showed willingness to work hard and learn that they'd let me do more sooner." Flora dropped her arms. "The family has separate laboratories at the house, but I got the impression that's for weekend and after-hours work, not weekdays."

"It does sound like an odd setup," Linda said.

"It is. Can we go to the university library now?"

"Sure thing. I'll take you inside, introduce you to a couple of the most helpful clerks, and then abandon you to your esoteric research on Greek sculpture."

CHAPTER SIXTEEN

Flora left work early. She strolled home along side streets, off the Campo, enjoying the bustle of late afternoon shopping. Women called to each other as they collected fresh vegetables and meat for the evening meal; people fell into conversations with local merchants who just might be family members. She passed a tiny piazza full of pigeons, who congregated around her sandals in case she had bread crumbs. Flora remembered standing still near San Marco in Venice, where pigeons would alight on the shoulders and arms of willing tourists, posing for pictures.

The little Madonna was coming along nicely. Since the painting was dry enough, she'd taken the painting with her to work on in the apartment. Yesterday, Flora had reluctantly entered Ernst's room for something other than basil from the porch: to eyeball the room as a second painting studio. As sad as being near his uncollected things made her, she couldn't help noticing that the lighting was perfect. She cleared his desk near the north window, carefully stacking his things on a nearby shelf.

She let herself into the apartment, dumped her keys on the little table near the door, and crossed to the kitchen to make some coffee. While it brewed, she entered Ernst's room, opened the shutters, and sighed. It seemed so wrong that he wasn't here, chatting with her as he watered the plants on the balcony or chopped vegetables for their evening meal in the kitchen.

Her little coffee pot bubbled and she hurried to turn off the burner before the hot coffee spewed out of the top. With her canvas bag in one hand and a steaming mug in the other, Flora returned to Ernst's desk and laid out her tools and the little Madonna canvas. She felt like Ernst was there, leaning over her shoulder, egging her on . . .

She'd just uncapped her tubes of paint and started mixing a rich brown when the doorbell rang. Who could it be at this hour? One of the Lorenzettis usually came in the morning, if they came at all, to check on the apartment or make minor repairs. Linda was still at work. They didn't know their neighbors very well.

Flora opened the front door. Her heart plummeted when she saw a middle-aged couple. European, but not Italian. The man with iron gray hair that curled in a way Flora recognized and the woman with a resigned expression on her face. She was not surprised when they introduced themselves as Mr. and Mrs. Mann from Munich. Ernst's parents.

"May we come in?" asked the father, who had Ernst's eyes.

Blessing the high school teacher who'd made her take German for two years, Flora answered, "Of course."

Ernst's mother moved tentatively, as if her whole body hurt. Flora guessed that grief had slowed her down. She was slender and looked fit enough, but her face was so sad.

"The police sent us here, after we picked up Ernst's wallet, cell phone, and laptop at the Questura. We wanted to see where he lived and pick up his . . . more personal things," she said with a little smile.

"I understand," Flora said. "Why don't you put down your bags and come into Ernst's room. I am using his desk right now to work on a painting. His room had the best light." She felt a little embarrassed, as if she'd been caught trespassing.

They followed her and stood still in the middle of the bedroom, taking in all the details of the unmade bed, books strewn on the floor, a German newspaper crumpled on a nearby chair.

"Ernst was never very tidy," said his mother. Her eyes filled with tears.

Mr. Mann showed interest in her painting. "You too are a conservator?"

"Yes. I have similar training to Ernst's, but not as much chemistry. We both worked at the Restauro Lorenzetti. He was so helpful to me, such a good colleague."

He sent her a keen glance. "Do you have any ideas who might have pushed him off that balcony?"

His wife sat down on the bed and fingered a discarded shirt with shaking hands.

"No, I don't. I was at work at the time. Many of us worked on Saturday mornings, just to catch up. The Restauro was awfully busy, had lots of clients." Flora hoped Ernst's parents didn't think she'd had anything to do with it.

Mr. Mann's mouth drooped, but he nodded at her. "He told us he had two good housemates, that you all got along. The other girl . . . Linda . . . is not here?"

"She's still at school. She's a graduate student at one of Siena's universities."

Mrs. Mann spoke. "Do you have any plastic bags, or maybe a box, for Ernst's things?"

"I'm sure we do. Let me look." Flora fled from the room, wanting to escape their devastated faces for a moment. In the kitchen, she grabbed a handful of plastic bags from the box near the stove and returned to help them pack.

The parents chose only a few items, a book or two that Ernst had dog-eared and clearly read multiple times, a couple of sweaters in good condition, small personal items such as his watch. So many young people used just cell phones these days to tell time, but Ernst loved his watch. Flora had noticed Ernst's silver-and-gold watch many times when he checked it to see if it was lunchtime yet, or shoved it up his arm when he painted. She guessed it had been a present from his parents, because Mr. Mann wore one just like it.

The Manns prepared to leave, consolidating their bags into two that could be easily carried. Mrs. Mann asked, "Were you and Ernst good friends?" The hopeful look in her blue eyes said she really wanted to know.

"Yes," said Flora gently. "We were friends. We had so many good conversations, and we cooked meals together. Your son was a wonderful man."

"You will write to us if you learn anything from the police?" Mr. Mann handed over a scrap of paper with his email address.

"Of course."

Their departure left Flora shaken and sad. How awful to lose a child, especially an only son. The wrong order of life events. She had lost relatives, even a friend or two through car crashes or ski accidents, but the bowed-down posture of these parents sobered her. They will never recover, she thought.

As Flora reheated her coffee in the tiny microwave, a renewed surge of resolve came over her. If the police can't discover who murdered Ernst, maybe I can. I knew Ernst as well as anyone. Surely, if I look hard enough, I can find a motive.

CHAPTER SEVENTEEN

Flora found her workplace empty without Ernst, especially after the distressing visit of his German parents. She was so used to Ernst strolling around, sipping coffee, stopping to chat every now and then. Not that he wasn't a hard worker, far from it. Ernst had been especially dedicated to his work, determined to do every project with precision and expertise. In between bouts of work, he paced the long corridor between their workplaces when he needed a break from the painstaking restoration, leaning over a painting and in-filling tiny areas, or when he was problem solving.

"Flora, what do you think?" he'd say. "I've made two mixtures of green on my palette; come and see which you think is the better match for this bit of landscape."

She sighed. Mourning Ernst wasn't going to catch his murderer. What could she do, besides keep her eyes and ears open to everything around her? She and the police had both looked in Ernst's desk at the Restauro, and the scene-of-crime police had gone over the apartment, presumably collecting fingerprints and any physical evidence to be had. Flora didn't know for sure what they had touched, because she'd been out in the street talking to Rizzo and Bernini at the time.

While she sipped her coffee, Flora pondered how she could help the police find the murderer. She made a list of every person she'd seen with Ernst since she'd arrived in Siena. Except for an electrician who'd come to the apartment during

Flora's first two weeks, everyone on the list was either a Lorenzetti, an employee of the Restauro, or a neighbor. Not helpful; her list was the same as the police's. The neighbors were just acquaintances, people the three roommates passed at the mailboxes or in the elevator. None could have any motive to push Ernst Mann off a balcony. And none of them had a key.

She couldn't remember any party at the apartment either. Ernst, Linda, and Flora tended to socialize in cafés and bars around the Campo, along with a good portion of the Sienese. Between Ernst's and Flora's overtime and Linda's schoolwork, the off hours of the three roommates rarely intersected. The three of them didn't socialize together as Flora would have preferred.

Flora refilled her mug with fresh coffee, stuffed the list in her purse, and began her morning's work. She was grateful to be almost past the scut work—mixing gesso and applying gold leaf to picture frames. Since Beppe had given her the copying assignment, she'd moved between gesso mixing, painting the second Madonna, and cleaning yellowed varnish off old paintings. That meant applying Q-tips soaked with the brain cell–destroying solvent, toluene, and sitting under the fume hood. That would be tedious and smelly work, but at least it meant actually touching the painting instead of only the frame. Maybe in a week or two, the family would allow her to do the delicate in-painting of restorations, matching original colors and brushstrokes—exactly what the course in Florence had taught her only a few months ago. She supposed she should be glad that she was advancing faster than Costanza and Graziano at the other end of the lab. The other man, Stefano, had already been promoted to actual painting.

Sun poured in through one of the high windows, increasing Flora's desire to be outside walking in the early morning freshness. A lower window, cracked to allow some air into the studio, wafted sound and smells into her workspace: catcalls of work-men, grinding of gears as large vehicles slowed in the narrow streets, the clang of a garbage can, the meowing of a hungry cat. Espresso, newly steamed and fragrant, mixed with street odors of diesel while the mildew from stacks of slightly damp manuscripts in the neighboring room tickled her nose.

Flora put down her paintbrush and rubbed her temples. There was one more picture frame with gesso to prepare, and she couldn't avoid it any longer. She collected the ingredients, poured some water into a plastic cup, and concentrated on making the pseudo-plaster the right consistency, somewhere between Greek-style yogurt and toothpaste. It must be spread-able on tiny sections of relief, the curlicues and floral elements of elaborate gold frames that had suffered damage over time. Usually she did several applications, building up layers that were allowed to stiffen and dry. Then she scraped off excess gesso with a scalpel, sanded the pseudo-plaster additions with at least two grades of sandpaper, and covered them with micro-thin layers of gold leaf.

An hour later, a thought came out of nowhere. Even if she couldn't identify anything sinister about the people Ernst had known, Flora did have something to investigate.

What had Ernst been about to tell her the day he was killed? What had he meant when he said, "The other day I saw . . ."?

He'd been talking about Pietro, his lack of focus, and his family's business methods. She could ask questions of the other employees. But which ones, and what, exactly? And if the Loren-zetti family was doing something illegal, how could Flora figure out which employees were "in the know" and who were in-nocent? Costanza, she was pretty sure, was fully in the family's confidence; Flora could not risk asking her, "Hey, Costanza. Have you noticed any illegal activities at the lab lately? Such as suspicious shipments going in and out, or some fancy accounting to hide additional income?" No, Flora would have to leave that kind of questioning to Bernini and his colleagues or risk putting herself in harm's way.

What else around here seemed off kilter? There was Marco's peculiar behavior when he'd snatched the photographs of Greek statues out of Flora's hands. Ernst's *Burlington Magazine* article on the Getty kouros in California . . . were all these things connected?

Flora reviewed everything she knew about archaic Greek marble sculpture, especially Archaic Period kouroi. That would hardly occupy her all morning; what she remembered from one college course could probably be summed up in a few pages. Let's see: not very many statues had survived antiquity; fewer than twenty were intact. The rest were in pieces, distributed across three continents and at least twenty museums. The British, the French, and the Germans had excelled in collecting Greek and Roman artifacts before the countries of origin established any laws prohibiting such removals. Lord Elgin—he was the guy who looted not only the Parthenon friezes and *metopes* from the Acropolis of Athens, but also some rare sculptures from Turkey.

Behind her, through the wall, she heard one of the Lorenzettis bang a file drawer shut. Beppe? His wife? The ever-obnoxious Pietro? Flora didn't always know who was there since there was another entrance at the rear of the building. Beppe only came through the front door when he wanted to check up on his employees. Then he'd pass though the inner door to his office.

Back to kouroi. The pictures she'd seen in the library showed a wild mixture of styles, from flat and skinny young men, still blocky and poorly detailed, to realistic athletic men with robust, rippled abs and rounded thigh muscles. Marco's statue looked somewhat like the Getty kouros, but also like half a dozen other examples she'd found in sculpture books and recent journals.

What if Marco's statue was based upon an original that had been illegally excavated? One that nobody in the art market had ever seen before, because it has been recently pulled out of the ground?

Flora chose a new piece of 600-grit sandpaper, the finest grade. While she sanded the corner of the frame she was repairing, she thought about Marco's work. He obviously cared about getting the details right—hence the pile of printouts and photos she'd glimpsed but not been allowed to examine. The real question was the intent of the sculpture: was it destined for a museum shop as a replica of an ancient work? Or were the Lorenzettis planning to sell it as an original, which would make it an illegal forgery? It would be interesting to hear what Marco said when she asked him if they had a buyer lined up. But she must be very careful and act as if she believed the family business was totally legitimate. Never mind how much money a good forgery would bring into the family business . . . or how crazy it would be if the Lorenzetti family dabbled in more than one kind of forgery at a time.

A burst of Italian alerted her that at least two people were in the family office, only a few feet behind her. She'd have thought the walls in such an old building would be thicker, but maybe there was some kind of ventilation grill behind her bookcases that let sound through.

She halted mid-sanding and listened.

"So, the American girl visited our home lab the other day?"

"Marco, that fool, took her there. Showing off his prowess as a sculptor. And so he must have taken her around the studios, shown her the storerooms . . ."

Two male voices, she thought. But the sound waxed and waned, like a cell phone with erratic reception. Probably they were moving around the office.

". . . hardly a problem . . . there was nothing to see . . ."

". . . you can't be sure! There's always a next time . . . he really must listen to reason about that girl . . ."

"*A next time* . . ." So they weren't worried about her suitability for their precious Marco at all! They sounded more concerned with what she might have seen in the family laboratories. Maybe the original of the sculpture Marco was copying? That was an interesting thought. If she could prove the presence—however briefly—of an original antiquity in the laboratory, that would give credence to the trafficking in illegal antiquities as one of the Lorenzetti family's extra activities.

And where was that statue right now?

She stood up and moved closer to the wall, but the voices faded again.

Her cell phone rang. Flora scrambled to pull it out of her tight pocket.

"*Pronto.*"

"Signorina Garibaldi?" asked a hesitant male voice.

Flora smiled. "Sottotenente Bernini. What can I do for you?"

"I have a few more questions for you. And, um, I'd like to ask you a favor. Can you take a coffee break, or maybe lunch, in the next hour?"

Surprised that Bernini wanted to meet her outside of work, Flora glanced at her watch. Almost eleven thirty. That was way too early for an Italian lunch, but perfect time for coffee. And she could go outside and get away from this stuffy place for half an hour!

"I can stop for coffee anytime. Is the Bavaria bar on the Campo okay for you? In about fifteen minutes?"

"That is perfect. See you." He rang off.

Flora closed her flip phone and slipped it back into the outer pocket of her shoulder bag. Another interview? Surely, they'd covered all the important aspects of Ernst's murder. Something he'd forgotten? Or something she'd forgotten to tell him?

Or maybe the young policeman had another agenda.

CHAPTER EIGHTEEN

Vittorio Bernini crossed the Campo to the bar Flora had chosen. It boasted a facade built of tawny tufa blocks and a green-and-white marble door frame. The upscale café and restaurant was perched in a prime people-watching location. Sooner or later, everyone passed by the Birreria Bavaria. Those who could afford the high prices stopped in for a Cinzano or an espresso.

Bernini chose a chrome-edged table near the back, away from the bustling bar. He wanted Miss Garibaldi to feel comfortable, relaxed, and chatty. That might be difficult; Flora had displayed some wariness of him as a policeman who was investigating the murder of a close friend. But what did she think of him as a man?

Don't be ridiculous, he chided himself. *She's hardly had time to think of me as anything except a nuisance! Give her some time.*

Now he watched her approach, stepping delicately across the cobblestones like an artist using a tiny brush to add the last highlight to the last flower on a finished painting. She wasn't tall and thin like a model, but she had all the right stuff in a petite and beautifully proportioned form. All that, plus wavy reddish-brown hair, a delicate nose, luminous dark eyes . . . and a sweet alto voice that snuck right under his guard. Bernini stood to pull out a chair for her, thinking as he did so that he was in danger of losing his objectivity.

"Thanks for coming," he said. "Espresso all right, or would

you like something else?"

"Espresso is fine," she said, eyeing him carefully. She placed her heavy purse between her toes on the cobblestones, disturbing a pigeon with designs on the crumbs left by a previous patron.

Bernini waited until the coffee had arrived. Flora added two sugars and stirred, releasing her spoon with a clatter.

"Miss Garibaldi . . ."

"You may as well call me Flora."

"Then you should call me Vittorio. That is, except when my boss is around."

She chuckled. "I get it. Then, you are always Sottotenente Bernini."

That chuckle made Bernini's heart skip. "Yes, that's right . . . Flora."

Her eyes danced. "Well, Vittorio, what did you want to ask me?"

Bernini grinned. "First of all, have you noticed any unusual activities at either the State Archives laboratory or the Lorenzetti home studio?"

"What do you mean, 'unusual'?"

"Anything out of place, anything that indicates a member of the family is dabbling in ways of making money other than restoring paintings."

"Ah." Flora sipped her coffee and then put the cup down. "Funny you should ask that. I have been wondering if what I've seen is normal or something I should report to you . . ."

"And?"

She leaned forward. "Nothing unusual at the State Archives, except what I already told Captain Rizzo about access to the accounting rooms being restricted and the way the family manages keys. What struck me as odd was the way Marco behaved when he took me to his sculpture studio." Flora described what

had happened, including the kiss that she'd felt was half normal
lechery and half obstruction, a way to keep her from studying
the kouros photographs.

Bernini took a few notes. He looked at her directly. "And
what do you think he might be trying to hide?"

"I have very little to go on," admitted Flora. "But I did
wonder if the family has, or had, an original Greek statue in the
laboratory that Marco is copying. Apparently, his cousin in
Chiusi began the statue, but then he died in a motorcycle accident. What if both the sculpture project and the photographs
of the original statue passed on to Marco?"

"Did you see the original ancient statue?"

"No. Just the photographs. I have no idea where that statue is
now."

"Where the statue is now . . ." echoed Bernini.

They looked at each other. Bernini took a deep breath and
lined up his spoon with his napkin. "Well, that all makes asking
you this favor a little easier. Or at least, I hope so. My boss
thinks his old friend Beppe might be dabbling in the illegal
antiquities market. In fact, we think the Lorenzetti family could
have been smuggling antiquities from Sicily to Switzerland for
years, but there has never been solid proof. We don't usually ask
civilians to help the police, but in your case . . ."

"You want me to spy on the family for you."

"Ah . . . yes. That was what we had in mind. You are ideally
placed to observe the comings and goings of the Lorenzettis,
whom they visit, who visits them—"

Flora interrupted him. "From Sicily? Wouldn't the family
need to have contacts in Rome and other parts of Tuscany to
move things north successfully?"

Bernini relished talking to someone so quick on the uptake.
"Indeed, yes. You can perhaps pick up who these contacts are
by working in the same office. The captain thinks the wall

between your work area and the family office is not very thick—"

"He's right about that. I overheard some chatter today. Two people were talking about me."

"Who?"

"I couldn't be sure; the voices were muffled. I thought at first it was about how unsuitable the 'American girl' is for their precious Marco. Then I realized they were afraid I might have seen something I shouldn't have at the family studios."

"Excellent!" Bernini smiled at her. "Then we're on the right track. At least at the State Archives, the family seems to trust you, and with the additional interest from Marco—"

"I don't think Costanza trusts me. Marco likes me, yes. Or he likes kissing me. I'm not so sure about my own feelings."

This frank statement made Bernini grin. "No?"

"No. He kisses like a leech."

Bernini threw back his head and laughed. "Could you bear to go out with him if you can avoid the leech?"

Flora gave a Mona Lisa–like smile. "I can do that, all in the name of justice. But Marco is a suspect in the murder, isn't he?" She shuddered, presumably at the idea of dating a possible murderer.

"Let's just say Marco's a maybe. If the family *is* involved, we think his older brother or his father is more likely. It could still be someone from the outside."

"I agree with you. Marco doesn't act like a criminal; he's too self-absorbed."

Bernini looked at her. "Don't forget, selfishness and supreme self-confidence are the key characteristics of criminals."

Flora's eyes sparkled. "And of many academics I know!"

Bernini raised his eyebrows. "How is that?"

"Some of my professors have never had a job outside of academia. They've always been tenured faculty. And in American universities, that means they can say and do pretty much what they want without consequences."

"Some of our politicians are like that."

"You can say that again."

A beautiful woman with a touch of cynicism in her makeup. Bernini liked that. "Going back to Marco . . ."

"Marco lives in his own world, but when he comes out of his reveries about sculpture, he's surprisingly considerate. And I don't think he has that much self-confidence. He is the butt of all the family jokes and none of the Lorenzettis think he is on the right track." She slanted her eyes at him. "What about me? Aren't I a suspect?"

"You never were, really," Bernini said. "You lack motive, and one of the neighbors said he saw you leave the apartment that morning while Ernst was smoking a cigarette out on the balcony. You didn't return until lunchtime, so you couldn't have pushed him over the railing."

"Well, I'm *so* glad you don't think I did it! Okay, the Lorenzettis don't like me as a potential daughter-in-law, but they know I'm a hard worker. That I'm very keen to advance in the business . . . unless I discover I'm working for a bunch of murderers." She gulped.

"That goes without saying. If we find something concrete in the way of evidence, you will get out of there, *immediatamente.*"

"Would the Carabinieri help me relocate until I find another job?"

"We'd certainly do whatever is possible."

Flora's smile was a little thin this time. "Okay. I really do want to find out who killed Ernst. And if the family is trafficking in illegal antiquities, I want to know that too. I already have a feeling I'm not going to be in this job for too long."

"But long enough for us to finish this investigation." Bernini knew it would be a juggling act because the local police were more interested in solving the murder, whereas the Carabinieri

Art Squad's objective was to recover stolen works of art and shut down clandestine excavations. But the conflicting aims of the different branches of the police meant the investigation might take a while, and that made his heart glad. He said, "I hope we won't finish too soon."

Her blush told him she understood his meaning. Her downcast eyes focused on her hands for a moment, and then she smiled at him.

"I think I can play up my interest in the restoration business without seeming too nosy about transportation of artworks or outside contacts. What else do I need to do?"

"Make yourself ubiquitous. Offer to run errands. Stay late when you can without raising their suspicions . . ." He outlined more ideas and she listened with flattering attention, while pigeons nibbling on biscotti crumbs gathered around her feet.

Flora drained her coffee. "One thing. Can you protect me if I get into trouble while I'm snooping around? Or going out with The Leech?"

"Yes, if we coordinate our efforts. I can't protect you if you don't let me know where you are or where you're going, though. Shall we trade cell numbers?"

CHAPTER NINETEEN

"Signorina Flora?"

"Yes, this is Flora Garibaldi."

"It's Marco. I would like to know if you will have dinner with me this evening?"

Flora gripped her cell a little harder. This was the second time Marco had asked her for dinner, and she had no excuse ready. In fact, it might be a good idea to say yes.

"Okay. What time?"

They arranged to meet at a posh little restaurant on the north side of the Campo. It was called the *Tre Porcini,* and it had a reputation for some of the best pasta in Tuscany.

Flora went home early to change into a fresh shirt and put on a little makeup. She enjoyed her walk through the streets of Siena with the lights just coming on and the rattle of louvered shop doors being rolled down for the night. Her favorite streetlamps jutted out from brick walls on elaborate metal arms, decorated with scrolls. She tested herself, trying to identify the coats of arms on the oldest building facades.

The inhabitants of the city were out in force, meeting friends and colleagues for drinks and chat, or parading around the Campo in their best see-and-be-seen fashions. Glasses clinking and waiters shouting filled the air, competing with the luscious smells of roasting meat and garlic-laced sauces.

It was only seven thirty. No one would actually eat dinner until at least eight o'clock, but it was good to be early to secure a table. Her rendezvous with Marco was set for 7:45 p.m.

Flora mulled over her recent encounters with Marco as she crossed the Campo, stepping carefully on the uneven pavers in her heeled sandals. First, his obvious interest in further acquaintance at the family lunch on the day of the murder. Second, the visit to his studio where he'd kissed her to stop her from looking at sculpture photos. What was Marco after, exactly? She couldn't read him. On the one hand, he seemed like a classic Italian playboy, ready to put the moves on any plausible young woman. On the other hand, Marco had a ruling passion: his sculpture. Flora suspected that for Marco, carving marble was what he lived for, not chasing girls. She planned to butter Marco up a bit and then ask all sorts of questions about his family. Maybe she could pick up some information that would help Bernini and Captain Rizzo.

She turned a corner onto a tiny side street, brick-paved and slightly sinister with its dim lighting and houses leaning inward across the pavement. A single lantern illuminated the arched entrance to the restaurant, shedding yellow light on the potted plants lurking in the shadow of the old building. Flora ducked her head to pass under the low arch into the dining room.

Marco, looking smug and full of anticipation, sat at a choice table in the middle of the room, facing the door. He stood to greet her with a cheek peck and pulled out her chair with a charming little bow.

"Cara Flora, I am so glad to see you. And so happy you agreed to have dinner with me."

"I'm glad too. But don't get your hopes up that this is going to be a long evening together. I'm exhausted; I need an early night."

Marco's expressive eyes said that wasn't quite what he had in mind. He smiled gently and poured her a glass of *vino rosso* from an open bottle. "You have been working too hard, Flora!

Surely my father is not that strict a boss."

"Not that strict, true, but he's not my taskmaster. Pietro is! He keeps piling on extra assignments. And he is not clear about which ones he wants finished first, and—"

"Basta!" Marco laughed and held up one hand to stop her flow. "I know my brother's methods, believe me! He drives me crazy in exactly the same way. Pietro was a bully when we were young; it started with him swiping a bicycle I got for Christmas one year."

Flora grinned. "So, is your father a bully too?"

"Not like Pietro. Papa is much more *simpatico*. He likes to avoid trouble in the family, especially with my mother. No one likes to make Gia mad."

Flora stored up these tidbits about family dynamics to tell Bernini. She eyed Marco's handsome face, alight with sincerity and warmth. She relaxed a little and sipped some wine. The waiter brought a tray of antipasti—marinated peppers and mushrooms studded with olives—and a crusty Tuscan bread, still warm from the oven. Suddenly ravenous, she picked up her fork and speared an olive. "Yum. These are delicious."

"Now, have you decided on your pasta? I recommend the *arrabbiata* or the *carbonara*."

"Neither. I want *tortellini alla panna con funghi*."

"You're not on a diet if you eat cream! How refreshing."

Flora smiled at him. "I am always on a diet, and I am always breaking it. I can't resist cream sauces or chocolate. Or red wine." She took another sip and admired the rich red color through her glass.

"You are slender; you don't need to worry. Now, my sister-in-law is always complaining, and truth to tell, she is getting a little plump."

Flora chose this as the perfect opening to ask more questions about Marco's family. She leaned forward and said, "I know

121

about your immediate family, but not your uncles and cousins. You told me there's a cousin in Chiusi?"

"Yes, that's Raffaelo. He is a sculptor like me—"

"On your father's side of the family, right?"

"Yes. My uncle Stefano is Beppe's brother and father to Raffaelo. And then there's my uncle Niccolò in Orvieto and Fabio in Roma. Fabio's son Luigi works for us in packing and shipping."

Flora found this confusing. She asked Marco to draw a family tree for her.

"Here," he said, pulling a pen out of his shirt pocket and drawing on his napkin. "Grandpa Pietro had four sons: Beppe, Fabio, Stefano, and Niccolò. Beppe has three children, as you know. Fabio has a daughter, Paola, in addition to son Luigi. Raffaelo and Carlo are the sons of Stefano, and Niccolò has no children."

"Thanks. A little diagram always helps me see relationships more clearly. What does uncle Fabio in Roma do?"

"Oh, he owns an antiques shop in the center. Near the Pantheon."

Antiques shop! Aha! Now she must tread carefully and not show too much interest.

"And the other uncle, Niccolò? In Orvieto?"

"Niccolò runs a restaurant for tourists. He charges much money." Marco grinned.

"I know a little bit about your father's family, how they've always been famous painters. What about your mother's family?" Flora kept her gaze fixed on Marco's face.

"Oh, she was a Brunetti before she married Papà. A farming family in Vescovado di Murlo. Mamma does her best to ignore her origins. She's always going on about how the Lorenzettis were rich in the past, how rich and important we will be in the future. I am so sick of it."

"Doesn't she realize there's more than one kind of success?" prompted Flora.

"Oh, I think so. But mine is to become the best sculptor I can be. That kind of success won't be measured in euros. If I make it, my success will be in the form of excellent reviews from art critics and gallery owners. Maybe someday my work will be in an art museum." Marco sighed.

Flora found this information illuminating. So that was why Gia acted so important! She'd been born into a poor, struggling family. She'd advanced in the world only when she married a Lorenzetti. Gia worked hard to promote her status as Beppe's wife and her role in the family business . . . and Marco was a true artist, obsessed with his medium and his ambitions.

Their pasta dishes arrived. Flora turned the conversation back to Marco's sculpture until the bottom of her plate shone and the last lick of cream sauce disappeared. The waiters served plates of arugula and tomato salad with a balsamic dressing.

"Marco, I am going to Rome soon. I must buy presents for my family, especially for my mother's birthday. Does your uncle sell Greek vases, you know, the little replicas for tourists?"

"Oh, yes, certainly. He has many vases, and some statues too. But maybe you cannot mail a statue?" He chuckled. "There are some original Roman lamps as well . . . perhaps she would like one of those?"

Flora pushed her wine napkin over toward Marco. "Write the address for me, would you? It sounds like just the sort of place I should visit." And where there were original Roman artifacts, there might well be other antiquities—valuable ones. Stolen ones?

As Marco scribbled the address on the paper napkin, Flora chattered on about her mother's fictitious collection of small antiquities and how she, Flora, always took something home to add to the mantelpiece. "Last year, in Israel, I bought her a tiny

Dead Sea Scrolls jar. It was correct in every detail, and even had a fake scroll inside. She loved it."

The address napkin secured in her purse, Flora concentrated on being charming and attentive without outright flirtation—a delicate balance, so open to misinterpretation. Marco lapped it up, and his smile broadened as his hands drew pictures in the air of his next sculpture. She resigned herself to a sticky embrace when he walked her home.

". . . a new finish for my sculpture, to make it look really old. See, first you bury the marble in cow manure . . ."

Flora realized she'd not been paying attention. "Wait, Marco, go back a bit. What finish for your sculpture? I don't understand."

His expression showed skepticism. "You are an art historian, of course you understand 'patina.' We adjust the surface with different processes to mimic aging. It is done all the time, on paintings, on marble, on metal figurines."

She gulped. "Ah . . . you mean your client wants it to look ancient?"

"Of course. He has a garden, designed like a Roman villa from about 100 A.D. He wants sculpture in it that looks as if it had been made back then. So, I scrub the surface with a weak acid and then bury it in manure for a month or two to acquire the staining of antiquity."

"Acid and then manure." Flora's mind churned feverishly. The process he described sounded so much like the article she'd read in the university library about how the Getty kouros could have been faked. Did Marco's client know he was buying a modern replica, altered to make it look ancient, or was Marco feeding her a line? What if it was a deliberate forgery sold as an original—for much more money? And how could she possibly find out?

During the main course of veal and vegetables, Flora tried a few more tentative questions, but Marco was much more interested in hearing about her family back in Chicago. Or so it seemed.

So far, so good. The date was going well and she felt no fear of her companion. She couldn't see him as the murderer—he had no subtlety in his makeup. Marco's attitude toward Flora was warm and mildly lecherous, like a slightly stupid satyr. He clearly found his life as an artist absorbing and easy, except when he clashed with his brother or father. Then he acted like a small boy, wheedling and making excuses. But the occasional gleam of shrewdness in his eyes gave Flora pause. Was he really the pushover he appeared to be? What if Marco turned out to be a really good actor? He might be planning to repeat their entire conversation to his family.

She rather hoped not.

Marco interrupted her uneasy reflections by handing her the dessert menu. "Uh, Flora, I should have mentioned this before, but my father keeps me rather short of cash. Is it okay with you if we split the bill tonight?"

Flora's smile was warm with relief. So this wasn't a "date" in the traditional sense, not if she was paying too. "No problem, Marco."

CHAPTER TWENTY

Flora managed to arrange a three-day weekend off the very next Friday. Vittorio Bernini had offered to drive her to Rome in his private car. He also said he'd book hotel rooms, plural, and put them on the Carabinieri account so she wouldn't have to pay a thing.

She felt a mixture of apprehension and excitement as she scurried around the apartment, throwing necessities in a small carryall and a larger purse than she usually carried. It would be good to get out of town—did she have any clean underwear? Maybe the trip would help her shake the depression and jumpiness that had dogged her since Ernst's death. Where were her black walking shoes? Under the bed, naturally. Would Vittorio take her out for dinner after they'd visited the antiquities shop? Was she falling for him and his beautiful hazel eyes? The shiver of anticipation she felt said maybe, yes. But what a stupid thing that would be, falling in love with a policeman—one who was investigating the murder in which she was still involved. Pack an umbrella? No, it wouldn't rain in Rome, not at this time of year . . . ha, ha, ha. Her mouth twisted as she remembered the street performer and his squirt bottle spraying the unsuspecting tourist.

Flora zipped her carryall shut, dropped it by the front door, and crossed to the tiny bathroom to freshen her makeup. She'd opted for a mid-length skirt and a crisp white blouse, wanting to look businesslike rather than seductive.

A honk outside the window alerted her to Bernini's arrival. Flora scribbled a note to Linda—"Gone to Rome, back late tomorrow. Flora"—and dropped it on the kitchen table, weighted down with the pepper shaker. Linda often stayed over with her boyfriend, but if she were at home, she'd appreciate knowing whether Flora was in or not. Neither of them felt comfortable in the apartment since Ernst's death, even with occasional police patrolling outside.

Flora grabbed her bag and ran down the rickety stairs. Bernini greeted her with a look that said she didn't look too businesslike to him, and took her bag from her. "Hop in," he said with a grin. "I got you a cappuccino. Sugar packets are on the seat, if you want sweetening."

"How kind!" Flora said, her spirits rising. This cop was considerate as well as attractive.

Bernini strapped on his seat belt and gunned the little car. It zoomed toward the southern gate of the city, the closest exit to the autostrada leading to Roma. "I figure we'll get there in time for lunch—there's a trattoria that makes *pizza bianca* and veal that's out of this world—and then we can wander over to the antiquities shop. I think we should pose as a courting couple to allay suspicion."

Flora glanced at his trousers, obviously civilian, and his tight shirt open halfway down to reveal a gold chain. He looked like any young man on vacation, thoroughly Italian, and not in the least like a policeman. "Of course. I am your fiancée from Pisa, and you are going to introduce me to your parents this weekend," she said with a wicked little grin.

"Ack!" said Vittorio, lifting one hand off the wheel. "The last time I tried that, my Mamma hated the girl I brought home!" He told Flora about that time in his life, about his first real job in Pisa that had led to clashes with another officer and his applying for a transfer. How the girlfriend had left him for another cop in the same division. "It seemed like everything about that job was a disaster."

"I feel that way about parts of my past—not worth repeating. So were you ever engaged?"

"No, never. No girlfriend ever lasted long enough." He glanced sideways at her. "What about you?"

"Never engaged. Not even close." Feeling a little shy, Flora looked out the window at the line of laundry suspended on the wall just below the second-story window on her right, and at the looming archway. They shot through the arch, and Flora noticed a grim but ornate building with a sign that read, "Ospedale Psichiatrico."

"An insane asylum? Here?" she asked.

"About two hundred years ago, yes. Now it's used for conferences."

"How appropriate," responded Flora, thinking of tenured faculty in art history who behaved oddly in the seminar rooms and halls of her old college. Some of them surely belonged in a psychiatric hospital!

They passed through the Porta Tufi and out of the city. Bernini reached for his cigarettes, and Flora took them from him so he could focus on the road. She lit one for him with the lighter sitting in the tray between them.

"Now tell me about your date with Marco. What did you learn?"

Flora settled back in her seat and gave him a mostly truthful account of her evening, leaving out the prolonged kiss and grope at the inner door of her apartment that Bernini could not have observed from his car across the street.

"I had the feeling that Marco decided I was getting a bit nosy about the family and that he deliberately changed the subject to my family."

"Hmm. How much did you ask about the marble patination process?"

"Only if he'd done it before, and if his client was a rich man. Then I let it go. I was afraid he would find my questions suspicious. But I'll find an opportunity to accompany him back to his studio. Hopefully he will show me the process." Flora finished her cappuccino and tucked the cup in the side pocket of Bernini's car.

Bernini nodded his approval, but Flora saw his mouth quirk. He said, too casually, "Did Marco try anything?"

"You mean, a goodnight kiss from The Leech? A quick one, and then I was safely inside." She watched the effect of her lie on his face, which softened in profile as he smiled at the steering wheel. Was Bernini a little jealous? And if he were, how did she feel about that? A little pocket of warmth grew in her belly.

"I wonder what we'll find in Fabio's shop," he said, after a pause to navigate a small traffic jam near the autostrada. He accelerated onto the ramp and changed gears.

Flora was glad he had changed the subject. She wasn't quite ready to explore her feelings for Bernini. Good company, charming manners—but he was a cop, investigating the murder of her best friend from Italy. Flora's intuition said, *Not now. Not until the investigation into the murder and the Lorenzettis' activities was complete.*

Better to ruminate on what she knew about distinguishing genuine antiquities from good forgeries, which was not much. Her strengths were painting and paper restoration, with a little book binding on the side. She'd acquired some secondhand knowledge about ceramic restoration from a colleague. But she didn't know enough about Greek Archaic sculpture to make an intelligent purchase, or about vase painting either. "Vittorio, do you know anyone in the Art Fraud Squad in Rome?" she asked.

Vittorio glanced at her, eyebrows raised. "We think alike,

Flora. And I do know someone. I'm going to call my colleague
Astorre Orsoni when we stop for gas. He can meet us at the
shop and then we'll talk with him afterward."

Flora thought about this. "Is he as good as you are at looking
like an ordinary citizen? Or will the shopkeeper and his staff
spot him right away as a cop?"

"Good point. He looks like a cop, always, even when wearing
ordinary clothes instead of a suit. It's something about his bearing—he comes across as too inquisitive. His nose juts out like
the snout of a hunting dog. And his hair is cut too short." He
grinned at Flora. "I'll tell him what we're doing and we will
meet him afterward. He can send someone else to check out the
shop at another time."

They made good time into the city of Rome, and Vittorio found
a parking spot near the Piazza Rondanini. Granted, it wasn't a
legal parking spot, but he put a police pass on the rearview mir-
ror.

"Lunchtime, Flora! The restaurant is about ten minutes walking from here."

Flora rose from the low seat and grabbed her oversized purse,
slinging it across her body to deter pickpockets. Rome was
notorious for gypsies—bands of kids working together to sur-
round, distract, and rob unwary pedestrians. If she walked with
a companion, Flora liked to put her purse on the inside. She
remembered how her friend Luisa had suffered a robbery by
motorcycle, when the cyclist zoomed close to her purse side
and snatched the bag off her shoulder. Flora had no intention
of being such an easy target.

Here they were again: the ubiquitous scooters ridden by many
young Italians—even women in tight skirts and high heels—
who drove with one hand on the handlebars and the other press-
ing cell phone to ear. Flora stepped closer to Vittorio to avoid

one that zipped between her and the wall next to her. He responded by tucking her free arm through his and slowing his pace to hers.

"Now we look like an engaged couple," she teased.

"Hmmph." He turned down a narrow alley and they passed a pizzeria. The cook was spinning the dough in the air, showing off for a couple of young girls who giggled their approval. Another few turns and they had arrived.

A hand-painted sign welcomed them to the Trattoria Tivi, and a placard informed them that today's specials were *pasta amatriciana* and *saltimbocca alla romana* (veal in Marsala wine).

"Ooooh. Pasta with spicy hot sauce." Flora eyed the cute little tables covered with white cloths tucked in among pots of geraniums. "Let's sit outside."

Vittorio agreed, and they chose the table that boasted a tiny bit of shade from the overhang of the roof.

They decided on the specials, along with a green salad and a bottle of house white wine. Flora marveled, not for the first time, at how Italian natives appeared to take wine at lunch in stride without getting sleepy. She planned to have only one glass, since she wanted to stay alert for the antiquities shop.

The food was excellent. Two glasses of wine and a double espresso later, they were ready to pay their bill and walk to the antiquities shop.

Flora took Bernini's arm, partly for show and partly because the wine coursing through her veins affected her footing on the cobblestones.

Idiot! You were going to stick with one glass! It could have been her mother speaking in her head. Flora was developing her own monkey-on-the-shoulder that commented on her every move.

Flora recognized the street when they turned a corner and saw the Pantheon ahead, its gorgeous skylighted dome gleaming in the sunshine. Strings of tourists meandered in and out of the portico, navigating around postcard stands, cars, and scooters. To her right, she noticed a tourist shop selling marbled paper souvenirs. Fabio Lorenzetti's shop crouched right behind it. The crumbling brickwork on the exterior provided a sharp contrast to the rich interior: beautifully displayed Greek vases set against velvet backdrops and statues on plinths. Roman lamps, Egyptian faience, and Etruscan gold jewelry were arranged in waist-high cases along the sides of the shop. A very tasteful and expensive store.

Vittorio Bernini whispered to her, "Go look at the statues while I distract the proprietor."

Flora appreciated his effort to give her clear field so she could really examine the antiquities without interruptions. She watched as he squared his shoulders and looked around for Fabio Lorenzetti, who was not immediately visible. Out of the shop, or just in the back somewhere? Bernini lurked by a case of expensive Etruscan and Egyptian-style jewelry.

Flora wandered toward the Greek section at the back of the shop. She spied two kouroi close together. As she approached, her breath snagged in her throat. One of the kouroi looked so much like the one she'd seen in Marco's studio! She examined it carefully. Same robust musculature, with rippled muscles in the abdomen, same delicate fingers on the left hand. The curls on the forehead reminded her of fat wood shavings, just as they had on the statue in Siena.

Could this be the original? Or a second copy?

She thought the modeling of the feet was different, but she couldn't be sure. Too bad she hadn't thought to take a photo with her cell phone during her visit to the studio with Marco.

But she could do it now, here in Rome. She glanced over her shoulder at Bernini, who was talking rapidly to a stringy young man behind the jewelry case. She whipped out her phone, pretending to check her email while she tapped the settings that turned on the camera feature with the flash off. Flora angled her back toward the two men and snapped two photos of the first kouros.

Then, holding her phone covered by her hand against her skirt, she moved closer to the second statue. It too was a kouros, but a bit taller than the first. The workmanship was similar, but not identical. And the surface appeared much older, pitted and stained with ocher and gray. If that was a faked patina, Flora had no idea how it was accomplished. Flora snapped two more photos and slipped her phone into her purse.

She compared the surfaces of the two statues. The smaller kouros' marble showed fewer pockmarks and pits. It was almost pure white in places, as if it had been scrubbed with a brush. And maybe dipped in acid? She'd eat her paintbrushes if that surface was original. The second kouros, the larger one, struck her as a better candidate for long-term burial at an archaeological site. The patina was much more varied, with little spots of color that might come from contact with lichen or water or mud.

"The signorina is very interested in Greek sculpture, yes?"

The new voice at her left ear startled her. Flora turned and gazed into the face of a middle-aged man who looked like her boss.

Fabio Lorenzetti.

CHAPTER TWENTY-ONE

Had he seen her take the photos?

Flora wasn't sure. She met the eyes of the proprietor and said, "Yes, I am always interested in Greek sculpture. I was an art history student at New York University, and Greek art fascinated me. But you have so many lovely things . . ."

She moved toward the vases, Roman lamps, and Etruscan jewelry displays, and Fabio Lorenzetti followed her. Flora felt his breath on the back of her neck and hoped her color had not risen. Where was Bernini when she needed him?

Bernini met her at the Etruscan jewelry counter and smoothly took over the conversation. "Signor Lorenzetti? I have heard of your wonderful shop from your brother Beppe in Siena. He told me you have especially fine vases from Sicily. I am interested in fifth-century painters in the red-figure technique for my private collection."

Fabio thrust out his chest and captured Bernini by one elbow, drawing him into a small alcove. "But of course, I have these vases. I depend on Beppe to send me good patrons such as yourself, Signor . . . ?"

"Esposito," said Vittorio smoothly.

He smiled at Flora and turned toward a particularly fine wine crater.

Flora let out a long breath of relief. Then a thought struck her, and she glided back to the statues, looking for labels that she had neglected to find when she was hell-bent on sneaking photos. The two kouroi were unlabeled, but a small sign said, "Antiquities from the Southern Mediterranean." How very helpful, she thought. That could mean anything: mainland Italy, Sicily, Greece, coastal Turkey, northern Africa, or some other unknown location! She debated asking questions and decided that would be too dangerous, especially since she was not a serious buyer.

Flora decided to check out other antiquities for provenance. She cruised around the shop, avoiding the proprietor and Bernini, and read labels. The vase labels said, "Etruria," or "Rome." Near displays of Greek and Roman jewelry, she noted provenances of "Rome," "Cerveteri" (that might be an Etruscan tomb), "Bologna," and "Central Italy" (meaning they had no clue where it was from!). A fine, mixed bag.

As she stood near a large *lekythos,* Vittorio Bernini materialized at her elbow and whispered in her ear: "Let's go." Out loud, he said, "Thank you for your time, Signor Lorenzetti. I have seen several items I'd like to consider further. I shall return." The last sentence had a slight emphasis that only Flora caught and she smiled to herself. *I bet you will return, with several officers!*

Once outside, she let her breath out in a long sigh and took Bernini's arm. They walked briskly for several minutes. Flora made a couple of comments about Fabio's antiquities, but Bernini told her to save it for the wine bar so Orsoni could hear everything.

Near the Piazza Navona, he ducked into a twisty side street and led Flora into a basement bar. It was dim and smoky, and perfect for a conversation that people didn't want overheard because the tables were scattered and separated by partitions. Enough conversation created a distinct white noise without forcing patrons to shout in order to communicate. Bernini lifted a hand at a tall, skinny, red-haired man who didn't look Italian and—here she disagreed with Bernini—certainly not like a policeman. It wouldn't matter if this guy wore a uniform or a business suit. If Flora had met him elsewhere, she'd have assumed Orsoni was a graduate student in philosophy or art. A harmless, intellectual sort.

Bernini introduced them. Astorre Orsoni took her hand and fixed piercing blue eyes on her face. "*Piacere.* Do sit down." He slid into a booth and Flora followed him, leaving Bernini to sit facing them.

They ordered espressos and water, and while Flora gulped water to steady her nerves and quench her thirst, the two cops exchanged small talk until the coffees were delivered by a short, harassed-looking waiter. Orsoni thanked him and turned to Flora.

"Now, tell me what you observed about our friend Fabio Lorenzetti's establishment."

Flora launched into a detailed description of what she'd seen and thought as she'd toured the shop, finishing with her survey of provenances—or rather lack thereof—on the labels. "I haven't been in many other antiquities shops recently to track how precise the labels are, but my favorite one in Siena certainly gives more information than this one does."

"Yes, I do agree with you there," Orsoni said. "We are almost certain that at least some of the goods in Lorenzetti's shop are stolen antiquities from sites such as Morgantina in Sicily, but we have no proof. Without a really good reason to search the back premises, we cannot do so, nor can we examine Fabio's paperwork without more information."

Bernini said, "Sounds like what you need is another chart of links between tomb robbers and dealers."

Orsoni laughed and drained his espresso. "Ah! You remember that story! Signorina, he is referring to a discovery the Art Fraud Squad made two years ago in a Rome apartment. It was an 'organigram,' a diagram of the players in the illegal antiquities trade, from southern Italy to Switzerland." He sketched it on a napkin for Flora. "There, at the top, Robert Hecht was the man with all the connections. Down here, at the bottom, are two of the *tombaroli* who actually talked to the police."

Flora was stunned. "I bet you don't find that kind of evidence very often! What was the guy thinking of, to write all of this down?"

"You can be sure he didn't plan on that piece of paper ever being read by the police!" Orsoni grinned wolfishly. "Unfortunately, this is only one network, and our cleanup didn't begin to capture all the people involved. As soon as we locked up some of the key players, the others rearranged themselves and disappeared. Trafficking continues, and we are just as far from stopping it as we were three years ago."

She crumpled her napkin, hesitating before she spoke again. Bernini nodded at her. "Lieutenant Orsoni, the part I didn't tell you yet is about the statues, the kouroi."

"Yes?"

"I think one is probably an original Greek Archaic sculpture, but the other has a very odd surface. I believe it may be a forgery, but I can't prove it. And I am no sculpture expert, so I can't decide just on stylistic grounds."

Orsoni's eyebrows snapped together. "Ah, yes. The other piece of the puzzle. The production and trade of forgeries. These pieces surface from time to time on the art market, fetching ridiculous sums."

"Like the Getty statue," said Flora, referring again to the scandalous purchase by the California museum of a kouros that no one knew for sure was real or fake. "What was that, eight million dollars they paid?"

"Nine," said Orsoni with a groan. "The horrible part of that story was that even the scientists disagreed: one group said the patina could not have been forged; the other said it could if you buried the marble in some kind of mold."

"The truth will probably never be known," Flora said. "Though I do wonder if any forger would take the amount of time that must have taken to create the complex surface described in the Athens publication—what was it called?"

"*The Getty Kouros Colloquium*," said Bernini. "I think."

"You'd be surprised," Orsoni said. "A real artist, a forger at the top of his craft, has his pride. Why not take years to create a masterpiece, particularly if you have plenty of money from lesser sales of forged antiquities in your pocket?"

"Tell him about Marco Lorenzetti," Bernini reminded Flora, filling her water glass.

"Oh, yes. Well, Marco—that's Beppe's middle son—is working hard on a statue that he said is a special commission. And he was looking at photos of other Greek kouroi that I saw lying around his studio . . ."

They talked about Marco's work and the fact that Flora didn't know if Marco and his father planned to sell the statue as an original or a legitimate copy.

"Does he have a client in mind?"

"Yes, but all I know is that it is a man who wants an authentic-looking Greek statue for his garden."

Orsoni shook his head. "The real problem is that we can't be there at the point of sale. Most dealers never write down anything but the purchase price, not the buyer's name, or how the artifact was labeled when it was sold. It would be so nice to know if an artifact was labeled 'ancient original' or museum-quality 'replica.' And the prices are all over the map. Provenance papers can be faked too. It's like sliding around on rigatoni—all slippery and changeable."

Flora leaned forward. This was the kind of stuff she really cared about, how forgers got away with the terrible crime of faking works of art and fooling collectors and museums all over the world. She found this much more compelling than the age-old problem of stealing antiquities from illegal excavations, perhaps because she felt so helpless to prevent trafficking. But forgery, that was an area where she could make a contribution with her conservation training. The academic journals were full of articles on how scientists and conservators had worked together to identify forged paintings. They used pigment analysis to identify supposedly ancient pigments that had modern ingredients, or special X-ray techniques to find underpaintings or additions.

"I see two areas we could check out," she said to Orsoni. "One, the stylistic criteria for judging between an original kouros and a fake—"

"What are they?" interrupted Orsoni.

"Er, it's very tricky stuff, as you know from the Getty investigation. The art historian studies characteristics such as how the hair and abdominal muscles are rendered. Oh, and the Getty kouros caused an argument about feet—they looked later than the hair and other details."

"But isn't it true that ancient sculptors mixed styles, just like modern artisans who want to create something new?"

"Yes, of course, Vittorio," Flora said, turning to Bernini. "That was one of the key arguments defending the Getty statue as authentic. That, plus the idea that just because you can't find a plausible predecessor for a newly discovered work doesn't mean there wasn't one. There are so few intact statues left compared to what existed originally. But remember, I am no sculpture expert; my field is painting."

Bernini asked Orsoni, "Do you know anyone who *is* a recognized sculpture expert we could consult? You said you have photographs—we could send them as email attachments."

"I'll check with my colleagues," Orsoni promised. "Flora,

what else do you suggest?"

"Well, the whole process of marble patination is a new field—both for forgers of sculptures and for curators and scholars who want to distinguish between a patina formed over thousands of years and one faked in a lab. I was intrigued by the patina in Fabio Lorenzetti's shop, the one I thought might be fake. It had a pitted appearance, like one of the acid-bath ones I've read about. Are there any examples we could look at of truly fake . . . that sounds funny . . . I mean, documented fake patinas on marble for comparison?"

"Yes," said Orsoni. "I can help you there. Our lab has fabulous examples of acid-bath treatments to burial in manure. A whole range of surfaces, just for you." His smile grew sly and oily, like a street vendor trying to sell a knickknack to an unwary tourist. "For you, Signorina Garibaldi, all these things for a special price!"

Flora laughed. But her elation was short-lived.

Bernini interrupted. "Orsoni, this is fascinating stuff, but our real focus is on the trafficking question. We need to get proof if the Lorenzettis are part of a chain of traffickers from southern Italy to the north." He glanced at Flora apologetically. "My boss, Captain Rizzo, was adamant that that was the reason he approved this trip to Rome."

"But—" Flora began.

"Don't worry, Flora. We can see the faked patina samples. But the rest of our time must be spent on ways to get that proof for Rizzo." Bernini turned back to Orsoni, and the two men discussed how the team in Rome would follow up on Fabio's activities.

Later that evening at the hotel, Flora accessed her email on her netbook and shot off a short message to her friend Lisa Donahue, an archaeologist living in Boston. She described what she was working on without naming names, and asked if Lisa knew any Greek sculpture experts Flora could email with some photo attachments of what she'd seen in Fabio's shop.

Then she took a blissfully long, steaming shower. Refreshed and changed into fresh pajamas, she returned to her computer. Flora was startled to see Lisa had replied almost immediately. She glanced at her watch and realized Lisa was just beginning her workday across the Atlantic, so it wasn't surprising to find her online.

"Hi, Flora! Long time no hear from. I can do better than give you an email address; one of the most famous scholars of Greek sculpture is in Rome now, working at the Villa Giulia. Her name is Assunta Vianello. And here is her email . . ."

Flora thanked Lisa and zapped off a quick email to Dottoressa Vianello, requesting an appointment at her earliest convenience.

Wrapped in the terrycloth robe provided by the hotel, she sat cross-legged on the bed and wrote down every single thing she could remember about Greek sculpture from the Archaic Period. She did better this time, after her long session in the Siena's University for Foreigners' library, and complemented by some scribbled notes she'd stuffed in her bag just before Bernini had picked her up for this trip.

Flora knew she was no sculpture expert, but she hated to appear like a complete novice in front of the Dottoressa. The least she could do is come up with a list of intelligent questions about how to assess kouroi: What are the essential features of each subperiod? How do hair styles change over time? How about musculature? Stance—that weird Egyptian stance with the left foot in front of the other? And the most important from Flora's point of view: How common was it for Archaic sculptors to mix different styles in one statue? The discussion about how the Getty Museum's statue had hair curls from one period and

141

feet from another revolved around one statue. Were there others equally eclectic?

She recalled a conversation she'd had with Lisa Donahue at a conference they'd both attended in Philadelphia. Lisa, as a Classical archaeologist and part-time potter, was fully convinced that ancient people were not "primitive" in their crafts. On the contrary, she said. Even early, handmade pottery showed extraordinary skill in the evenly thick, smooth walls and decoration created without a potter's wheel. And styles in shape and decoration displayed human ingenuity in every single culture she'd studied. "It's crazy to call someone 'primitive' just because they lived in a village in Peru or China three thousand years ago and produced art we're not familiar with. Some early cultures are incredibly sophisticated in their technology," Lisa said. They'd discussed how styles were mixed in new artifacts because people, both ancient and modern, loved to experiment.

So, reasoned Flora, it made sense that a Greek sculptor might make each statue unique, blending old and new features. After all, each piece was individually carved. It wasn't like using a mold to mass-produce relief pottery or metal ornaments. And those sculptors hadn't had access to photographs of other statues they admired. Perhaps they had done quick sketches on the spot, and then worked from memory.

Finally, she threw down her pen and got ready for bed. Tomorrow promised to be an interesting day.

CHAPTER TWENTY-TWO

It was an extremely interesting day. Assunta Vianello proved to be a tall, model-thin blonde with impeccable English. She'd been born in Sicily, she told them as they made their way into the Villa Giulia's Greek Classical galleries, but earned her graduate degrees at Harvard. So she too had a Boston connection.

"How do you know Lisa Donahue?" asked Flora, feeling a bit intimidated by the glamorous and assured sculpture expert.

Assunta laughed. "Conferences, just like you. Classical archaeology is a small world. Attend the same conferences in Rome and the U.S. for a few years and you know everyone. Now, here we are. I'm going to give you a crash course on what you should look for in fake Archaic sculptures."

Flora and Vittorio Bernini followed her, stunned at her fluent and unstoppable flow of words about each statue.

To Flora's delight, the Dottoressa confirmed much of what Flora had read. "The big problem is that we have so few complete statues left. So many of them are in fragments, and sometimes museums try to match the head from one statue to the body of another to make better displays."

"What about the types of marble we should look for?" Flora said.

"Funny you should ask. Look at this case." Assunta pointed to a nearby case that contained several small blocks of marble from various Greek and Italian quarries. "Now remember, we have limited information on which quarries were exhausted in

143

antiquity . . ."

Flora took notes. This stuff was gold, she thought. The information she learned here couldn't be easily found in textbooks; you had to search for it in obscure journals and densely technical articles.

"Okay, now we move on to the extraordinary business of producing fake sculpture. We have discovered several methods for imitating the patina on truly ancient marble: acid bath, burial in manure, weathering in an urban atmosphere . . . subjecting a piece to acid rain and other kinds of pollution over a period of years—"

Bernini interrupted her. "But would any forger really take years to produce a forgery? Wouldn't he take shortcuts to get his fakes on sale as quickly as possible?"

Flora remembered the same discussion in Rome. She waited for Assunta's reply.

"Most would not," conceded Assunta. "But the forgers who are already wealthy, who knows what they may attempt? They go to seminars, they follow the museum literature, and they study the science of conservation."

"And," said Flora, "I bet the good ones just love to fool the experts. It would be a triumph for a really good artisan to produce a statue or other antiquity that would fool collectors and art historians all the way to the auction house!"

Assunta smiled. "Yes, you are correct. A few individuals, a very few, are wily enough to wait for years, maybe a decade, to produce a masterpiece and then sit back and watch the fun as their baby goes to Sotheby's or Christie's and fetches a huge price. Do you remember a video produced by Nova in the early '90s called *The Fine Art of Faking It?*"

"Yes!" Flora stopped in midstride. "There was a painter, a German, who made a fake Grunewald . . . purchased by the Cleveland Art Museum, I think . . ."

"That is the one. The forger claimed that because he never signed the piece, he had no intention to deceive and was therefore not a forger."

"Ha," said Bernini.

From the way he avoided looking at the Roman scholar's figure, Flora guessed that he found the blond woman very attractive but was trying to hide that fact. Funny how well she felt she knew him already.

"Ha, indeed," agreed the Dottoressa. "Herr Goeller may not have made much money on the transaction when he sold his St. Catherine painting, but he certainly loved seeing his fake painting in a famous auction catalogue!"

Flora smiled, but inside she was wondering if her employers might turn out to be forgers who enjoyed a little fame along with the money. No, she decided cynically—Mamma Gia might enjoy some fame, but the rest of the Lorenzettis were all about money. They all lamented their lack of means at every opportunity. Beppe complained that his girls spent too much money, and Marco had hinted more than once that Flora could pay for their dinners out since he was perpetually short of cash. Besides, the kind of fame Mamma Gia lusted after was being known as the best, most important painters in Siena, and that could hardly happen if her men ended up behind bars.

She came back to the conversation when Bernini asked about Orsoni's mention of a collection of fakes.

Assunta nodded. "Oh, yes. We collaborate on that one. The collection is actually housed here in one of our storerooms. Come along and I will show you some of the best fakes in all of Europe."

CHAPTER TWENTY-THREE

Back in Siena, Flora found it very hard to concentrate on work. She decided to postpone work on the Madonna copy until she'd settled down. Even as she applied gold leaf and mixed gesso to yet another picture frame, her mind churned with scraps of conversation from the ride home and the implications of her growing intimacy with Lieutenant Bernini.

They'd discussed every tidbit of sculpture lore provided by Dottoressa Vianello at the Museo Nazionale di Villa Giulia. Flora took notes while Vittorio drove; she wanted to remember everything she could.

"What was that procedure with potato mold the American geologist tried?" she'd asked.

"Oh, yeah. Some professor had his students bury hunks of marble in a mixture of oxalates that produced a thick patina after three weeks. He said you could probably do it with mashed potatoes that had fermented a while."

"And to get the kind of crust on the surface that another geologist said no forger could imitate?"

Bernini laughed. "Expose a dolomitic marble to the weather for a few centuries. He claims you get a calcitic patina. Try proving that one in a laboratory when all you have is a few months to complete your forgery!"

"The problem is," she said, "that it's easier to prove how something could *not* be done than how it *was* in fact done."

"Right. Which is why chemists spend so much time arguing

with art historians. The scientists explain how varying conditions can produce different results with the same material, so then the historians accuse the scientists of changing their minds. Remember what that curator Marion True said about the Getty kouros? She was very upset when the second set of scientists contradicted the original geologist's claim that the patina was ancient."

"Yes, I remember. Ms. True concluded that scientists are no more objective than 'connoisseurs.' Sometimes, like when I read about some crazy controversy like the Shroud of Turin, I think True's right." Flora slid her notebook back in her purse.

"What do you mean?"

"Oh, there was a Russian scientist who set out to prove that the carbon-14 date for the Shroud was wrong by thirteen centuries."

"How could he do that?" Bernini raised his eyebrows as he downshifted for the Siena exit.

"The Russian couldn't accept that other scientists had dated the cloth to the thirteenth century instead of the first century A.D., when Jesus was crucified. So he built a silver box similar to the one the Shroud is stored in in the church in Turin. Then he put some linen in there and set the whole thing on fire so carbon would accumulate. His theory was that the fire that scorched the Shroud during its long history could have absorbed extra carbon and made the linen cloth's date appear much younger than it really is."

"And?"

"The carbon date on Kouznetsov's cloth came out younger, but not by thirteen centuries. The silver box he used was not the same as the one where the Shroud was stored. And the cloth samples he tested were not taken from the actual Shroud."

"His experiment was similar to what may have happened to the Shroud, but it wasn't identical—it couldn't be. So no one

147

took his result seriously," said Bernini as he negotiated a narrow street corner.

"Right. The Shroud story has lots of other examples of religious scientists who demonstrate bias: they want to prove the Shroud really is the burial cloth of Christ at almost any cost. They conveniently ignore any test results that don't fit their hypotheses."

"Doesn't sound very scientific!" Bernini said.

"Religion itself is unscientific."

At the end of the journey, Flora had stayed up half the night sipping Chianti and writing down everything she could think of.

During her library reading and subsequent searches online, Flora had researched not only patinas but other types of damage to limestone and marble sculpture from pollution and acid rain. Soft stone—limestone—was particularly vulnerable to the sulfur compounds in acid rain. Sulfur dioxide combined with water eventually changed into sulfuric acid, causing stone to pit, flake, or dissolve. The same thing happened to harder, dolomitic marble; it just took longer. Some of the most dramatic weathering occurred in heavily polluted cities like Athens, Greece, where the Parthenon temple on the Acropolis showed significant damage.

Flora took a sip of wine and thought about the forgery process. What would she do if she were a knowledgeable sculptor and wanted to fake an ancient marble statue? First, do her homework. Obtain marble from a quarry that had not been exhausted in antiquity, carve it with tools only available in antiquity, and patina it with multiple layers of mold and weathering. Say, bury it in the back yard for a few weeks and get some cats to piss on it, providing an acidic environment. Then dig it up and expose it on a windy, rain-swept hillside for a few more weeks in a place no one ever visited, preferably near a town with epic pollution, like Athens. She stared at this for a while and started a new page.

How to complicate your life as Flora Garibaldi: fall in love with a policeman who was investigating a murder at your place of employment and who might—no matter how eloquently he denied it—still consider you a suspect. Remain totally objective while continuing to work at said place of employment and wondering if your employers were (a) criminals engaged in digging up antiquities and spiriting them over the border into Switzerland, (b) art forgers, (c) murderers, or (d) all of the above. Refrain from calling your parents for advice for fear of worrying or angering them, resulting in both emotional and physical indigestion . . .

The screech of the outside door yanked Flora back into Monday morning at the State Archives compound. She discovered she'd overmixed the gesso so that it was beginning to harden. Silly Flora! That's what came of not focusing on what she was doing. Sighing, she dumped the hardening mess in her wastebasket and started again with fresh powder and water from the tap to the right of her desk.

"And how are you today, Miss Garibaldi?" Gianetta Lorenzetti stopped at Flora's desk.

"Fine, thank you," stammered Flora. She was surprised Mamma Gia took the time to greet her. Usually she marched down the center of the front room in a royal progress with one of her daughters, talking nonstop and completely ignoring the *stranieri*, the young foreigners who were employees of the family business.

They chatted about the weather for a few moments, and Flora had a feeling something else was on Gia's agenda. She was right.

"Now, Flora, I hear you've been dating my Marco. Of course you know he's engaged to be married to Catarina Brunetti?"

149

"I didn't know that, Mamma Gia, but it doesn't matter to me because—"

"Cousin Catarina has been his intended since childhood. She is my brother Guido's daughter from his second marriage. We will have the formal engagement party in September. Marco likes you, I can see that, but it is all for nothing because he must marry a well-known Sienese, a distant relative, and keep everything in the family, the most important painting family in all Tuscany . . ."

Flora let Gia's voice just roll over her since trying to interject anything would have been like lying down in front of a Mack truck and expecting it to stop. She wondered if Marco even knew about his family's plans for him—he had never mentioned his future. But he was a happy-go-lucky guy who lived in the present. So the Lorenzettis believed in arranged marriages to cousins? How interesting and old-fashioned. And how lucky for Flora that she wasn't one of those cousins; it sounded like the marriageable ones were bartered like goats or cows to the highest bidder.

Mamma Gia finished her pronouncements with a tight smile and a decisive nod. Then, just as she was about to sail down the room, Flora spoke.

"Mamma Gia—Beppe asked me to look up the original order for this painting frame I am working on. Is now a good time to come into the back office and find it?"

The older woman looked surprised. "Beppe gave you this to do? Very well, come along now."

Flora followed in her wake, relieved that Beppe's wife hadn't forbidden her access to the inner sanctum. Perhaps she would have a chance to poke around in the files a little and locate some of the buyer information Bernini wanted so badly.

They passed through the framing and packing rooms and through the door that led to accounting and filing. Aha, thought

Flora, as she saw the neat rows of filing cabinets. Everything she and Bernini wanted to know about the business was in there, if she could only have the time to search.

"What is the name on the order form?" asked Mamma Gia.

"Salvatore Turchetti," Flora said.

Mamma Gia marched over to a set of files labeled "Customers." The phone rang, and she turned away to answer it.

Flora sidled into the space vacated by her employer and opened the first drawer. She scanned as many names as she could before closing that drawer and opening the next one below. How fortunate that the name she sought was near the end of the alphabet. She pulled out a couple of files, looking for sculpture customers, but found only painting restoration contracts.

As Mamma Gia spoke into the phone, Flora opened the drawer labeled "S–Z."

"*What* are you doing? I didn't give you permission to go through the files!"

Flora turned around to face the irate woman. "Sorry, Mamma Gia. I was just trying to save you some time. Beppe is always asking us to be efficient and—"

"Never mind what Beppe says! I run this office and *I* say don't put your little fingers into our files unless I request it! Do you understand, Miss Garibaldi?" Gia's face set into a grimace and her voice resembled a growl.

"Yes." Flora decided she really didn't want to get on the bad side of this woman—ever. Or meet her in a back alley—Gia was almost twice her size.

Mamma Gia pulled out the correct file in about ten seconds and handed it to Flora, almost slapping it into her hands.

"Thank you."

"Go back to your desk, then."

Flora left the inner office, breathing a sigh of relief that the dragon lady hadn't actually breathed fire on her. But her mind raced as she passed Graziano and Lisa, noting their interested expressions as they realized one of their own had been chastised. Costanza looked more than interested; her expression reminded Flora of a cat with tuna. *Smug little know-it-all,* thought Flora. She's taking full advantage of her closeness to the family. Flora thought Costanza wasn't really that interested in Filippo as a lover—but she certainly wanted to have the status and money that would come with marrying into an old Sienese family. And she was far too interested in Flora's movements, especially lately . . .

Flora sat down at her desk with a thud. Surely it was a little odd that employees weren't allowed to fetch relevant files themselves. Was Mamma Gia one of those people who couldn't delegate responsibility, a micromanager who had to have control over every aspect of the business?

Or did she have something to hide?

CHAPTER TWENTY-FOUR

Vittorio Bernini slammed down the office phone. He hated office work; he'd much rather be outside patrolling the streets or investigating crimes. He had so much work on his desk that his head spun. His boss, Captain Rizzo, had assigned him two other murders besides the German restorer, Ernst Mann, and he hardly had time to breathe, let alone see Flora. This job drove him crazy, no doubt about it. Both the Polizia de Stato and his division of the Carabinieri were understaffed and overworked, and he felt ready to walk out the door.

He made two more phone calls concerning the Antonelli case and decided he needed a cigarette. Bernini hoisted his long form off the chair and wandered down the hall to a small porch he and his fellow officers used for smoking ever since the senior boss had declared all the offices smoke-free zones. Lieutenant Colonel Riccardo Bruno showed his modernism in strange ways, they all felt, and impinging on their God-given right to smoke wherever and whenever was one of them.

By some miracle, the little porch was empty except for a pot stand bearing a large ashtray. The solitude appealed to Bernini more than the cigarette, but this feeling didn't stop him from enjoying the rush of smoke into his lungs.

Flora had promised to look in the Lorenzetti files. Her objective was to find lists of customer names and phone numbers, or invoices, or anything else to show how the business operated. The difficulty was that many signs of legitimate trade (packing boxes, tools, contacts for transport companies) would be indistinguishable from those used for illegal activities. The same with the documents—how would one tell if a receipt described an illegal transaction? Or would there be no receipt at all? No, he remembered. Even crooked art dealers wanted a paper trail to prove their innocence. Papers could be, and were, forged or altered to make both the buyer and the seller look good.

Captain Rizzo appeared at his elbow. "The others are here, Bernini. Let's go get this meeting over with."

Bernini followed his boss to the so-called "meeting room"— little more than a closet with a table and six chairs. Major Esposito from the Carabinieri Art Squad and the two local officers from the Polizia di Stato, Mancini and Querini, were already there.

After some customary small talk and screeching of chairs, everyone sat down.

"Captain Rizzo, how goes the Lorenzetti case?" Esposito asked. His posture, knees apart and arms in his lap, was relaxed; his eyes flickered with alertness.

"We've made some progress, but not as much as we hoped. We finished checking out Signor Mann's contacts and interviewing employees at the Restauro. I've applied for a search warrant to take apart the family laboratory—"

"Good heavens, what's the hold-up? Doesn't the prosecutor know how urgent this is?" interrupted Esposito.

"We haven't successfully made the case that the Lorenzettis are trafficking, sir," Bernini said. "The prosecutor wants something concrete before he issues the warrant. But, I think I may soon have a scrap of evidence from Signorina Garibaldi."

"What's this?" Rizzo growled. "And why haven't you told me?"

"I'm juggling rather a lot right now, as you know. She saw some photographs in Marco's studio behind the family home.

The signorina thinks one of them is a stolen ancient Greek statue that Marco Lorenzetti is using for a model."

"And how does she know that? Is she clairvoyant?" Mancini sneered.

"He tried to prevent her from studying the photographs—by grabbing her and kissing her."

The men guffawed.

"One up for Marco! Those Americans need kissing!" laughed Querini. He scratched his balding pate.

"Okay, okay." Esposito held up a hand. "Where are these photos now?"

"Still in Marco Lorenzetti's possession," said Bernini.

"We need to obtain them. I will call the prosecutor and get on his case about the first warrant. What about the second search warrant for the laboratory in the Palazzo, next to the State Archives?"

"The Prosecutor promised it tomorrow or the next day," Mancini said.

Rizzo replied, "We've already been there and found nothing incriminating. All normal business records, packing supplies, a clipboard of jobs that Pietro Lorenzetti used to track objects in and out of the lab. And now that we have a Roman connection—" He bristled as Esposito interrupted him.

"But a more thorough search, when the Lorenzettis turn over all their keys, is what we need," broke in the major smoothly. "And you must go through all the files, again. Who knows what has been moved since your first visit? As for the shop of Fabio Lorenzetti in Rome, Orsoni has been in touch. I know all about that. His team will continue to investigate the statues and vases there, especially the ones without documented provenances. It's only a matter of time until we have enough evidence to prove trafficking from Rome to the north; now we need the link to Siena and other parts of Tuscany." Esposito turned back to

Rizzo. "What new evidence do you have on the activities of Beppe Lorenzetti?"

"Nothing solid, but we're working on it. I don't believe my friend Beppe is the ringleader," Rizzo said. "I think it's Fabio in Rome; Beppe is just a peon."

Major Esposito's dark brown eyes narrowed. "Paolo, *my old friend,* you mustn't refer to a suspect in a major investigation as 'my friend,' even if he is that! You display your obvious bias in his favor. Unless I see more action on your part, not to mention results, I will pull you off this investigation."

Rizzo turned purple and appeared to swell in his chair.

Bernini felt a little sorry for his boss. He'd just received a dressing down in front of his subordinate and two colleagues from the State Police, and it didn't help that Mancini smirked as he watched Rizzo's reaction. Unfortunately, Major Esposito was correct in his assessment of Rizzo's mixed emotions and how they were interfering with his performance. Now Bernini had a new dilemma: How could he help his boss while at the same time furthering his own fledgling career?

He said, "Major Esposito, the young American woman agreed to be our mole inside the State Archives lab. She's snooping in the business files whenever she gets the opportunity—"

"We will search those," snarled Rizzo, whose color was returning to normal.

Bernini replied, "Flora thinks there has been a recent shuffling of files. And she often sees family members carrying bulging briefcases home. We may still miss something, whenever we search."

Esposito nodded. "The ideal search would be both facilities simultaneously. For that, we need a larger team of men. I will see to it." He looked at his cell phone. "We have another meeting that will take about half an hour. Stick around, Bernini. I'd like to speak further with you." He took the two State Police officers away with him, leaving Bernini and Rizzo staring at each other.

Bernini, tingling with anticipation about what Esposito might have in mind for him, stubbed out his cigarette and waited for the explosion from Rizzo. It didn't come. His boss appeared to be waiting for him to take the lead. He sucked in some air and said, "Now I understand why you dislike Mancini so much. He is very difficult."

"You can say that again," Rizzo rasped.

"We're in a holding pattern here, sir. Miss Garibaldi is snooping in the files, I am making phone calls to our Roman colleagues in the Art Squad."

"Ah, the beautiful Signorina Garibaldi is at work! So who did you call in the Art Squad?"

Bernini chose to ignore the comment about Flora. "Giuseppe Morandi and Astorre Orsoni—Orsoni's the one I met with already. And Cesare what's-his-name."

"You told them about the Lorenzetti relatives in Chiusi and Rome?"

"*Si, certamente.* I am trying to find any direct links between the different branches of the Lorenzetti family and tombaroli down south or any evidence of transport activities that don't match their usual pattern."

"Ah, *bene, bene.*" Rizzo lit another cigarette and wandered over to the window. As he inhaled smoke, his tense shoulders visibly relaxed. "Not much of a view here. Why can't we have one of the Cathedral or the Piazza del Campo? What do you think Miss Flora will turn up?"

"Well, I'd be delighted if she found what the Americans call a 'smoking gun,' something like photographs of known stolen artifacts tucked behind a wall, a list of phone numbers of contacts who are not legal clients . . ."

"You watch too many movies. I suppose you expect to find a

nice, clearly written chart linking the Lorenzettis to known tombaroli in Sicily and art dealers in Switzerland?"

"I don't expect that kind of luck. But it would be nice to find something."

The captain ground his half-smoked butt into the ash tray. "What we do next is search the Lorenzetti compound as soon as we can obtain a warrant for evidence of transporting illegal antiquities. I'd like to do it while Beppe is out of town—he tells me he is going to Rome in about four days. It will take at least that long to obtain a search warrant by Friday—even with Esposito's intervention. Oh, and that reminds me. I had a call from the Finance Police this morning."

"What did they want?" asked Bernini, as his stomach lurched. Another branch of the police involved was not what they needed. It just slowed everything down.

Rizzo threw up his hands, scattering cigarette ash. "They want copies of any and all financial records we have from the Lorenzettis. As if we had them here—how likely is that? They think Beppe didn't declare all his income the past two years. That fool! I told him tax reporting was the last area he should take shortcuts."

Bernini sighed. Another complication in an already convoluted case. The glacial pace of the investigation made him wonder if his boss was really motivated to prosecute his old friend, no matter what kind of evidence they came up with. And to make it worse, Rizzo was dating that luscious-looking widowed aunt he'd seen at the Lorenzetti house! Pillow talk might result in some more tidbits about the family, but it also made Rizzo look bad. Sleeping with a member of a family under suspicion of murder was foolhardy at best.

"What you need to do, Bernini, is stay in close touch with Signorina Garibaldi and follow up on those phone calls with our colleagues in other cities. We need every crumb of information on business contacts for that family, whether it's the local ones or the branches in Chiusi and Rome. I still think Fabio Lorenzetti is the most likely to be the ringleader, no matter what Esposito says. And do they have relatives in any other city who are involved in the business in any way?"

"I'm on it, sir."

Rizzo's expression grew grim. "So, what do you think of my old boss Esposito?"

Bernini hesitated. "He's okay, I think. Not sure I'd like to work for him, though."

Rizzo sighed. "He's very competent, but he doesn't communicate well with underlings. He made my life hell by never really defining what my job was . . . oh well, that was a long time ago."

Captain Rizzo left, and a few moments later Bernini heard his booming voice haranguing another junior colleague down the hall.

Hmm. Rizzo had always surprised Bernini with his flashes of insight. Now, he clearly suspected that Esposito intended to poach Bernini away from him. Yet he didn't seem overly upset about the prospect. On the contrary, he had just given Bernini a friendly warning about the major's operating style. Maybe Rizzo also realized that Bernini was having doubts about him, Rizzo, as a boss. Had Bernini betrayed his concern about Rizzo's close connection to the Lorenzettis and Rizzo's obvious bias?

Bernini returned to his office with plenty to think about. Rizzo: how to keep him happy while exploring other opportunities with Esposito. Major Esposito: how to extract maximum information while remaining deferential. Flora: how to keep her happy and interested in him while solving a murder and investigating illegal operations. Bernini was glad his boss wanted him to keep a close eye on Flora, but leaving the real work to a woman not on the police force made him distinctly uneasy.

He made a new note on his "to-do" list. Call Flora at the earliest opportunity and see how she was doing, check Lorenzetti relatives in other parts of Tuscany . . . Orsoni was investigating Fabio and his antiquities shop in Rome, but Bernini could make some more inquires about the cousin Raffaelo Lorenzetti in Chiusi. Was he a painter, or some other kind of artist? Where was his workshop? What, exactly, was his role in the Lorenzetti Restauro business? That sort of thing.

Bernini stuck his head out the door to make sure no one was hanging about. He lit another cigarette because smoking helped him think. If the family was really trafficking in antiquities, they'd need stations on the way north for transferring goods. What about Bologna? Verona? Bolzano? Bolzano could be key because of its proximity to the Brenner Pass over the Alps into Austria. Then from Austria, it was a short hop to Switzerland, home of bank vaults and gateways to the auction houses of London and collectors in Europe and the United States.

He reached into his right desk drawer and pulled out two maps: one of Italy and another of Europe. Bernini grabbed a yellow marker and decided to do what he did best: put himself in another's shoes.

For the next half hour, he would be a smuggler of stolen antiquities and plot every viable route out of Tuscany to northern Europe.

And whatever his boss thought about Beppe, Bernini would keep an open mind. For his money, Beppe was just as likely a ringleader as Fabio, and Siena made a less obvious way station than Florence for antiquities moving from south to north through Tuscany.

Esposito stuck his head into Bernini's office. "I have to leave shortly. Can we talk?"

"Of course. Come in. Shall I close the door?" Bernini rose

and dumped the files off his one and only guest chair. "Have a seat, sir."

"Yes, good idea." Esposito sat and fixed his penetrating gaze upon Bernini's face. "You are too smart not to have guessed why I wanted to speak with you privately."

Bernini took a breath. "Perhaps you want to tell me about opportunities in the Art Squad."

"And would you be interested?"

"Yes, certainly. I was an art history major before I went into the police force. And I've remained current by reading a lot, as much as time allows."

Esposito smiled. "What about relocation? Would you be willing to move, say, to Rome?"

Bernini suffered a pang or two when he remembered Flora. But maybe she'd be moving away from Siena herself, when this was all over. "Rome is the home office of the Division for the Protection of Cultural Heritage. I'd be very interested in working there."

"Excellent. Write me a letter of interest and send it to me by email. Here's my card, and my direct phone numbers. Once I have the letter, we'll get you to fill out the transfer application. All right?"

"Great. Thank you so much."

CHAPTER TWENTY-FIVE

A few days later, Flora contrived to be the last person in the
State Archives laboratory at six in the afternoon. This was highly
unusual. The Lorenzettis tended to stay late—in fact, they kept
very peculiar hours. She felt a little uneasy about being the
Carabinieri's errand girl, but that worry was outweighed by her
desire to please Vittorio Bernini.

And why are you so keen to please this Italian policeman, hmm?

Go away, Mamma.

Voices and drawers banging shut made her realize people
were leaving. She pretended to be engrossed in the final
touch-up of the Martini copy, but she watched through her long
bangs as the others packed up to go home.

"Bye! See you tomorrow!" called Costanza to Graziano. Graziano turned in his chair to follow Costanza with his eyes. He
noticed Flora looking his way. "Hey, Flora, you're staying late?"

"Just want to finish this up," Flora said with a smile. "Pietro's
been on my case about working faster."

Graziano headed straight for the Archives door, but Costanza
stopped at Flora's desk to see what she was working on.

"And Pietro has given you some actual restoration work now,
I see. How nice for you."

Flora didn't like the acid tone of Costanza's voice. No way
she was going to tell her this was a special commission from
Beppe and that she was copying a painting, not restoring it.

"Well, this is what I trained for in Florence last semester."

"Really? I thought that program wasn't considered top-of-the-line in restoration work."

Fat lot you know about it, Costanza! But Flora didn't say this out loud.

Having failed to get a rise out of her, Costanza changed tack. "At least Pietro will approve of your obvious industry!"

"He's not here to notice," said Flora. She hoped her bitchy feelings toward Costanza didn't show too much.

Costanza tittered and waggled her fingers before pulling her sunglasses out of her leather purse. "Ta, ta, Flora! Don't work *too* hard!"

Flora made a face at Costanza's departing back and immediately felt better. She carefully painted in her secret symbol, the little wheel that only she could identify, while she waited for the lab to empty.

At six-thirty, she dropped her paintbrush into turpentine and stood up to stretch. Her shoulders were especially tight, and her neck ached from sitting in one position for so long. Were the Lorenzettis really all gone? Luckily, the only bathroom was in the packing area, near the entrance to the inner office. She'd walk back there with a ready-made excuse if someone questioned her.

The fitful light of early evening slanted down through the high windows, leaving a golden trail down the center of the long room. Flora tiptoed toward the back of the lab, listening hard for any noise from the inner office. She heard nothing. So far, so good. She'd really have something good to show Bernini now. Feeling smug, she advanced to the closed door of the accounting rooms.

It was locked.

Shoot! Now what? Flora looked around her, wondering if there was a spare key anywhere . . . she felt around behind a handy bookcase and found nothing. Too easy. Where would she hide a key? Flora remembered someone telling her during a long-ago Easter egg hunt that the way to trick people was to hide eggs either higher or lower than anyone expected. She bent down and groped under the bookcase. Dust brushed her fingers. Then her hand encountered something hard, covered with tape. She scrabbled with her fingernails. A key!

That was almost too easy.

Then she heard something tiny fall to the floor behind her, and the hair rose on her neck.

Was someone watching her?

Flora stood in the packing and shipping room and listened hard. A ping from the roof—a pigeon or a squirrel? An unidentified clang from outside the lab. The sound of metal grating rolling down—must be the gate blocking off the biccherne alcove for the night.

She heard the footsteps from the guard closing up the museum. There was only silence on her side of the hallway that separated the biccherne room from the laboratory.

Flora breathed deeply and her brain rumbled into operation again. She looked at the key in her hand. It must be an emergency key, a spare key that was rarely used but that the family wanted to remain accessible to a trusted few. Surely, that's why the Lorenzettis hadn't hung it in an obvious place, where non-family employees might notice it and take advantage of the opportunity to snoop in the files or abscond with office and painting supplies.

Flora slid the key into the lock of the accounting wing and turned. No problem—she was in. She walked straight through the first line of interconnected offices to the inner accounting chamber, the one directly behind Flora's own cubicle. She crossed to the file drawers she'd opened before, when Gia's back was turned, but this time she was thwarted. The files, like the door, were locked, and she found no key in any drawer she checked around that part of the room. Frustrated, Flora scanned the desk surfaces for useful documents. The printouts on Gia's desk looked like unsigned invoices, with names, institutions, and addresses. Invoices wouldn't help her—they were typed up before each transaction. Flora needed to find signed receipts showing what customers had actually paid, and for what.

On one of the other desks, she spied an old-fashioned Rolodex. Yes! She scooped it up and flipped through the first part of the alphabet. Names and phone numbers, but no indications whether the contacts were customers, suppliers, or colleagues. Well, this was far better than nothing because the police might be able use it to build up a picture of how the business operated. But she couldn't just steal the little name cards; someone would miss them and remember she'd been the last person in the office.

Was there a copy machine? Flora found it by the coffee machine, still humming from its day's work. Quickly she selected a chunk of cards from the middle of the alphabet, whipped them out of the metal holder, and placed the little cards face-down on the scanner. As she hit the copy button, she heard the heavy front door from the hallway across from the biccherne room slam.

Flora grabbed the printout before it had completely emerged and yanked hard. The single sheet ripped slightly. She stuffed it down her shirt and gathered the Rolodex cards in an untidy heap with trembling hands. Some were upside down, and all were out of order. No time. She mashed them into the Rolodex and fled through the open door.

When Maria, the Lorenzettis' daughter-in-law, approached, Flora was just turning into the bathroom in the packing room. Maria held a bundle of papers that Flora wished she could examine.

"Why hello! It's Flora Garibaldi, right? You're working late!"

"Yes. I had some painting to finish and my paints were all mixed and starting to dry out, so I stayed."

Maria Lorenzetti stopped. "Wasn't the inner office door shut?"

"I didn't notice," lied Flora.

A hard look. "Well, no matter. I will put away these files and lock up. I'm afraid you can't stay. Papà Beppe doesn't like employees here without someone from the family in the building."

"Okay. Good evening," Flora said as she escaped from further scrutiny.

Whew. Flora couldn't help wondering if Maria had already been in the building. Could she have lurked in accounting, exited through the private door that only the family used, and returned through the front door near the biccherne room?

Cut it out; you're being paranoid.

You have every right to be paranoid after a murder in your own apartment—a murder that appears to be connected with your employers.

Flora trotted down the main street and took a shortcut to return to her own neighborhood. She found herself in a warren of tiny streets south of the Duomo, twisty and shadowy as sunset approached. The buildings leaned inward as they had done for centuries, and the cobblestones under her feet were slick with rain from earlier that afternoon.

The sounds of the Campo faded as she moved farther away from it. Italian cities were never completely quiet, but this part of town came close. Sounds dwindled to a shutter closing above her, an alley cat's screech, and low voices from an open window to her right. Flora whipped around as she heard footsteps behind her, but the pedestrian disappeared into a courtyard half a block away. Hurrying now, she felt the classic tingle of unease between her shoulder blades—was someone following her?

Ridiculous. Nothing had happened at the lab, not really. No one knew about Flora's raid on the Rolodex. Unless someone *had* reported on her unusual lingering after hours to someone besides Gianetta Lorenzetti?

The ping of something metallic falling on stone behind her made Flora whirl around again. She was in time to see a dark figure duck into a doorway.

Thoroughly spooked, Flora picked up her metaphorical skirts and ran the last three blocks home.

No one came after her, and she managed to unlock the front door of her apartment building after fumbling with her keys and swearing at herself.

Okay, Mamma, I admit it: I shouldn't be here . . .

CHAPTER TWENTY-SIX

Costanza Brunetti smiled with satisfaction when she saw how spooked Flora was the first time she turned around.

Serves that American bitch right, she thought. She's had it awfully easy until now. She thinks she can waltz into our laboratory and be the darling of the boss after just two months? Ha.

Then Flora turned again, just a block or two ahead, and Costanza ducked into an arched doorway, trusting to her dark clothing and the bend in the medieval street to shield her.

She waited until Flora resumed her fast walk back to her apartment before following again. Costanza discovered she enjoyed this kind of work; the hide-and-seek aspect of it thrilled her. She knew her slim build gave her an advantage, and she'd always been light on her feet. Past partners said dancing with her was like holding a ball of cotton.

Before Maria had arrived at the laboratory, Costanza had been the one hiding in a supply closet to observe what Flora did after hours. Since Gia had given her a second key to the accounting department, Costanza chose the closet closest to Gia's desk so she could watch anything that transpired. Thus she saw Flora's raid on the file drawers and her clumsy actions with the Rolodex file and the copy machine. She thought of using her cell phone to take pictures; after all, a picture was worth a spoken report any day. But she sensed that Flora's hearing was as good as her own—she might hear the tiny clicks of Costanza's cell phone as she turned on the camera and turned off the flash.

Mamma Gia would believe Costanza's account. Costanza had Gia in her pocket now, all ready to accept her, Costanza Brunetti, as a permanent member of the Lorenzetti family.

As she traipsed back to her apartment, Costanza meditated on her next move. It would be awfully nice to have some money of her own in a bank account that Filippo never touched—or even knew about. An account that no one in the Lorenzetti family would know about. Pietro's wife Maria received a meager monthly allowance for housekeeping that left little room for impulse shopping or fun. Costanza hated the very idea. While marrying into the Lorenzetti family would get her out from under the firm rule of her father, Costanza was determined that her marriage would not be as restrictive as Maria's. No point in exchanging one overbearing ruler for another.

So how to fund such a bank account? Costanza knew a young man in another Sienese family, a family considered by the Lorenzettis to be their chief rival in the art market. The Bertoldis, of the Snail Contrada. They lived in another part of the city, but Costanza knew it well. She had dated men who lived in that neighborhood, knew its bars and restaurants.

What would Giovanni's father pay for information about Gia's spying on an American conservator, Beppe's selling of suspicious copies of paintings, Marco's patina experiments?

Costanza meant to find out. Marriage would never diminish the lifestyle she coveted and expected.

CHAPTER TWENTY-SEVEN

The next morning, Flora called Bernini at his office.

"Hello, Signorina Garibaldi," he said with a lilt in his voice.

"I have some news. I managed to get into the office files for the second time last night. I pinched some of the family's Rolodex of names and customer numbers."

"Excellent! Phone numbers too?" ·

"Some."

"When can we meet?" asked Bernini.

"I'm about to leave for work now. I can stop by your office. They don't expect me until nine thirty today."

Flora put away her cell phone, grabbed her purse and keys, and left the apartment on the run along Via Pantaneto. It was only eight thirty, but she wanted time to tell Bernini about being followed last night. She'd also like some assurances that one of his officers would keep an eye on her. It didn't seem likely, though. Bernini had told her the Carabinieri were based in Florence, with a minimal Siena operation, and the local police were short-staffed on a regular basis. So if Flora continued to participate in the investigation, she would probably have to protect herself.

Lieutenant Bernini met her in the lobby, saving Flora precious time.

"Coffee?" he asked.

"I can't. I have to get to work on time today because I've been cheating hours the last week or so. People like Costanza are starting to notice."

"Why does Costanza matter?"

"Costanza seems to be the office spy. She delights in report-ing any and every irregularity in our behavior to Pietro or Gia." She pulled the Rolodex copies out of her purse pocket and spread them out on his desk.

Bernini leaned over, almost touching Flora's arm. His eyes focused on the paper copies and he saw that many of the Rolo-dex cards were missing. "It looks like you grabbed only a third of the alphabet!"

"I know. I rushed because I felt sure that one of the family would return at any minute—they keep such irregular hours. So I grabbed the middle chunk and made copies of them. I put everything back, but the cards are now out of order. That might not attract notice, but if it does, Maria Lorenzetti knows I was the last one in the lab. And she suspects me of being in the in-ner sanctum." She explained about the locked files and how Maria had appeared just as Flora was making the copies in ac-counting.

Bernini said, "There will be an official police search of the entire office area within days. Hopefully the family won't notice a little disarray before then."

"If they use that Rolodex on a daily basis, they certainly will notice!" Her voice rose in pitch.

"Okay, I get it, I get it. Let's see what you got." He spread the copies out on his desk and together they sorted them into alphabetical order. "Huh. Names, some with addresses, some with just phone numbers. Probably all business contacts, but there might be other folks mixed in."

"Like office supplies vendors? Painting materials suppliers? Museum contacts?"

"Sure. And maybe shipping supplies, wood and stuff for repairing frames. I wish we had more information about who their actual clients are. Then we could weed them out and perhaps find the people who are links in the illegal antiquities chain." Bernini started a list of items that would interest Captain Rizzo.

"I was thinking we need signed receipts too. I saw some documents on Gia's desk that looked like ordinary invoices. But the ones I saw were incomplete—no records of goods or services received, and no signatures. I didn't get a chance to examine them all, and I didn't dare take them."

"Too bad. I bet they have an office safe somewhere. Have you ever seen one?"

Flora thought for a moment. "No. But I can nose around."

Bernini said, "I agree with you. The best kind of evidence would be copies of receipts given to clients. If we're lucky, they might have notations about what was purchased. And what the client thought he was getting."

"You mean, a note that says, 'original antiquity from Sicily, sold to Signor so-and-so, purchased for three million euros,' or something like that? Come on! The best we'll get will be 'Greek statue' and an illegible signature!" Flora scoffed.

"We can hope for more," argued Bernini. "Even incomplete documentation can help us build up an overall picture of transactions. Each buyer wants some kind of documentation that he's getting what he paid for. I agree that these people are too careful to put anything incriminating in writing, but it's far more likely that an original antiquity will be noted than a forgery. A forgery's documentation might say 'copy,' or nothing at all. Or just 'Greek statue' or 'Hellenistic vase.' " He scrubbed his hands through his hair.

"And the whole operation depends on the provenance papers," Flora added.

"Yes, of course. Unfortunately, many provenance papers are fake—just like the ones for the Getty kouros."

"I'd give my eyeteeth to see the 'provenance papers' for the kouroi in that Roman shop run by Fabio Lorenzetti." Flora gave a reminiscent shudder as she recalled Fabio sneaking up on her.

"We don't know yet whether those pieces are authentic or fake—that's in Orsoni's hands. And that's not the issue right now. We need to concentrate on the route out of Sicily and how the stuff gets to Switzerland."

"But forging originals is just as much a crime as stealing them!"

"Yes, but Major Esposito—that's the head of the Florence division of the Carabinieri Art Squad—believes the transportation contacts will lead us to everything else."

Flora gazed at Bernini, noting his obvious enthusiasm for anything connected to the Art Squad. She had a horrid suspicion he was more interested in advancing his career than in solving Ernst's murder. But she herself had split motives: to catch the murderer *and* find proof that the Lorenzettis were selling forgeries. "Have the local police gotten any closer to finding out who pushed Ernst over our balcony?"

"The State Police are working on that. They've conducted a house-to-house inquiry in your neighborhood, and we've eliminated most of those people."

"His parents came to visit me."

"Yes, I know. I sent them. I thought you would treat them gently."

"It was easy to treat them gently. Ernst's mother looked like a puff of wind would blow her over. And his father was so sad." Flora felt tears welling behind her eyes.

Bernini touched her arm. "It must have been hard on you."

"It was," Flora admitted, pulling out a tissue and mopping her eyes. "What about a motive for killing Ernst? Any progress on that?"

"We think it has something to do with trafficking. Ernst must have seen or heard something that made one of the smugglers very nervous."

Flora stared out the dirty window overlooking the street. "What if," she began slowly, "the piece of information Ernst had was about *painting* forgeries rather than the transport of original vases and statues from Greek cities to Sicily?"

"You mean the Lorenzettis are expanding their forgery operation to painting as well as sculptures?"

She looked at him. "Why not? Painting is what they do best. Remember the Martini in the lab on the day of the murder? Your boss showed considerable skepticism when Pietro tried to brush off the obvious resemblance between that painting and the other one Rizzo saw at the Lorenzetti home studio."

"True. We really haven't investigated that angle yet. Again, it all hinges on exactly how each painting is sold, and if it's being sold instead of restored and returned to a museum or church."

"There's more," said Flora. "The painting Beppe asked me to copy is one of the Martini pieces. I still don't know what will happen to it when Beppe sees it. I marked it with a special symbol in such a way that only I can recognize it. If he takes my copy away and sells it, we should be able to trace it."

Bernini grabbed his head with both hands. "Sheesh! This case is driving me crazy! It has too many arms, like an octopus! And we have no proof, no proof at all—for anything!"

Flora gazed at him with sympathy. At least he cared about doing his job well, even if Ernst's death or the forging of art works were not his priorities.

Bernini dropped his hands and looked at her. "Anyone else at the State Archives lab who is a good copyist, good enough to create a forgery?"

"Graziano is. I don't even know his last name, but Beppe gives him plenty of work."

"What about Marco? Is he involved in anything besides sculpting?"

"I doubt it. Sculpting is his passion, his whole life. But Marco is uneasy about what is going to happen to his current sculpture when it's finished. I haven't figured out if it's because he knows and wants to hide the information from me, or he doesn't know because his father and brother will decide."

Bernini rubbed his forehead. "You think they're going to sell it as an original?"

"That's one explanation for hiding the photos from me. Or maybe he didn't want me to realize he's copying something ancient, that he didn't just dream up that kouros in his own head."

"These Lorenzettis!" grumbled Bernini.

"I know. Um, there's something else I should tell you. I was followed partway home last night." Flora heard the tremor in her own voice.

Bernini pounced on her admission. "When was that? Where were you?"

"The Via San Martino neighborhood. It's a shortcut I take sometimes. And I'm not absolutely sure. There was someone behind me who ducked into a doorway when I turned around. But maybe he or she had some other reason for not wanting to be seen." Flora waited for his reaction.

"If you think someone followed you, it's probably so. After all, this is a murder case. And our primary suspects are your employer and his family. Now, are you sure you want to keep on with this? I need your help, but I freely admit I can't always be available to watch over you. Last night I was called out on a murder case right about the time you were walking home."

Flora twisted her hands. "*Another* murder case, you mean."

"Yes. Flora, I have not forgotten Ernst Mann. But I have to proceed according to my boss's priorities." Bernini looked

175

around to make sure no one else from his office was within earshot. He leaned closer to Flora and whispered in her ear, "My other big problem is that the captain is hopelessly biased in favor of his old friend Beppe and is doing his best to delay any prosecution of the Siena branch of the Lorenzetti family."

She nodded. "I had a feeling that was the case. And he seems awfully keen on Matilde, the sexy widow."

Bernini's eyebrows shot up. "You're right, of course. She's his mistress." He raised his voice to normal level as a uniformed sergeant passed his doorway. "Signorina, you should be more careful wandering around Siena at night. Not all neighborhoods are safe."

Flora sighed. "I plan to avoid that shortcut—that neighborhood is a little too isolated. I'll stick to my usual route along Via Pantaneto, where people are out until quite late."

"*Bene.*" He smiled at her. "If you can get into that back office again without arousing suspicion, look for anything that resembles a client list."

"Yes, I'll try. Oh! I meant to tell you. Pietro always carries a clipboard stuffed with papers around with him. I'd really like to see what he guards so closely."

"Good idea. I think we took a quick look at that clipboard on our first visit, but it wouldn't hurt to have another. There's probably new material he's added."

"Okay. See you soon." She gave Bernini a wan smile and departed.

CHAPTER TWENTY-EIGHT

That evening, Costanza arranged to meet her friend Giovanni Bertoldi at an obscure bar in a part of Siena she knew well but was rarely visited by the Lorenzettis. She dressed carefully in more conservative clothes than usual, a longish skirt and a blouse with a light sweater that covered her arms. Giovanni was one of those old-fashioned Italians who hated pants on women. He was also gay, which might explain his preference in women's clothing. He wanted to keep the different parts of his life separate—and his sexual preferences a secret from his family. This fact, gleaned by Costanza by yielding her body to another "friend," gave her a bargaining chip she could use now, or hold in reserve for when the negotiation became sticky.

Giovanni was waiting for her. Tall, slender, with curly black hair and flashing eyes. The way he took her hand and held it showed his appreciation for her toned-down appearance.

"Costanza, how nice to see you."

"Good to see you too." She recovered her hand and led the way to a table against the wall, swishing her skirt as she walked. "I'll have a Prosecco," she said before he could ask her what she wanted.

He returned shortly with a beer and a glass of the fizzy wine for her. "What's new at the Restauro?"

Taking a hefty swig of her wine, Costanza told him the story of the young German's murder and the interviews by the police. "The investigation is ongoing; the police don't know anything."

"Can't be good for the Lorenzetti family's reputation."

"It hasn't been in the newspaper much—only a couple of paragraphs. The German wasn't very important."

"Too bad for him. So, tell me all the family news." Giovanni's eyes gleamed. He loved gossip, the more salacious the better.

She obliged with a funny story about one of Gia's meltdowns, just to tantalize him. Gia had scandalized the entire family one lunch time by throwing food at Beppe and swearing with words even Costanza didn't know. Then, when she saw Giovanni shift in his chair, she nailed him with "Giovanni, I have some information I think your father will like. About the Lorenzetti family's 'extra' activities."

He leaned forward. "Oh? And just what would you like in return?"

"A little nest egg." She named a sum.

"That much? I thought you had Filippo firmly on the hook. When you marry, surely you will have a nice allowance?"

"The other brother's wife gets only a pittance, barely enough for housekeeping. I am not used to being deprived." She smiled slowly.

Giovanni laughed. "I'll bet you aren't!" His expression shifted from jovial to shrewd. "Well now, tell me what you know, and I'll tell you what I think the information is worth."

"I'll tell you half now, the other half when your father pays me."

"He doesn't operate that way. Try again." Giovanni looked smug. He was baiting her.

Costanza studied his face and his relaxed pose and decided he wouldn't budge. It was time to play her hidden card. "Does Papà Bertoldi know what you really do when you stay out all night? Which bars you visit, who you hang out with?"

Giovanni paled. "You little bitch!" Gone was the unruffled demeanor.

She waited.

He fidgeted and drummed his fingers on the table. After a long pause, he said, "This had better be worth it, Costanza." He drew out his wallet and extracted some bills. "Okay, cough it up."

She put her empty glass down, took the money, and began her recital. She described tidbits she had picked up from Filippo and later from Pietro, who sometimes let details slip when he forgot she was listening to conversations between Pietro and Beppe. About shipments coming in from Sicily and going north from the family compound, about Marco's patina project, about Flora's snooping and the police investigation. Costanza held back only the location of the receipts for transactions, the family's secret archive of information. She stressed that Beppe was the ringleader, the head of all the operations, and that Pietro was his right-hand man. Filippo was innocent, just a pawn on his father's chessboard. Marco too was a pawn in a larger game.

Giovanni stared at her. "My father will be interested, very interested, in what you say about our archrival. But I am surprised you would incriminate the family you hope to marry into. Your meddling could bring down the whole edifice the Lorenzettis have built up over the years."

"Only Beppe and Pietro will go to jail," Costanza assured him. "Filippo is like Marco; he's a patsy. Filippo does what he's told, and his work's all connected with the shipping side of the business. He doesn't know what he's sending out or receiving half the time; others do the packing and moving. I saw an organizational chart showing who is responsible for what. I can get it after your father pays me."

Giovanni's eyes flickered and his mouth thinned. "You imply that the police are investigating. What advantage will this new information be to my family, if the cops succeed in shutting down the Lorenzetti operations?"

"The police are having trouble finding proof. They still haven't done a thorough search of either the State Archives lab or the one in the Lorenzetti compound. Not surprising, since the murder of Ernst Mann took place in another part of the city. The police probably can't get a search warrant very easily. And by the time they do, everything that could help them will have been moved. So, what your family can do is discredit Beppe and Pietro. Start rumors in the art world that they are untrustworthy and dabbling in illegal activities. Refuse to deal with the Lorenzettis yourselves and encourage others to cancel their contracts. Build up Filippo and Marco as the only honest members of the Restauro and the family."

Giovanni shook his head in mock admiration. "You want to bring down the head of the family while feathering your own future nest? Costanza, you are even more a snake than I thought! What makes you think you can get away with this? What happens if you get caught?"

A brief shiver of doubt disturbed Costanza's usual complacency. "Leave it to me. Now, will you talk to your father?"

They parted without air-kissing or pretended good wishes. Costanza left the bar, wending her way through the narrow streets back to the Campo and the better-lighted parts of the city.

As she clip-clopped in her high heels, she thought over the conversation, reviewing what she had said and what she had held back. Signor Bertoldi would pay up, she was sure of it. He had hated Beppe Lorenzetti for years since their areas of black market operation overlapped. A Lorenzetti contract meant less business for Bertoldi and his family.

Costanza experienced a great thirst. She saw another bar, one she had never visited. She entered, ordered another glass of wine and a chaser of mineral water, and sat for the better part of an hour.

The wine calmed her nerves. She hadn't even realized she was nervous. Why should she be? Her plans always worked out.

Costanza checked the time on her cell phone. It was almost midnight; time for all good little girls to be in bed. She paid her bill and set off again, taking every shortcut through the city.

She found herself in a largely residential neighborhood, only about ten minutes from home. Costanza passed a dim alley. She never saw the figure who leaped out, or the wire that whipped around her neck, tightening.

Her last thought was that perhaps Giovanni had been right—she had miscalculated.

Chapter Twenty-Nine

Rizzo and Bernini met with their colleagues at the Questura after Costanza's body was removed. It was two in the morning, and Rizzo was exhausted.

Commissioner Mancini was beside himself. "Another murder, and you think it's connected with the first one? It didn't even occur in the same part of the city!"

"The victim was a niece and an employee of the Lorenzettis. She was also engaged to the Lorenzettis' middle son, Filippo," said Rizzo. He'd been torn away from a pleasant evening at Matilde's place. Maybe he *was* getting too old for this job; he'd lost his fascination for the chase and just wished the dead body would disappear.

"But why would anyone murder a young woman? There was no sign of sexual assault—at least, nothing obvious," Querini said.

"We don't know yet," said Bernini. "But Costanza was very close to the Lorenzetti family, and they're being investigated for two reasons: their connection with the first murder of the young German man, and also for probable smuggling of antiquities. She may have learned something that made her a threat to someone. Flora says—"

"What does the signorina say?" Rizzo snapped.

Bernini turned red. "She says Costanza has recently shown undue interest in Flora's activities. She may be collecting information for the Lorenzettis."

"Huh. Maybe she makes deals on the side. What a family! Well, we have to interview everyone again. Find out who Costanza Brunetti knew besides the Lorenzettis and her fellow employees at the Restauro." Rizzo groaned. "I just wish we'd get a break on this case!"

"Which one?" Mancini growled. "We could have two separate cases here. I refuse to believe the murders are connected until you find a motive and at least one suspect. Who, where, why."

"Oh, pipe down, Mancini! The rest of us don't need any instruction in detective work!"

Bernini said, "I'll go back to the Restauro first thing in the morning and start interviewing."

"It's Saturday tomorrow."

"Doesn't matter. Those folks work every day except Sunday."

"Do it," Mancini said. "Querini, you take the young lady's neighbors. I'll talk to her family."

"And I'll talk with the Carabinieri in Florence. Make sure they're in the picture. Can we go home now?"

"Wait," said Mancini. "When shall we meet again tomorrow?"

They agreed on four in the afternoon.

CHAPTER THIRTY

After the disaster of Costanza's murder, the Restauro employees suffered through another round of interviews and a thorough search of Costanza's desk and work area. The questions seemed endless to Flora, and she'd heard them all before. Who were the victim's friends? Who was she dating? Which parts of the city did she frequent? Any enemies at work? Et cetera, et cetera.

The combined forces of the police turned up very little about Costanza's activities. Flora regretted the girl's death, but felt some relief from her continual barbs and overactive curiosity about Flora's work and private life. On the other hand, her death spooked Flora. It hadn't happened in either Flora's apartment or her workplace, but it was too soon after Ernst Mann's. The two murders must be connected. She became increasingly convinced that the many-legged nature of the Lorenzettis' businesses contained the answers.

"What do you want me to do now?" Flora asked Bernini after her second formal interview.

"Carry on as usual for a few days, let people's emotions quiet down. Keep your ears open. Was anyone at the lab Costanza's roommate?"

"No, she lived alone. Preferred it that way, she said." Flora grimaced. "Her attitude suggested that she had male visitors, frequently." Flora thought Costanza had been promiscuous, but didn't like to say so.

"She certainly had a come-hither manner," Bernini said.

"And she dressed very provocatively."

"So you noticed!" teased Flora.

"Be hard not to."

So they all settled into a wait-and-see mode. The police came and went, and Flora and her colleagues worked hard, trying to finish Costanza's workload as well as their own assignments.

The city's mood was lazier, to match the relentlessly hot weather. Everyone seemed to be waiting breathlessly for the second Palio on the sixteenth of August. In the meantime, Siena was choked with tourists licking gelatos, buying souvenirs, and cluttering up the Campo so residents could barely cross it without stumbling into clumps of overheated foreigners pretending they were having a good time in the stifling heat.

The Sienese braced themselves for the second annual invasion: Europeans on holiday. People all over the continent left their jobs, often for the entire month of August, driving to the coast in droves and to favorite hotels that tourists rarely used. These families would also fill Siena, but they were generally better dressed than the Americans, and far more leisurely. Instead of thronging the monuments and churches, they preferred the open-air cafés and restaurants and the endlessly fascinating sport of people watching while sipping every kind of beverage, gesticulating, and smoking. Italy had not yet joined America's anti-smoking crusade.

Flora bided her time, plotting how to peek at Pietro's papers. To her disgust, Pietro developed the annoying habit of clinging to his clipboard at all hours. Two days ago, Flora almost managed it by sidling up behind Pietro while his clipboard rested on Costanza's empty desk. She glanced down at the pages and saw enough to realize she had been right about what he was carrying: the top page had a list of paintings, assigned personnel, and notes such as "awaiting second coat of varnish."

Then Pietro turned around, scooped up his clipboard, and

scowled at Flora. "Something you wanted, Signorina?"

"Just wanted to check on supplies. Has that new order of paints come in yet? I could sure use some—"

"The box is in the packing room. You may as well unpack it and put the paints out where everyone can access them."

Who does he think I am? His personal secretary? Flora snarled to herself. This guy was definitely old-fashioned when it came to women. Despite his father's approval of her painting, Pietro continued to treat her like a bimbo assistant who did only menial tasks and wasn't worth training to do anything else. So much the better, she thought. Let Pietro Lorenzetti continue to underestimate Flora Garibaldi from Chicago.

Flora pulled out her brushes and turpentine, rags and palette, and plunked them on her desk, ready from her return from the packing room. She stomped down the hallway and unpacked the paints on the communal supply table, taking the ones she needed for her next assignment. At least Beppe and Pietro had agreed that she could do in-painting now, after seeing her early work on the Madonna. Flora was a full member of the legitimate restoration team. She picked up her new painting from the assignment shelf. It was a small book cover with exquisite colors and minute printing. She'd have fun with this one.

Flora turned her finished copy of the Martini so it faced the front door and shoved it over to the corner of her worktable. She could hardly wait until Beppe passed judgment on it. She wondered whether he would give her more copying assignments. She set to work on the book cover, mixing burnt sienna with a touch of vermillion to get the exact shade of the priest's robe.

The front door banged just before midday, and Beppe strolled over to Flora's desk. He noticed the little painting immediately. "So, where is your copy, Miss Flora? I want to see it!"

"You're looking at it," she replied. She stood and fetched the original canvas to put next to the one Beppe was looking at.

"Amazing!" he exclaimed, as he realized he'd been fooled. "Pietro, come and look at this!"

Pietro rushed over from Graziano's station and stopped next to his father. The two men gazed at Flora's copy in silence, their stances with one arm akimbo identical.

"Well," said Beppe finally. He turned to Pietro, waiting for his reaction.

"Well, well," Pietro said. His eyebrows lifted and he almost smiled. "Miss Garibaldi, I owe you an apology. That is a very fine painting."

"Yes, indeed." Beppe peered closely at her work, his gaze going back and forth between the two paintings.

"Shall we show it to Luigi?" asked Pietro.

"Definitely."

Beppe picked up Flora's copy and Pietro grabbed the original Martini.

"Nice work, Flora," said Beppe, using her Christian name for the first time. "We'll probably have another assignment for you soon."

I just bet you will, thought Flora. Where would her copy end up? How would it be sold? And who the heck was Luigi?

CHAPTER THIRTY-ONE

Marco invited her to visit his sculpture studio again a few days later when the family wasn't around. He chose late afternoon, right after siesta time, when everyone ran errands and then returned to the office until six or seven. Pietro himself rarely took a siesta. He preferred to keep an eye on the work and the comings and goings of his employees.

As they hustled over to the Lorenzetti compound, Flora told herself to stay alert for anything unusual and to avoid sticky entanglements. That was easier said than done, with Marco behaving like an over-large puppy dancing around her and begging for affection.

"The statue is finished now. You'll see," Marco boasted as he took her arm and they walked around the house to the back courtyard. Marco, dropping the key in his eagerness, finally unlocked the studio door between the two flower pots. He gestured for her to enter, saying he wanted to show her everything he'd accomplished since her first visit.

"See? I am beginning a new piece here. It's a fountain with Eros figures. But the kouros is in back, beginning the aging process." Marco's satisfaction with himself and the high quality of his recent work was palpable.

"Oh, I'd really like to see the finished statue!" said Flora truthfully. She followed him to the back of the lab and exited the back door to a walled-off alley. To the right, near the service entrance to the family compound, was a large manure bed.

Parts of the kouros's arms and legs showed.

"Okay. What we do is bury it for three to six weeks in a mixture of vegetable matter and used cat litter. The scraps of veggies begin to mold and they make a pretty patina, and the acid from the cat pee helps the process along." Marco used a small trowel to pull rotting vegetation away from the statue's right hand. "See?"

Flora peered at the hand, noting its delicately mottled surface. "Looks like it's aging by the minute. And it's quite a pungent mixture," she said, resisting the urge to hold her nose.

"Glad you approve," Marco beamed at her, bouncing a little on his heels.

"Do you turn it over at some point, or just pile the, ah, shit higher?"

He laughed. "Oh, yes, just like a roast of veal. When it's half cooked, we flip it so the patina will be nice and even. Just in case the soil mixture is a little different lower down. And to make sure everything has been covered for as long as possible."

"So what does it look like at the end? When the patination process is complete, I mean?"

Marco took her back into his studio at the front of the building and extracted a small boy pulling a thorn out of his foot from a lower shelf. "There! An ancient Roman boy, circa 100 A.D."

Flora recognized the little statue as a copy of one she'd seen in a museum. She leaned over and examined the surface closely. It showed a complex, uneven surface, with patches of mottled white and brown, pitted in places. Totally convincing. I wonder if . . . then she felt Marco's hands on her waist.

"Marco, cut it out."

"But it's been weeks now. You know how patient I've been. I want us to be a couple; I want to be your lover!"

Flora removed his hands from her waist. "Marco, you are a

very nice man and I like you. We can have fun together, go out for meals and stuff, but I'm just not ready for anything more right now. Besides, I think it's dangerous to become too friendly with a member of the family that employs me. What if we had a relationship, and it went wrong? I could lose my job." She expected sulks, but Marco responded with a resigned shrug.

"I suppose you are right," he said, stuffing both hands in his pockets. Then his disarming smile returned. "But I have lots of time to change your mind!" Flora guessed that Marco had never been turned down by a woman he wanted, so his optimism was hardly unfounded. Besides, he knew very well that he was attractive. He probably hoped Flora would come around, and he clearly hadn't thought about the fact that if things went wrong, Flora would be the one to leave, not him. Marco would never be out of a job—unless he infuriated his family once too often.

Flora shook her head, smiling. He was quite irrepressible. And she really did like him—as a person, not as a potential boyfriend. But the last complication she needed right now was a love affair with one of the prime suspects in a murder case. Not that she believed Marco was the one; Pietro was a far more likely character. It might even be Beppe, but he seemed such a family man, so genial, so fond of his grandchildren and daughters-in-law. Could he really be a murderer?

She tucked away her suspicions and returned to asking questions about the patination process. "So, Marco, who's the client for your beautifully antiqued kouros? You said something about a guy who wants an ancient-looking statue for his garden, right?"

"A friend of Papa's," answered Marco without any attempt to hide information from her. But he didn't give her a name, either. "Papa says his friend is very rich and can afford the best."

If this client can afford the best, thought Flora, then he can afford a real antiquity looted from Sicily. Or a forgery passed off as one. She probed a little more. "So do you have other clients for this special work? Making replicas of ancient statues, I mean?"

"Not yet, but I will. Papa says soon I will have as much work as I can handle. Look, Flora." Marco shoved aside some debris on his worktable and pulled out some smaller pieces from his shelves. Dancing girls, animals, fish—everything a rich gardener might want.

Flora remembered the Roman villa at the Getty Museum in Malibu, California. A museum garden would be a perfect location for these pieces of Marco's—if they were sold as modern copies. She'd never seen such good patinas on marble before.

"I think I could sell these as replicas for tourists to buy at museum shops, don't you? The smaller ones especially," boasted Marco.

"Then why don't you?"

"My father and brother say we can make more money if we sell my statues to private clients."

Hmm. Then the million-euro question was, sell them how? An authentic Greek sculpture, excavated from a legitimate archaeological site, would immediately become property of the state and go straight to a museum like the Villa Giulia in Rome. A looted sculpture, dug up at night and secretly shipped north, would have false provenance papers, claiming a vague source such as "Southern Italy." For Marco's work, there were only two options. Sell it to a museum or a collector as a legitimate replica, with a receipt saying something like, "copy of an original marble copy of a lost Greek bronze statue made by M. Lorenzetti of Siena." Or sell it as a forgery, with a vague, made-up provenance. Flora's gut told her that however it was done by the Lorenzetti family, it would involve more lies than truth.

Then she had an idea. "Marco, do you sign your work? I mean carve your initials or a date or something on each piece of marble?"

"I did at first, but Pietro told me to stop doing that."

Bingo. Authentic-looking sculptures with no signatures. Not exactly the smoking gun they were looking for, but highly suggestive. Flora remembered something that she'd meant to ask Marco. "Marco, do you remember when Captain Rizzo came to Sunday lunch the day of Ernst's death?"

"How could I forget that day?"

"You looked angry. Why were you angry?"

Marco sighed and fixed her with his beautiful brown eyes. "My family makes me angry. Frequently. My father and older brother have so many things going, and they don't like anyone poking their noses into the family business. I thought they were being rude to the captain."

Good answer, thought Flora, but not entirely convincing. She tried another question, "Another thing: your father liked a copy of a Martini painting that I finished this week. He asked Pietro if they should 'show it to Luigi.' Who is Luigi?"

"Oh, poor Signorina Garibaldi! There are two Luigis. Cousin Luigi who works at the State Archives, and Luigi Turchetti who owns an art gallery near the Campo. It was probably Turchetti; he sells copies of paintings that we make for the tourist business."

"Oh," said Flora, a bit disappointed. Well, she wasn't going to solve all her mysteries in one afternoon. "Marco, is there a bathroom here? I drank too much coffee."

He grinned and directed her to a tiny bathroom down the hall, opposite his father's studio.

When Flora came out, she noticed that the door to one of the storage rooms was unlocked. Glancing swiftly toward Marco's studio, she pushed it open. Her breath caught in her chest.

A Greek statue stood on a low, wheeled platform with a rope handle. A kouros. Not just any kouros, but an original ancient statue with a strong resemblance to the one Marco had made and was now subjecting to the patination process. As she stepped closer and looked at the surface, she remembered Assunta Vianello's commentary on surfaces. *"Once you have seen the original, it's hard to imagine how you could be taken in by one of the cruder fakes. An ancient surface is uneven, pitted, discolored. It bears little resemblance to the surface created in an afternoon's soaking in acid . . ."*

Marco stepped into the room. "Flora, let's go. My father would be furious if he saw you poking around."

Flora didn't care. Her brain buzzed with excitement. "Marco, is this statue the original, the one you used as a model for your own kouros?"

He looked uneasy, but not particularly upset. "Yes. It just arrived from Chiusi, from my cousin's studio. I saw it last spring, studied it and sketched it, and took many photos."

Flora stared at him, strongly tempted to question him, to ask about the provenance of this exquisite statue that surely was the "smoking gun" the Carabinieri for the Protection of Cultural Heritage sought. She could hardly believe that Marco was innocent, yet his attitude suggested just that. To him, the statue was something to imitate, something to recreate as his own work of art. Just like she'd told Bernini, Marco didn't care what happened to it, or whether his family activities were illegal. Even if she was wrong about him, she couldn't afford to antagonize anyone in the Lorenzetti family.

She said, "It's absolutely gorgeous. No wonder you wanted to copy it!"

Obviously relieved that she asked no questions about where it had come from or how it ended up in Chiusi, Marco pointed out some of his favorite features—the style of the curls around the archaic face, the beautifully detailed stomach muscles, the delicate feet. As she listened to him, Flora realized how cleverly

Marco had modified those details just a little, to make his own kouros unique.

Inside, Flora squirmed with impatience. *I've got to call Bernini!*

They stayed a little longer, and then Marco checked the time on his cell phone and said he had an appointment. "We'll go out the back."

He had just closed the door and was about to lock it when a truck pulled up in the alley. A medium-sized, plain brown truck, with a roll-up door on the back.

Two men hopped out of the cab and exchanged greetings with Marco. The shorter man unlatched the back hatch to the truck and lowered a ramp. Taking Flora's hand so she was forced to accompany him, Marco led the way to the storeroom where the statue waited. One of the men grabbed the rope handle of the cart and the other man pushed. Before Flora could do anything to stop them, they had maneuvered the statue outside. It was hauled up the ramp and deposited inside quicker than Flora thought possible.

"Marco, do you know if—"

"Hush. These men work for my father."

Flora desperately wanted to memorize the truck's license plate when the ramp was raised and the hatch lowered, but Marco's tall body blocked her. Had he done it on purpose, to prevent her from obtaining that information?

She looked up into his shuttered face as the truck drove away.

Marco's eyelashes flickered, and she realized he wasn't quite as innocent as she'd supposed.

CHAPTER THIRTY-TWO

To Flora's consternation, Marco walked her all the way back to her apartment. They scarcely talked on the way, probably because neither of them could think of a safe topic for discussion.

Flora whipped out her cell phone and called Bernini as soon as she had unlocked her door and shut herself inside. He didn't pick up, so she called the Carabinieri office.

An underling answered, and she struggled to make the urgency of her call understood. In a few minutes, Captain Rizzo answered the extension.

"How sure are you that the statue was ancient?" said Rizzo, who had no idea where Bernini was.

Flora sighed. "I'm no sculpture expert, but I'm about ninety percent sure it was ancient. It had all the hallmarks of an ancient kouros, and the patina was totally believable—complex and pitted. It closely resembled authentic statues I saw in the Villa Giulia Museum in Rome recently."

"Describe the truck to me."

"Plain, brown, no markings. I couldn't get the whole license plate, but it had an eight and a four in it."

Rizzo groaned. "Any idea what direction they took?"

"The truck took a left out of the alley. That's all I saw because Marco Lorenzetti steered me in the opposite direction, back toward the Campo."

"Great. Thanks, Signorina Garibaldi. We'll be in touch."

Flora wished she were a cop herself so she'd be in the information loop a lot sooner. But she was only a civilian, and a half-foreigner at that. She really didn't expect to hear from Rizzo again, but Bernini would call. When? Where was he, and what was he doing? Then she spared a thought for Marco. What was he up to? Was he actively helping his father, or just trying to protect Flora from getting herself into deeper trouble? Maybe he was as conflicted as she was at this moment and had no idea of what to do next.

The next morning, after a restless night, Flora lurked at her desk at the State Archives laboratory and fumed. Bernini had not called. She'd left two messages for him since waking up that day.

Fine. What next? She sipped her ever-present coffee and reviewed her options. She suspected that the Lorenzetti family had several stashes of information connected with different parts of the business. Maybe it was because different people were in charge of each operation, maybe it was insurance against loss. So, what would she do, if she were a Lorenzetti? Spread the files around so that if some interfering employee—or visiting cop—found something, duplicates existed elsewhere. But that could be cumbersome, keeping track of everything and laying your hands on what you needed at any given time.

She agreed with Bernini that the Lorenzettis must have a safe somewhere because the papers she'd seen so far were either innocuous or incomplete. The receipts and shipping records must be hidden, because they were the documents most likely to detail any wrongdoing. So, Flora would wait until people were out of her immediate area and start poking around. Inside the accounting office made the most sense, but perhaps the family wouldn't keep a safe where it was expected to be.

Behind a file cabinet? Too inconvenient and too heavy to

move if you wanted to get in and out in a hurry. How about behind a painting? The staff made a habit of hanging works in progress on the wall at different stages of restoration in order to step back and look at them, check color matches and brush-strokes for accuracy.

But some paintings were permanent fixtures. Flora glanced around at the paintings she saw every day. An original Lorenzetti (of course), yet another Martini, two miniature book covers, and some other art works she couldn't identify. Her gaze returned to the Martini—just the right size to conceal a safe. And the frame wasn't so huge that she would be unable to lift it off the wall.

Flora waited until Pietro and Maria had disappeared into the accounting suite at the back of the lab. Then she nipped over to the Martini, which was hanging over Ernst's former workstation. If she got caught, she planned to say she wanted to temporarily remove the Martini and replace it with the painting she was currently working on so she could study it from a distance. She slid out of her sandals and climbed onto Ernst's chair and then to the top of the desk in her bare feet. The painting seemed stuck to the wall. Flora pulled a bit and it dropped into her hands, almost overbalancing her in the process. Eureka! A small wall safe, conveniently placed at a height that Flora could manage easily—if only she knew the combination.

Footsteps announced that someone was returning to her part of the lab. Flora rehung the painting with trembling fingers and hopped down from the desk. She didn't have time to slip her sandals back on so she stood on them, pretending to look for a pen in Ernst's top drawer. Uh, oh. She'd forgotten to bring her own painting with her to make her story more plausible . . .

Pietro and Maria passed her without a second glance, heading out of the lab for lunch.

Whew. Flora really should wait until no one was around, but

then she risked being caught at a time when she clearly had no business being on the premises. But her gambit to stay late had worked once. She decided to delay on one of her projects, a re-varnishing job that was supposed to be ready by the next day. Then, after everyone left, she could slap on the final layer and try to break into the safe while it was drying.

Five thirty, and people still lingered. Everyone had work to fin-ish, and Pietro seemed to be everywhere at once. Annoying man! Why was he such a micromanager? Flora spent most of the afternoon on a less urgent gesso-and-gold-leaf application until Pietro complained.

"Miss Garibaldi, I see on the schedule that the Palazzo Pub-blico painting assigned to you is due to be returned to the museum tomorrow. Have you finished it?"

"Ah, almost. One more layer of varnish to go. I was planning to stay late to finish it."

"But you are working on a frame for a different painting just now!"

"Yes, while the first layer of varnish dries. The retouching of the surface turned out to be more time-consuming than I'd thought."

"Very well, stay until it's complete. But try to manage your time better in the future."

Flora stuck her tongue out at him as he turned his back. Gra-ziano, who was cleaning brushes at the sink, saw her do it and smirked. Another weasel type, she thought. Ever since Co-stanza's death, she'd felt Graziano's gaze following her. They rarely spoke, except about work-related tasks. Flora had always felt Graziano didn't like her. Was he suspicious of foreigners? Maybe he was gay and disliked women.

An hour later everyone had departed except Flora and Pietro. Since Pietro knew she was working late, he made an exception to the rule about employees staying after family members were present.

"I have to return after dinner, Flora, so I will lock up then and set the alarm. How long do you think you'll be?"

"Another half hour or so. Not long," said Flora.

"Okay. Make sure you slam the door that leads to the hallway opposite the biccherne room."

"I will."

Alone at last. Flora lost no time in crossing to Ernst's desk and removing the Martini painting. She wanted to make sure the safe was really locked before she hunted for the combination. She reached for the knob and twisted, and to her amazement the door popped open. Someone had forgotten to check that it was locked! What luck. She gazed at the contents inside and debated how much to take without making it immediately obvious that the safe had been robbed.

A small rustle made her jump and she whirled around, almost falling off the desk.

There was no one there.

Chiding herself for being a ninny, Flora grabbed a double handful of papers and jumped down onto the floor so she could spread out the papers on the desk.

Five years of tax records. Old invoices, last year's packing lists. Everything except what she was really looking for. Frustrated, Flora opened an unmarked manila envelope. There they were! Receipts for the last several months, with names, addresses, and phone numbers. Flora extracted the sheets she wanted and folded them so she could stuff them into her deepest pocket.

She was about to reassemble the pile of documents and put them back into the safe when she heard a whoosh behind her.

Pain erupted in the side of her head and darkness engulfed her.

CHAPTER THIRTY-THREE

"Uh . . . uh . . . uh." She heard someone groaning.

She opened her eyes. Her head felt like a rotten melon, and she was the groaner.

Underneath her lay a lumpy surface that slid and rumbled. She must be in some kind of vehicle. A truck? A swerve threw her to the side, and a ridge on the metal wall collided with her shoulder.

The pain produced a string of curses she didn't know she knew.

Her arms strained against rope bindings. Someone had tied her up and thrown her on a pile of sacks. At least she hadn't been gagged or blindfolded. Flora struggled and felt the rope loosening. A few minutes of squirming and twisting and her hands slid free. Lucky for her, the kidnapper had not bothered to tie her feet, and he'd done an overly hasty job on her hands as well. She stood, rubbing her wrists and stomping her feet to bring back the circulation.

Was there any kind of window? Oddly, yes. A narrow aperture on the upper wall, toward the back. She shifted a small footstool over to the window and grabbed at the metal ridge running from floor to ceiling to hoist herself up. Her astonished gaze fell on rock escarpments and a stunning view of the valley behind them. It certainly looked like the South Tyrol region and the Dolomites! And the road must be the Brenner Pass! What was she doing here? How did she end up in the back of this truck?

She tested her arms and legs. Except for the lump on her head, her limbs worked smoothly.

Flora's head ached and she found standing difficult as the truck swayed back and forth. She slid down the wall of the truck until she was seated, legs stretched out for balance. She waited until the dizziness passed and looked at her surroundings. Around her were large and medium-sized wooden crates, tied with rope. Some kind of shipment going north, and she was part of it. Who was the driver? Pietro maybe, or one of his minions.

She needed to pee, urgently. She saw nothing available to serve as a toilet. She crept forward and pounded on the wall separating her from the driver. "Hey! Let me out!"

Loud radio music was her only answer. The truck sped on.

Shrugging, she grabbed a sack and threw it over to the other side of the truck from where she'd been sitting. She crossed to the sack, slid down her pants and crouched, leaning against the vibrating wall to keep her balance. Nothing to wipe with, either, not even a tissue from her pocket. Hoping for the best, she pulled her pants back up and resumed her precarious seat, bracing herself as the vehicle continued to sway and rattle at every curve in the road.

They traveled higher and higher, and time passed. She couldn't tell how long she hovered, waiting, but her thirst increased with every mile. Finally, she felt the truck exit from the highway and slow down.

Get out of the truck. Run away from the driver, whoever he is.

She had a plan. She didn't know how she'd made this decision, but it didn't matter. At the first opportunity, when the doors opened, she planned to jump on top of the driver. She hoped there was no second man—she assumed it was a man who'd abducted her. Then she'd run like hell.

The truck slowed further, turned left, and rattled to a halt.

She rose, positioned herself on one side of the roll-up door, and waited.

An unbearable pause, so long that she feared the driver had left the truck to buy a drink or a meal. Then the door rolled up.

A squat, dark man she'd never seen before reached for her. She stepped back from the truck bed edge, out of range.

"Hey! Miss! Where do you think you're going?"

She took two running steps and launched herself at his chest, succeeding in knocking him down and using his body as a cushion for her own fall. Another yell, punctuated with gasps for air, greeted her effort. The man lay in the middle of the street, totally winded and clutching his stomach.

Flora didn't stick around to hear what else he had to say. With a parting kick to his stomach, she took off down a narrow side street.

Street signs appeared in both German and Italian. She was definitely in the transalpine region of Italy near Austria and Switzerland.

Bolzano? suggested her foggy brain. If so, she'd been here before; she might recognize landmarks.

She ran despite the rising nausea in her throat from the head injury and the pain in her shoulder, passing a tent full of beer drinkers and a German band. The revelers looked at her curiously, but no one stopped her. Rounding a corner, she saw a square, and a sign reading Piazza Erbe. She knew it! She *was* in Bolzano. She'd visited the city when? Three years ago? She remembered a central square and the fabulous museum that housed the body found in a glacier. The Iceman, the ice mummy found in the mountains between Italy and Austria. The one that international scientists had argued over, dissected, imaged, and studied for years. And now it had a museum all its own—after the border dispute was settled in Italy's favor.

"Hey, stop! Miss!" yelled a man behind her.

It sounded like the driver. Flora had no intention of stopping. Her path became a zigzag through more narrow streets, right and left, then straight, then left and right. Her breath rasped in her throat and her chest was on fire.

"Flora! Flora Garibaldi!" The man shouted again.

Flora? Not for the first time she thought: What a silly name. Her parents should have done better for her.

"We did, you ninny," said a remembered voice in her head. "I wanted to call you Daisy, but your mother objected."

Her father. Scraps of memories of her childhood flitted through her head as she ran faster. Dodging cyclists and a motorcyclist hell-bent on shaving off a corner—or a piece of Flora—she passed a trattoria, a newsstand, and a wine shop. At the corner of Via Museo she took a right for the Archaeological Museum. Lots of tourists would be in there . . . a good place to hide from her pursuer.

The entrance of the museum loomed. A large sign next to the doorway decorated with iron scrolls said, in four languages, "South Tyrol Museum of Archaeology, Home of Ötzi the Iceman." Flora darted in the front door and zoomed past the ticket booth. It took the one guard on duty moments to realize that someone had just dashed by him and skipped paying. By the time he gathered his wits, Flora was halfway up the stairs to the second floor.

She sped through the archaeological exhibits. Case upon case of stone knives, ceramics, maps of Austrian and Italian sites, signs pointing to the Iceman exhibit on the upper floors. Clumps of tourists blocking her way.

Up, up she went, almost losing her balance at the top of the last staircase.

Hide. Hide.

Where? She remembered the room containing the mummy, small and shriveled and isolated in his special climate-controlled case. Not there. Too many tourists near the entrance, and no place to hide inside.

Aha! A tall case in the corner, part of the exhibit that described what the Iceman ate and drank before an arrow in the back took his life. She remembered that the first X-ray had totally missed the arrowhead; it took more advanced imaging a few years later to find it. At first, the research team had believed the Iceman had died from exposure, trapped on a mountaintop during a blizzard, covered by a glacier and hidden for centuries. Then the researchers realized that the Iceman had been shot and wounded, and had traveled or was carried to the mountaintop where he died about five thousand years ago.

Flora slowed down so she'd be less conspicuous. The case she was aiming for stood on a plinth, a solid mass of wood from waist height down to the floor. Glancing around to make sure no one was watching, Flora slid behind it, crouched down, and tried to quiet her breathing.

How was she going to get out of here? The museum staff would require payment, and Flora had no purse, not even a handful of coins. As she lay on the floor, her hands surveyed her pockets and found a pair of sunglasses. Not much, but better than nothing. She untwisted her hair from its ponytail, letting her hair fall around her face in an untidy mop, and put on the dark glasses. Now she'd wait for a nice, large family group.

Miracle of miracles, they came. A surge of noisy tourists, with a grandma in a wheelchair. Perfect. They gathered around the case, chattering in French about the Iceman model dressed in full traveling garb (leggings, cape, and medicine bag), and Flora stood up and followed the group closely as they moved on to the next case. More people poured into the room, clearly part of a tour group.

It was so easy to blend in. The French family never noticed her, or if they did, they thought she was just part of the tide of humanity advancing on the elevator.

Flora nipped behind the wheelchair just as she spotted her pursuer climbing the last flight of stairs. The doors closed before he saw her, and the car sank toward the first floor.

CHAPTER THIRTY-FOUR

Her luck held. Flora exited the museum with the large French family and ducked into the first side street she saw. Just in case the truck driver was still behind her, she looked for a family restaurant or pizzeria where she could lick her wounds and recover while she figured out how to get home.

Ahead, she spied a small pizzeria with an open door. Following the aroma of garlic like a little dog, she entered and took a tiny table as far back as she could. Another family enjoying a late lunch effectively screened her from view to any casual passersby. Just to be sure, Flora held up the menu in front of her face. Then she remembered that she had no purse to pay for her meal!

Wait. Emergency cash pouch . . .

That bump on the head was affecting her short-term memory. She reached into the waistband of her pants and found the little travel pouch where she always carried extra cash. Fifty euros. She heaved a sigh of relief. Enough for a meal, but probably not a train or a bus back to Siena. Never mind, sustenance first, then maybe her mind would work properly.

She ordered a *piazza bianca* with arugula and a bottled water.

"Wait," she asked the waiter as he turned to go back to the kitchen. "Could you spare a couple of aspirin? I have a terrible headache—that's why I didn't order wine."

"Certainly, Signorina."

He brought her three aspirin and a pitcher of water. She

drained the first glass and refilled it. She drank half of that glass also.

As the aspirin took effect, Flora watched the entrance to the restaurant. No one she recognized appeared. Her brain turned over like an engine greased with molasses while she waited for the aspirin to take effect.

Suddenly, she remembered her visit to the safe behind the Martini painting. The documents with names and addresses that Bernini wanted! She'd had them in her possession! But she'd never had the opportunity to examine them or memorize anything, and now they were gone!

Someone stuffed me in that van and shipped me north. What were they going to do with me? Nothing good . . .

Who was the driver? Must have been some employee she hadn't seen before. A singularly inept kidnapping, since he hadn't tied her up properly or managed to prevent her escape. Maybe the man was just that, a driver, instead of being an experienced thug. A guy who worked for Pietro or Beppe who had never kidnapped anyone before. Pietro—or maybe Graziano—had knocked her out and passed her onto the first person heading north, to get her out of the way.

The safe. Was the discovery of the safe the reason for Ernst's murder? Had he seen some of the same documents Flora had tried to steal? She wished she'd had more time with those papers.

No point in returning to the State Archives. Flora's job was kaput, and the Lorenzettis would probably throw her out. And chances were good the family had moved anything valuable to another location—or else made sure the safe was properly locked. But first she had to get home to Siena with practically no money.

The pizza, piping hot and fragrant, arrived. She burned her mouth on the first bite, but it was worth it. Nothing like garlic, tomato, basil, and cheese for reviving a fugitive. As her tummy filled, she became aware of the conversation of the couple at the next table.

". . . so we go to San Gimignano first?"

"Yes, we can visit cousin Elettra and then go on to Rome in a day or two."

San Gimignano! That was a stone's throw from Siena. If Flora could hitch a ride to the most famous medieval hill town in Tuscany, she'd have enough money for the rest of the way to Siena by bus.

Chapter Thirty-Five

Hours later, an exhausted Flora arrived in Siena. She didn't remember much of the trip; she'd dozed for most of it and worried for the rest. Her head hurt, and her thinking was mushy.

Wait until you get home, Flora. Rest, eat, rest again. Her mother's voice. For once, Flora agreed with her good advice. She didn't trust her sore head and woolly brain to make sense of anything until after a good night's sleep.

Her waking dream included a merry-go-round with Beppe, Gia, and Pietro riding horses, gesticulating and complaining to Flora about her poor riding abilities. Bernini rode the horse next to her, up and down, up and down, but he disappeared before the carousel stopped. Pietro scowled and slid off his horse to come talk with her. He grabbed her arms and—

Flora woke with a jerk as the car exited the highway at Siena. The kind couple who'd agreed to give her a lift dropped her right at her front door instead of a more central place. Perhaps they had noticed how terrible she looked; her clothing was torn and filthy after her surprise truck ride, and she figured her face was pale and sweaty after her exertions and the excruciating headache that came and went.

"Thank you so much!" Flora said to the Moscatos. "You've no idea how grateful I am to be home so much quicker than I'd planned."

"Piacere," said the man. "No problem, as you Americans say."

Flora waved goodbye and dragged herself up the stairs.

For once, Linda was home.

"What on earth happened to you?" she said, eyebrows raised all the way to her hairline.

"You won't believe it. I was knocked out, kidnapped from the office, thrown into a truck, and driven north over the Brenner Pass to Bolzano."

"What! This sounds like a thriller plot to me! Shall I get you a drink? I want to hear the whole story."

Flora half fell onto the couch and kicked off her shoes. "Have we got any aspirin? My head is killing me again."

Linda brought a tall glass of ice water and bent over to examine Flora's head. "That is a nasty bump you have there, but the bleeding has stopped." She probed gently with her fingers and Flora yelped. "Sure you don't need to see a doctor? Or, at least put some ice on that?"

"I think I'll be okay, but my brain doesn't seem to be working well."

"Whoa! Then you might have a concussion! I think you do need a doctor."

Flora rubbed her eyes. "How about a bag of ice, for starters? My vision is okay, and Signora Moscato—the wife of the man who drove me home—said my pupils weren't dilated or different from one eye to the other. I think if I get a good night's sleep, I don't need a doctor."

"Hmm," Linda replied as she returned to the kitchen for a bag of ice and a dish towel to wrap it in. "I might have to wake you up a couple of times to check on your eyes. Your pupils might change overnight if you're really concussed. Here you go. Now tell me."

Flora accepted the ice pack and held it to the lump on her head while she told her story. "I'd never seen the driver before, but I'm guessing he's an employee of the Lorenzettis. Pietro is the most likely person to have conked me on the head. He must have seen me, after all."

"So what were you looking for in the safe?"

"Receipts of transactions. Names and addresses of clients. The Rolodex I copied part of before only had phone numbers and names, but no indication whether the people were clients or suppliers or colleagues. The papers I found in the safe—if I can find them again—did appear to have extra real information about who paid what when." Flora told her story.

Linda shuddered. "Do you think they planned to kill you, whoever kidnapped you?"

Flora thought about it. "Maybe. But they could have done that so easily here, in Siena. I think maybe they just wanted me out of the way. Perhaps because a big shipment was coming in, or some other major deal was about to take place."

"Well, I think you should call that nice young policeman, what's his name?"

Flora grimaced. "Sottotenente Bernini. I tried several times; he didn't answer. He's totally tied up with trying to get the different branches of the police to work together. I'll call him again soon. First I need to check out something at the lab. By the way, Linda, you can't repeat any of this to anyone, got it? It might be dangerous."

"Don't worry; I'm not interested in playing Superwoman, even if you are. Bernini is going to be pissed at you if you act without police support."

"Probably. But the police aren't very interested in the possibility of the Lorenzettis making and selling forgeries. I am. And I think I know where the proof is."

Linda frowned. "What about the murder of Ernst? Didn't you tell me the DNA results showed lots of people in our flat, including half the Lorenzetti family? Stands to reason, since they are our landlords."

"Yes. That's why they have no real evidence yet of who pushed

Ernst off that balcony. I know it wasn't you; you were away that weekend."

"Gee, thanks. So glad you don't think I'm a murderer!"

Flora gave her a weak smile and rubbed her sore head.

"Thanks for your help, Linda. I'm going to bed."

Chapter Thirty-Six

After ten hours of sleep, Flora felt so much better that she decided the best medicine for her aching head was fresh air and a long walk. After three aspirin and a cup of coffee, that is. Then she discovered she had no purse. No purse, no cell phone, no keys. Where was her purse?

Flora clutched her head and thought hard. She hadn't had her purse on her when she looked for the safe. So the person who conked her and threw her in the truck had never had it. It must still be in the desk drawer at the lab!

She gazed out the window. How could she bear to go back into that den of criminals? For that is what they were. She still didn't know which one of the Lorenzettis was Ernst's murderer—or Costanza's—or who was her kidnapper, but that didn't matter right now. She didn't trust or want to meet any of the family right now. All right, she would go to the lab, try to get in without keys, and retrieve her purse and a couple of small personal items. She reckoned the chances of anyone hitting her on the head in broad daylight with lots of other employees around were vanishingly small. Then, once she had her phone again, she would call Bernini, or go visit him in his office. He needed to know what had happened, the sooner the better.

As she descended the stairs to the cobbled street, she debated the wisdom of telling so much to Linda Maguire the night before. But Linda, despite her occasional ditzy behavior, had never betrayed a confidence. Losing Ernst had brought them closer together. And, in Flora's current state of mind, she needed a female ally.

Not for the first time, she wished she could talk with her father. His common sense and total support of her always made her feel both cherished and taken seriously. Problem was, he couldn't keep anything Flora-related away from Flora's mother. She swooped down on anything to do with her precious children.

The air was fresh and cool. Usually, Flora couldn't think of a place she'd rather be than in Siena, Italy, on a perfect summer morning. The hint of crispness spoke of the approach of autumn—soon, but not yet. If only she were a tourist, with many days of sun-soaked hanging around the Campo ahead of her. Instead, she was embroiled in a murder, along with probable trafficking and forgery, and she was out of a job. Well, technically they hadn't fired her yet, but they would at the earliest opportunity. And that meant getting another job—without a reference from her current employer . . . damn! She'd think of something.

Aha, a post office! Didn't post offices in Italy have pay phones? She hurried in and checked. There was one, in the corner. But when she approached it, she saw that the cord had been ripped out of the wall. Everyone used cell phones these days; why should the city of Siena replace broken pay phones?

Flora exited the post office and picked up her pace. She wanted to get the visit to the lab over with and call Bernini. As she neared the courtyard of the State Archives, a garbage truck blocked her way. Flora nipped around to the side and almost bumped into Graziano, who'd clearly done the same thing from the other direction.

"Ciao, Flora! Stupid truck. That driver doesn't need to park here in an entrance."

"True, but he won't listen to us."

Graziano peered at Flora's face. "Hey, you look tired today."

"I had a busy weekend."

"Ah. Have you been on any interesting trips lately?" Graziano's dark eyes gleamed with a touch of malice.

Flora stumbled on the lowest step of the staircase leading to the State Archives. "Er—no," she said, but her brain caught fire with the distinct impression that Graziano *knew* about her sudden and disastrous trip to Bolzano. And if that were true, what else did he know? She cursed herself for not finding out more about this young man who was almost certainly another nephew or second cousin or friend of the Lorenzetti family. Flora recovered and added, "I'd love to travel right now in this perfect weather, but I don't suppose I'll get the chance."

Was she imagining things? Maybe she'd misinterpreted his manner, but her gut said otherwise.

Wait a minute—if Graziano knew about Bolzano, so did the entire family. Would they even let her in the building today?

Graziano was waiting for her. That in itself was odd—Graziano had never waited for Flora before. Okay, then, she'd brazen it out at the Restauro just long enough to get her things.

They entered the building with his keys since Flora didn't have hers. No one said a word. Perhaps not everyone knew that she'd raided the safe and gotten caught. People in the lab treated her normally, which meant basically ignoring her.

Flora pulled the purse out of the lower drawer and checked for her phone. Thank goodness, everything was still there. But the phone's screen showed the ominous "!" next to the battery logo, meaning the battery was dead. She couldn't call Bernini, not on this phone.

"I didn't expect to see you here." Beppe's voice came out of nowhere. She hadn't even known he was in the building.

She turned. Beppe and Pietro stood a few feet away. Pietro glared at her, arms crossed. Graziano stood next to him, an expression of glee on his sallow face.

"I, um . . ." Flora took a deep breath. "I came to retrieve my phone and personal things. Then I'm leaving for good. I'm resigning."

"No, Signorina Garibaldi, you are not resigning, you are being fired! We don't employ people we cannot trust." Beppe wore an injured expression on his broad face. Pietro had uncrossed his arms and was opening and closing his hands. No doubt he'd prefer to throttle her instead of letting her go. Beppe continued, "You have five minutes to pack up your personal things. Then I will take your keys and you will leave this place!"

Flora, fuming with all the things she wanted to say, handed over the Restauro keys. A crazy part of her wanted to tell them what she thought of their bullying tactics and boast how much she knew about their business. But that would be fatal; the Lorenzettis didn't have any idea how much she knew or proof that she was already in cahoots with the police. She just had to get away, and quickly, before any of them found an excuse to keep her there.

Feeling dizzy, she packed her personal belongings quickly. It only took a few minutes, since most of her painting supplies were already at the apartment. Cheeks burning, she walked out of the lab and crossed the biccherne room. The big door to the outside world slammed behind her for the last time, and Flora held the iron railing as she walked slowly down the marble stairs.

Now what? She was really out of a job. Tears ran down her face, making her feel even more foolish. Why was she crying over being fired by a bunch of crooks? She'd already known the job was over; getting fired was no surprise. But the trio of Lorenzettis lining up against her made her feel vaguely guilty, as if she had really done something wrong. What should she do? Her head ached, and she was hungry. Okay. Go get some sustenance—she'd forgotten to eat breakfast—and plan the next step.

She dragged her weary self to the outdoor café where she'd seen the street player only a few short weeks earlier. Now, it was half-filled with Europeans on holiday and native Sienese taking coffee breaks. The sounds of conversation in at least three languages and the clink of glasses formed a soothing background for Flora's uncomfortable thoughts.

Flora desperately wanted wine but knew the state of her head made that unwise. She ordered coffee and a tomato and cheese sandwich. She planned to wait until she was calmer and then walk over to the Carabinieri office to find Bernini. When the waiter brought her order, Flora had started a short "to-do" list:

See Bernini. Tell him about her abduction and what she'd seen in the safe before she was knocked unconscious. Ask if the family studios had been thoroughly searched yet, and when.

Look for a new job. Who could she ask for a reference among her former employers?

Where? Back in Florence? Or maybe Rome.

She paused for a restorative sip of coffee and another bite of her sandwich. Uh, oh. She wasn't just out of a job, she was probably out of an apartment as well. Even if the Lorenzettis did not evict her right away, Flora had no intention of renting from them any longer than she had to. She added to her list:

Find a new place to live, just for the time it would take to finish helping Bernini solve this case and obtain a new post.

The act of writing had calmed her down and her tears had dried. Flora shook out two aspirin pills from the little box in her purse and swallowed them. She finished her coffee and glanced at her watch. Only eleven-thirty. If she hurried, she could find Bernini before he took a lunch break.

A ten-minute walk brought her to the police station. She asked the uniformed sergeant at the front desk for Bernini. He told her Bernini was out, probably for the day. The sergeant's extreme youth and flirtatious manner put Flora off. She didn't want to tell this young man her business. Was Captain Rizzo available? No, she was told, he was in Florence for the day.

Flora felt her heart plummet. She asked if she could use the desk phone to call Bernini because she had important information about the Lorenzetti case and her cell phone was dead. After a few nosy questions, the young officer grudgingly handed over the phone. Flora assured him that Sottotenente Bernini had given her his cell number and told her to call anytime.

Flora punched in the numbers eagerly, only to be met with Bernini's answering service. She left a message that she needed to speak with him urgently.

Then, having nothing better to do with her time, she wandered through the quiet neighborhoods away from the Campo and chose another café to continue her meditations. Just as well to stay away from the places she usually frequented. She didn't want any of the Lorenzettis to find her, either on purpose or by accident.

If Bernini wasn't available, then—oh crap! He would try to call her cell phone but wouldn't reach her because the battery was dead! She rose from her table and asked to use the café's phone. Bernini was still unavailable, so she left a second message about her cell phone being dead. Flora finished the message by saying she would return to her apartment to charge up the phone, and that if she didn't hear from him soon, she'd call again.

Then, over yet another coffee, she pulled out her notebook again and did her best to list everything that had happened, every bit of evidence linking the Lorenzettis with (a) the death of Ernst Mann, (b) the possible trafficking of stolen antiquities, and (c) the likely faking of at least one Greek statue.

What did her kidnapping mean? The Lorenzettis certainly

had something incriminating in that safe. And one of the ac-counting people may have asked questions about the Rolodex cards being out of order and Maria had figured out it had to be Flora. Her two attempts to snoop had labeled her as a troublemaker, and so they had removed her from the premises.

Flora had told Linda that getting Flora out of the way at that particular time probably meant the Lorenzettis had a major shipment coming in or going out, or another kind of deal taking place. They hadn't wanted Flora snooping around.

What could she do to help the police now? As Bernini had explained to her at one of their meetings, the combined forces of the Carabinieri and the Polizia di Stato were focused on solv-ing Ernst's murder and proving links between the murder, the Lorenzettis, and illegal antiquities. The possibility that the same family was forging artifacts to sell on the black market was a lesser concern. If Flora could find something definitive to show Marco's statue was destined to be sold—or maybe had already been sold—as an original antiquity, then she would make a contribution. She wondered if Captain Rizzo had succeeded in stopping the truck carrying the original statue.

Fortified by more caffeine and another aspirin, Flora packed up her notes and headed home to recharge her cell. She'd give it an hour and then call Bernini again. As she hurried home, she continued to review what she knew.

Unfortunately, a forger was not an obvious criminal when he worked in his studio, creating his sculpture or painting. He was just a copyist or a restorer until someone caught him passing off his own work as an original Greek or Roman antiquity—or an Old Master painting. And what about all the legitimate artists who sold replicas to museum shops? How many of them did a little illegal trade on the side, say, signing ancient names to Greek vases instead of stamping them "replica" for the tourist trade? Dottoressa Vianello had confirmed Flora's idea that very few people in the business of copying art were lily white; it was too easy to slip over to the dark side and earn extra money if your work was so good that even experts couldn't distinguish your replica from the real thing.

Flora arrived at her apartment. She glanced around her to make sure she wasn't being followed, and let herself in the front door. Once inside the apartment, she plugged in her phone and changed her clothes. A plan took form in her mind.

She concluded today was her last chance to learn anything about the Lorenzettis before the police took over. Bernini and his boss Major Esposito would surely do something when they found out about her kidnapping. And she was *persona non grata* now; the family would probably throw her out of the apartment this week. She was running out of time.

Her best chance of proving forgery would be a piece of paper documenting the sale of a Lorenzetti-made statue or painting as original art. Where would the Lorenzettis be likely to hide those documents that had been hidden in the safe? Answer: somewhere in the rectangular building at the Lorenzetti compound. In a set of files that had not yet been discovered.

Flora would continue to call Bernini's number every hour or so. She planned to walk over to the Lorenzetti family's house when they were most likely to be at dinner. Marco'd told her they usually ate around eight p.m. She even knew where he kept the spare key to his lab. He'd reached under a loose brick when he'd thought she wasn't looking. Would he have been equally careless about the key to the file cabinet? Or maybe there was no key . . . maybe since the cabinet was in the family lab, no key was necessary.

With her cell phone partially recharged, Flora punched in Bernini's number.

"Bernini here. Leave a message."

What use was giving Flora his phone number if he never

answered? She put away the phone and set off. She'd walk the streets, get a bite to eat, and wait for the friendly dark to hide her raid on the family compound.

Hours later, Flora sat at her meal in yet another piazza, in a little trattoria she'd never visited before. Time to go. Nervousness stole her appetite, so she left half the basil and tomato pizza on her plate and paid her bill. She'd eat later after she'd broken into the files . . . if she succeeded in finding them. At least her head felt clearer and she was no longer dizzy. Flora stood, purse slung over her body, and set off for the Lorenzettis'.

As evening fell, Siena took on a magical atmosphere as people strolled and chatted. The pigeons retired to their roosts in the eaves of medieval *palazzi,* and the stray cats slunk around to the backs of restaurants looking for scraps. The air cooled enough to make her wish she'd brought a sweater or a hoodie. And she felt like a thief in her light-strapped shoes, a cross between Mary Janes and sneakers.

Darkness fell like a thick theater curtain as she crossed town. So much the better, she thought. *And what a good thing I'm dressed in a dark shirt and pants.*

Flora let herself into the side gate of the Lorenzettis' back garden. She snuck around the corner of the house, pausing near a bush so she could peek into the dining room without being seen. Sure enough, the family was at dinner. Flora tiptoed toward Marco's studio, again circling to the back where she had seen Marco extract the spare key. It was there.

She let herself into the silent hallway and stepped over piles of cardboard packing material and paper rubbish. With a tiny penlight that she shielded with one hand, she explored the studio building more thoroughly than she had on her previous two visits.

There was a tiny room, more like an alcove, behind Beppe's studio. Why hadn't she noticed it before? Probably because of all the cardboard rubbish stacked in the hallway that partly blocked the door. The alcove was nearly dark except for faint light from a small window above her head. Below the window was a tall file cabinet, partly blocked by more boxes.

Flora tried the file cabinet. Locked. She looked around. Where would the family hide the key? Somewhere not too obvious, but where they could all find it. She cozied up to the cabinet, feeling around the back, thinking it might be taped to the metal. No luck.

Was there a hook on the wall? None that she could see. Flora risked another quick look around with the tiny penlight. Okay, somewhere else in the alcove.

The tall windowsill beckoned. She reached up with her fingers and found nothing but cobwebs and a dead beetle. *Ugh.*

Wiping her hands on her pants, she looked around the dimly lit room. There was no other furniture, but she identified scraps of marble discarded by Marco and a stack of packing boxes.

Then she remembered the bookcase at the State Archives. People tended to repeat ideas they thought were clever. What about the underside of the file cabinet? She knelt on the dusty floor and reached under, scrabbling around with both hands. Found it! Good old duct tape, worked every time!

Flora stepped out the back door of the studio building and listened. Clinks of silverware and laughter indicated that the family still sat around the table. She would risk a quick look at the files.

Stepping back inside, Flora clicked the little light back on and opened the top drawer. Files, neatly labeled with last names. The drawer below had unmarked files, fewer of them, but stuffed full of papers. She checked the other drawers and found nothing interesting, so she returned to the top two. She extracted a few client files, glanced quickly through them, and stuffed them into her purse.

The unmarked files contained lists, a map, and a diagram in one of the folders. She held the diagram up to her light and gasped. It showed names of people and cities ranging from Sicily to Austria! Surely this was the kind of thing Bernini and the Carabinieri sought! She clicked her light off and stuffed those files into the front of her shirt.

Good idea to check on the family again before she let herself out into the garden. Flora ducked into Marco's studio at the front of the building and peered toward the house. She could still see people sitting around the table, but there were not as many of them. She counted swiftly. Marco, Pietro, Filippo, Beppe, a young woman Flora didn't recognize . . . where were Maria and Gia? They must be clearing plates or fetching something from the kitchen—

The sound of footsteps behind her froze Flora in her tracks. An overhead light clicked on and a voice said, "I guessed it was you in our studio building, you sneaking little thief."

Flora turned.

Gianetta Lorenzetti. Her broad face contorted and her black eyes filled with hate. She bore no weapon, but she didn't need one. Gia's arms and legs looked like tree-trunks next to Flora's. "This is what comes of hiring foreigners! I suppose you have a good explanation for why you're here at this hour?"

Flora gulped. "I was waiting for Marco—I wanted to surprise him. He left the door open, so I just walked in."

Gia cocked her head and gave a nasty smile. "A likely story. Marco brought a guest home for dinner, a young lady friend. The one he'll marry, since she is my niece by marriage."

"I—I—"

"Never mind," Gia continued, circling around Marco's newest block of marble to get closer to Flora. Fortunately, its sideways bulk took up substantial floor space and its height prevented the stout woman from hopping over it. "I know why you're here. You want to snoop around and poke into our business! Well, you won't get the chance this time!"

Flora stalled for time. "You mean, when I looked in the accounting files at the State Archives? You know I was just trying to help because Pietro asked me to find an invoice—"

"Don't play games with me, young lady!" Gia moved fast for someone twenty years older than Flora. "You're coming with me, and you will explain yourself to my husband!"

That didn't sound like a good idea, especially with important documents stuffed in her clothing. Flora moved to keep the block of marble between her and Gia. She glanced at the front door of Marco's studio, the one leading into the courtyard and the family home. It was bolted shut. She didn't think she could unbolt it and run through the door before Gia caught her. It would have to be down the hallway past the alcove and out the back door.

"I don't know what you're talking about. I'm not snooping, I just wanted to see Marco."

"You know perfectly well what I mean. You robbed our safe at the State Archives laboratory!" Gia pulled a long kitchen knife from her apron pocket.

So she does have a weapon. What can I use against a knife like that?

Flora sidled closer to the hallway door, keeping the huge block of marble between them. Her mind jittered as she reconsidered all her preconceptions about the Lorenzettis. It looked very much like Gia was fully informed about Flora's activities. And that the female of the species was the most dangerous member of the family.

"What safe?" she said to the enraged woman, hoping to tire her out.

Her pretended misunderstanding had an unexpected effect. Gia stopped moving and let out a tirade. "You know very well, you little slut! You thought you could waltz into our business and wreck all our plans! And charm my son Marco into helping you spy for the police! Well, you can't fool me. I'm the power behind the throne, the one who watches out for the Lorenzettis! How else do you think we've come so far? We will be almost as rich and respected as in the last century by the time we're through, and no one—especially a little nobody from Chicago—is going to stop us!"

Flora stood as close to the hallway door as she would ever be. She whipped around and darted through, making a run for the back of the building.

The hall light flipped on and Pietro stood in the doorway, blocking her exit.

"Ha! I knew it," said Pietro. "The spy in our midst! You didn't really think we'd let you get away after you were fired this afternoon, did you? We had you followed so we could see what you did next. And you behaved just as I predicted you would." He crept toward Flora, chucking his lit cigarette onto the floor. Then he saw his mother.

"Mamma, why are you out here?"

"Someone has to do your job, Pietro! I saw a little light moving around in the studio so I came to investigate."

Flora stood at the door of the little alcove, her head turning back and forth between the two Lorenzettis as if she were at a tennis match.

"Go back inside, Mamma. I will take care of this little bitch and make sure she causes no more trouble."

"I will stay and make sure you do it properly this time. You never can seem to carry through on the tough jobs. Like that German boy; I took care of him."

Flora gasped. "You? You pushed Ernst over the balcony? But why?"

"He knew too much about the business. Always snooping around in drawers. Just like you."

Flora realized how easy it would be for Gia, the landlady who had a key, to come into the apartment. Even if Ernst had seen her, he'd have thought she was there on a legitimate errand, checking on the apartment.

"He was innocent. You murdered him!"

Gia sneered. "Stupid foreigners. You have no business coming here in the first place! I always said we should only employ family members! And I am the one who persuaded Marco to woo you in order to keep an eye on you. He was happy to do it, and he reported everything you said and did to me."

So that's why Marco's advances felt odd to me. He was acting. At least some of the time. But he does like me; he was trying to protect me from finding out too much.

A whoosh and a rustle behind Flora made Gia shout. "Pietro! There is a fire behind you!"

Pietro's lighted cigarette had fallen on top of a pail of rags to the right of the back door. They ignited so quickly that Flora knew they must be soaked with solvent. And there were all kinds of cardboard boxes and piles of paper lining the hallway.

"Go out the front, Mamma!" yelled Pietro. "Get everyone to bring water!"

Gia Lorenzetti, knife raised and at the ready, didn't budge. Pietro advanced on Flora while the fire surged up and nearby rubbish ignited. Flora stepped backward into the little alcove and slammed the door.

As she braced her feet against the bottom of the door and pulled the doorknob with all her might, she wondered just how long she could hold the door against two large, angry Lorenzettis.

But no one tried to come into the tiny room. Instead, she heard Pietro and Gia shoving things against the door. They meant to trap her inside!

She pushed back and discovered that they'd used marble scraps or packed crates to block her escape while they dealt with the fire. But the heat coming through the door and shouts and running feet from the side of the building meant the fire was already out of control.

"Let me out! Let me out!" she shrieked, pounding on the door.

She thought she heard Marco's voice. Surely he wouldn't let her burn to death, even if his horrible mother would be delighted. She yelled again.

She tried the door to Beppe's office. No luck. Then she turned her little light back on and looked up at the window. It was too small. But it might provide air if she couldn't get out in time.

Flora rocked and shoved the file cabinet closer to the window. The room was so tiny that once she had it in position, she was able to brace her feet against the wall and haul herself on top of the cabinet.

The window was painted shut.

Smoke curled under the door.

Screaming again, Flora scrambled down and tried the door. It was so hot that she could barely touch the wood. The door was totally blocked from the outside.

As she coughed in smoke, she felt a little draft on the back of her legs. Where was that coming from?

Flora dropped to her knees, remembering the primary school lessons in Chicago: "Stop, drop, and roll!" She had no room to roll because of all the boxes, but she scooted closer to the side of the building where the little draft now blew on her knees. She lowered her head to the floor.

The wood and fiberglass structure had a tiny gap at the bottom of the wall. A miniscule amount of clean air leaked in while the room behind her filled with smoke. Alternately coughing and yelling for help, she kept her face to the gap.

"Flora, I am coming for you!" yelled Marco. He was on the other side of the wall.

"Hurry!" screamed Flora.

"You fool, don't go in there! The building is all on fire!" cried Gia.

Flora's head spun as another coughing fit took her.

She heard someone running into the hallway.

Marco! But she couldn't hear him moving the pile away from the door.

More shouts. Sirens coming. Smoke stifling her . . .

It wasn't enough air, after all.

CHAPTER THIRTY-SEVEN

Flora felt hands under her shoulders and knees, lifting her.

She tried to speak and coughed instead. She coughed until her throat felt raw.

"Stay quiet, Signorina. Let us move you outside into the fresh air. Then we'll find you a drink."

The two men carried her out to a low bench in the Lorenzettis' back garden.

Flora lay in a stupor, listening to voices and the hiss of water on the fire.

"It's almost out . . ."

"Did you move the young man's body already?"

"Had to in order to get the girl out. She was unconscious."

"I'm not now," Flora gasped. And coughed again. She felt as if her entire body was full of smoke, that she would never get rid of it.

Faces appeared above Flora. "Here, drink this," said a young policeman she'd never met.

She gulped the water down and held out her glass for more.

Vittorio Bernini put a hand on her shoulder. "That was an awfully close call, Flora. When you're feeling better, I have a few questions to ask you." His voice was gentle.

Flora struggled to a sitting position so she could take the refilled glass of water from Bernini's colleague. "What about Marco? Is he okay?"

She saw Bernini shake his head at the second cop as he

opened his mouth to speak.

Bernini said, "I'm sorry, Flora. He died from smoke inhalation. Trying to save you."

Tears filled her eyes and ran down her face, mixing with the water in her mouth. "He was . . . the only decent member of that family!" A new fit of coughing claimed her.

Bernini guided her to a green and white lawn chair and she sat down, shivering. Someone dropped a blanket over her shoulders. The other young policeman refilled her glass with fresh water a second time.

Flora sat like an automaton, sipping water and staring at the remains of the studio building. The cool water tasted wonderful but did nothing for the rawness in her throat. She longed for ice. Then her attention focused on Captain Rizzo and Lieutenant Bernini, who were questioning Pietro only a few yards away. The Lorenzetti parents sat on another bench, distraught and silent except for Gia's muffled sobs.

". . . I don't care why Signorina Garibaldi was here, I want to know why you trapped her in that room! You came very close to deliberate murder!" Rizzo roared.

"I wasn't going to kill her!" Pietro said sullenly.

"We just wanted to keep her from escaping until the family could question her, the interfering little bitch," cried Gia. "She is a thief and a snoop! I wish we'd never hired her—Marco would still be alive!" She buried her face in her husband's shoulder.

"Yeah," said Pietro. "She broke into the safe at the office, and she probably came tonight to find more private correspondence."

"How do you know she broke into the safe?" Bernini asked Pietro.

"I saw her! She—" Pietro shut his mouth and glared at his feet.

"When did that happen?" Bernini took out his notebook.

"Two days ago, in the evening. I saw her climb on a chair to get at the safe—"

"And then what happened?"

Pietro hesitated, glancing over at Flora. "Well, I—"

"He hit me over the head and he and his confederates threw me into a truck. They drove north to Bolzano, where I escaped and found a ride back to Siena." Flora stood and walked closer to the family group.

Rizzo turned stern eyes on Bernini. "I thought you told her not to attempt anything on her own without our help?"

Bernini grimaced. "She's a stubborn American, sir. Impulsive too. I tried to keep her out of trouble, but . . ." He shrugged.

Flora made a face at Bernini. "It's not his fault," she said to Rizzo. "I take after my mother—and she's an Italian from Siena. Dad always said he couldn't keep *her* from doing anything she'd set her mind to."

Bernini put his hands on Flora's shoulders. "Why didn't you call me?"

"I tried. Several times."

"I never got your messages. My cell's been on the fritz the last two days."

Rizzo ignored this discussion. He asked Flora, "Did you succeed in taking any documents from the safe?"

"Yes, but the kidnappers took them from me before I got thrown in that truck."

Both men turned back to the Lorenzettis.

"Wait," said Flora. "I've got a much better haul this time, from the locked file cabinet in the studio building."

She pulled the lists and diagram from her smoke-streaked shirt.

"Holy Madonna!" exclaimed Bernini as he got a close look at the diagram. "Look, Captain. It's a chart of the entire opera-

231

tion, from Sicily to Switzerland!"

The two policemen stared at the paper. "Dominic Underhill, art dealer . . . Salvatore Benni in Firenze . . . Lorenzetti in Siena . . . Lorenzetti in Roma . . ." Rizzo looked up, his swarthy face full of fierce delight. "We've got them now!" He scrabbled through the other papers and held up one. "Phone numbers! We can use the numbers to obtain addresses! This will be a major roundup of illegal antiquities dealers. A triumph, an absolute triumph."

Flora smiled, but inside her natural cynicism broke through. Would they really catch all of them? Surely not . . . just like in the Medici scandal, a few men would evade capture, move to another city, set up again with a new network. Each one of them had uncles, nephews, brothers, who were all in the business to make money.

"What's this?" said Bernini, peering at another piece of paper. "It looks like a receipt."

Heart beating, Flora stepped closer so she could look over his arm. It said:

"I acknowledge arrival of original Greek statue of young male nude, a kouros, from Restauro Lorenzetti. Provenance: Morgantina, Sicily." She looked for a date—it was two days ago. She glanced at the signature. Illegible!

All three of them groaned.

Flora said, "I bet it's the same kouros that Marco showed me recently. It was resting in a trough at the back of the workshop in a false patina mixture of moldy plant materials. Here, I'll show you."

The trio rushed to the back of the studio building.

The trough was empty.

CHAPTER THIRTY-EIGHT

"You don't know how much this hurts me, to see you here accused of so many crimes," said Rizzo to a dejected Beppe Lorenzetti.

Beppe sat on an uncomfortable folding chair at the interview table. He knew the tape recorder was running, and that nothing he could say now would redeem him or his family. He looked up at his former friend. "I didn't plan on this, my wife becoming a murderer, so many of us going to jail—"

"You mean, you didn't plan on getting caught! How long did you think you could meddle in so many illegal activities without someone betraying you? Without our police forces finding proof of your trafficking, your forgeries, your murders?"

"That Costanza, who would have thought our own niece could be an informer to the Bertoldis." Beppe reflected that his ulcer had known before he did, that the house of cards he had built over the past five years was about to tumble down.

Major Esposito and two other officers entered the room. Esposito nodded at Rizzo to continue his questioning.

"We'll get to her. Now, start at the beginning. You know we can reduce your jail time if you cooperate, if you name your accomplices."

Beppe sighed. "Where do I start?"

"With the trafficking of antiquities. Tell us who and where, every single detail about your transactions. We have the file cabinet and all its contents, so don't think we can't check what you tell us."

Beppe shrugged and began his recital. It took a long time. He named contacts from Sicily to Switzerland, filled in the blanks on the organigram, and described the roles of various relatives in the operation.

After a long pause, during which Captain Rizzo's eyebrows seemed permanently fixed to his hairline, Major Esposito said, "Is that all? Have you left anything out?"

The chastened head of the Restauro Lorenzetti hesitated. The faces of his sons flashed through his head. Could he protect any part of his business, keep anyone out of jail? Filippo was essentially innocent. Pietro and Beppe had kept him out of the picture as much as possible, as if they anticipated the day when the Lorenzetti family would go down. He said, "Pietro was my right hand, but my younger sons, Filippo and Marco, they were not involved in the planning, the arrangements, for either shipping antiquities or selling the copies as forgeries—"

Major Esposito barked, "You expect me to believe that? That two of your own sons were unaware of your operations?"

Beppe spread his hands and looked directly at the major. "This is true. We are a traditional family. The father and the oldest son have always been responsible for the family business. We keep our duties compartmentalized." He waited for their reaction.

Esposito and one of his officers exchanged glances. "We'll see what the analysis of all the documents show. But it is extremely likely that all the men in your family will go to jail, at least for a time."

The thin, gray-haired officer asked, "Did your son Marco really not know how you planned to sell his sculpture as an ancient original?"

"He may have suspected as much, but I was careful to discuss it only with Pietro. I wanted to protect Marco; he lived only for his art. He was the least worldly of all my family."

Esposito nodded at Rizzo. "Okay, Captain, you can join your colleagues in the interviewing of the wife. We have some more questions for Beppe here."

Shoulders bowed, Captain Rizzo left the room.

Beppe felt a wave of grief for his demented wife and his dead son. How could it all come to this? What would his grandfather have said? That the Lorenzetti family would go down in shame would have killed him.

Gianetta Lorenzetti had to be restrained. Two female officers sat on either side of her after the struggling woman was handcuffed to two chairs and a leg of the table. Now she could not move unless she took nearly all the furniture with her.

"Let me go! I must be with my Beppe!" She screamed and shouted for a good five minutes before they convinced her she wasn't moving from that room.

Bernini observed her disheveled appearance with something approaching loathing. If she pulled one more stunt, he'd order a straitjacket for her. How could this woman, this mother of three children and two grandchildren, have hidden her true nature so successfully? They'd already heard her raving about the stupid foreigners, Flora and the young German, how she had pushed one to his death and conspired to kidnap and kill the other.

"So first Costanza was your spy, and then you recruited Graziano? Each one was supposed to tail Flora and report back to you?"

Gia's eyes burned with rage. "Costanza! I spit on her! She may be related to my side of the family, but I disown her!"

"She's dead," said Bernini. Of course Gia already knew this, since during her raving she'd revealed that she'd hired a hit man to follow Costanza. The man had sat in the bar, right behind Costanza, and overheard the entire conversation with

Giovanni Bertoldi. Then he followed her and killed her in the street. The police had not yet extracted his name, or his contact information. Very likely he would get clean away.

"How is Graziano related to you?"

Gia said nothing.

"A second cousin on the Brunetti side," said one of the female officers.

What a family! Bernini thought. "Gia, you can't escape. Tell us again why you murdered the young German."

She glared at him, hair from her bun straggling over her shoulders. "He found the safe, just like the American girl. He snooped in other people's drawers, in our accounting files. Stupid boy! He thought he could bring us down! Us, the Lorenzettis, the most important painting family in Siena!" Her voice rose again and she struggled, trying to get her hands out of the handcuffs. The weight of the two female sergeants kept her from rising to a standing position.

Rizzo entered the interview room. Bernini nodded at him and sat down. This was his way of saying, "Take over. I can do nothing with her."

Rizzo paced a bit and then turned and looked directly at Gia. "Gianetta," he said softly, using her full name for the first time. "How could you do this? How could you involve your family in two murders, all for the sake of more money? Didn't you have enough already? Why, when you married Beppe, your standard of living rose dramatically. How could you be so foolish?"

The gentleness of his tone seemed to enrage Gia Lorenzetti. Her eyes blazed, and she drew herself up behind the table. "You are such an idiot, Paulo! You will never understand what is required to succeed in the art world! It wasn't enough for us to succeed, we had to be the best! And we had to provide for all our children, our grandchildren! Our sons, they are not yet ready to run the business." Her protests turned to insults, and she threw her torso back and forth, straining against the handcuffs bound to the furniture. The two female officers grabbed her arms, but they couldn't hold her still. One looked at Rizzo helplessly.

Rizzo opened the door and motioned for two beefy male officers to enter. "Take her away. Give her some water and take her to a cell. We'll get nothing more out of her now."

Bernini helped the two men refasten the handcuffs behind Gia's back.

When they were alone, Bernini and Rizzo looked at each other.

"Sit down, Vittorio." Rizzo lowered himself heavily into the nearest chair.

Bernini sat facing Rizzo, surprised at his boss's use of his first name.

Rizzo rubbed his forehead. "I'm getting too old for this; this case has just about killed me. It's time for me to retire, leave the whole shebang to you young folks. I hated having to arrest Beppe. I don't want to do this anymore. I don't want to discover that any more of my old friends are criminals." He stared at Bernini. "I hear you've been offered another position. Esposito called me."

Bernini clasped his hands in his lap, surprised again that Rizzo didn't seem to mind his defection. But why should he, if he was leaving the police for a quieter life, perhaps with Matilde Lorenzetti? "Yes, sir, with the Carabinieri in Rome. But what about you? Where—?"

Rizzo read his mind. "I am not going to move in with Matilde. No, that relationship has run its course. My wife and I will move to a small house outside of Florence, in the countryside." He suddenly looked ten years younger. "And I, I will grow grapes. My son wants to join me and make some wine. We have big plans." He stood up and offered his hand to Bernini.

Bernini shook it and smiled. "I am sure you will find running a vineyard rewarding. I'll stop by in a year or two and sample your wine."

"We'll be ready for you. Good luck to you, Vittorio. You will go far, I think."

CHAPTER THIRTY-NINE

Two weeks later, Flora met Bernini for coffee in their favorite bar in the Campo. Flora had a list of questions for him, but she didn't pull it out of her purse until she took a long look at his face.

"A café macchiato," she said to the waiter, who was hovering.

"An espresso, please."

Vittorio's eyes showed strain, and the shadows below spoke of sleepless nights. He needed a vacation, soon. But his expression as he gazed at her showed a mixture of hope and uneasiness.

He smiled at Flora. "Out with it."

"What do you mean?"

"You have questions."

"Well, of course I do! I haven't seen you for two weeks! I want to know what happened! Did Gia break down? Is Beppe still in prison? Did—?"

Bernini laughed. "One at a time, Flora! Yes, the entire family is in prison. We have all the hard evidence we need now to shut down the Lorenzetti trade in illegal antiquities for some time."

"Not permanently?"

He smiled. "You know that old myth about soldiers springing up out of a field?"

"From dragon's teeth. As fast as you cut them down, they grow back . . ."

"Exactly. We can't possibly round all of them up. Italy will

239

always have smugglers and crooks in the business of stealing antiquities and selling them to willing buyers in Europe and the United States. And even farther away than that—we know of collectors in China who will accept anything they can afford. The amounts of money involved are just staggering."

Just what Flora had concluded. "And the forged statues?"

Bernini shook his head as he added sugar to his espresso. "Marco Lorenzetti is gone, but it was his cousin Carlo in Chiusi who started the sideline business. He sold several statues—as originals—before he died in a motorcycle accident two years ago. Pietro and Beppe were eager to take over that branch of the family endeavor and roped Marco into it. I don't think Marco fully understood what he was getting into."

"You're right. He was basically straight—he wanted to make legitimate replicas for museum shops. All he really cared about was sculpting for the sake of sculpting. He paid little attention to what his brother and father did with his products. Marco was always thinking about the next piece of marble. A true artist." She sipped her coffee. "What about Gia? She is the actual murderer of Ernst Mann. But I suppose in a way, the entire family is guilty of that act."

Bernini's expression sobered. "Gia Lorenzetti is a sad case. Her history explains some of her obsession—and her inflexible attitude. Her original family, the Brunettis, were poor farmers on the outskirts of Siena in a little town called Vescovado di Murlo. She grew up scrimping on everything. She never went to university. She met Beppe at a local dance. Then, like many wives who move up in the world upon marriage, she out-Lorenzetti'd the Lorenzettis."

"You mean, she was prouder of her new family, more ambitious for them, than the Lorenzettis themselves?"

"Yes, exactly that. She wanted all the wealth and prestige the family originally had centuries ago. She wanted to be somebody—and to never have to worry about money again."

Flora sighed. "Too bad she had to murder two people to get what she wanted."

"Her sons and husband may be released after some years served, but she will stay behind bars, probably in a special facility. They are doing psychiatric tests now."

Silence fell as they both sipped their coffee. Flora focused beyond Bernini's shoulder on her favorite view of strolling shoppers and Sienese families enjoying the Campo.

"You haven't asked about Fabio Lorenzetti and his Roman shop," Bernini reminded her.

"Oh! What did you find out? I mean, what did your colleague Orsoni in Rome find out?"

"Fabio Lorenzetti was part of the chain of smugglers who transported original antiquities from Sicily to Europe. The extended family had contacts with all the major dealers and auction houses, in Paris and New York as well as Switzerland." He leaned forward, his eyes bright. "Now, you'll enjoy this, Flora. One of his contacts was a guy north of Florence who had a swimming pool full of Greek vases. They used the pool to treat the vases, to remove the encrustations. The entire villa was stuffed with looted antiquities."

"Incredible!" Flora chuckled as she imagined the scene.

"It gets even better. This man also had a studio at the top of his house, stuffed with more antiquities. And a desk that contained another Rolodex file." He grinned.

"With names and addresses, the works?"

"You bet. That file saved us heaps of time in pinning down where the crooks lived."

"Amazing what people think they can get away with." Flora's gaze fell on the wonderful lines of the Torre del Mangia and the Palazzo Pubblico and the pigeons parading on the pavers in front of the café-bar. How she would miss this place, despite the recent memories of horrible events.

When she looked at Bernini again, she saw that his gaze was fixed upon her face.

"You are out of a job, Signorina Garibaldi," he said with a slight smile. "But I bet you have not been idle. Where will you go now?"

Flora made a face. "My family in Chicago wants me to come home. They seem to think I have a talent for finding trouble wherever I go."

Bernini's smile deepened.

"But I told them I'd fly home later, after I get settled in my new job." She took a deep breath as she confronted the sadness in Vittorio's brown eyes. "In Rome. I have a position in the conservation laboratory at the Villa Giulia museum. I leave next week to look for an apartment."

Vittorio lit up. "Rome! And at the Villa Giulia, no less. But how wonderful! Captain Rizzo is retiring, to start a wine business. I am moving to the Carabinieri's Art Squad in Rome. They think it will be a good fit for me. I am sure it will be."

Flora's heart took a bound. "That sounds like the perfect job for you! Then we can see each other there. In Rome."

"Yes." He smiled back at her. "How did you manage it? I mean, you surely couldn't get a reference from the Lorenzettis!"

"No, I couldn't. I wrote to my professor in Florence and told him what had happened. He was happy to phone the head conservator at the museum in Rome and sing my praises."

"Good for you! I was fortunate as well. Major Esposito of the Carabinieri division for the Protection of Cultural Heritage liked my work, so he recommended me for the transfer to Rome."

"Congratulations! Is it a job you wanted?"

"Yes, very much so." He stood and pulled his wallet out. "Let me walk you home."

Vittorio paid for the coffee and they strolled across the Campo. Flora took a small street that went past her favorite art gallery. She made a point of looking in its window once a week or so to see what was new. This time, she almost forgot to look because her mind was full of Bernini's news and the possibilities it offered for a continued relationship.

As if he could read her mind, he took her hand and held it as they approached the gallery. "Treasures of Siena" said the sign above the door. Flora automatically glanced in the front window. What she saw there made her trip slightly.

"What is it?" Bernini asked.

Flora pointed. "That little painting. The Martini. I have to see it close up."

Bernini pushed the door open, which set off a chime inside the shop. A young man with shiny black hair and soulful eyes appeared. Flora asked to see the painting, so he lifted it off its stand and placed it on the counter. When Flora reached for it, he stopped her, asking her not to touch the painting.

"Humor her," said Bernini, pulling out his badge and displaying it.

The shopkeeper shrugged and handed Flora a pair of gloves. She slid them on and held the painting up to the light.

"There, Vittorio. You see? That's my painter's mark." Her forefinger hovered over a small green wheel, almost lost in the folds of the blue-green drapery of the Madonna. "It's my work, my painting."

"Impossible!" said the young shopkeeper. "That is an original Martini! Why, my boss bought it only last week . . ." He stopped as he noticed their serious expressions.

"I am afraid, Signor, that your boss was hoodwinked. It's a copy, painted by this young lady while she was employed by Restauro Lorenzetti."

The young man gasped, and his eyes no longer looked soulful. "The outfit that was in the news last week for fraud?"

"And art forgery," said Flora. "Don't worry, it's not your boss's fault that he purchased a fake. Or mine, since I painted it as a copy." She spared a thought for Herr Goeller somewhere in Germany. "How was I to know the Lorenzettis would sell it as an original?"

"Tell Signor Rizzardi that all we need is proof of purchase, and any documentation he was given," Bernini said. "For now, I will take the painting. Here is my card. Tell him to call me as soon as possible."

Bernini took Flora's hand again as they left the shop.

"I really can't believe it!" said Flora, shaking her head. "It's so brazen! That painting is a copy of one housed in Florence, in the Pitti Palace. It was on loan here. Surely someone would have noticed!"

"Not soon enough to prevent the sale."

" 'It's all about what happens at the point of sale,' " Flora quoted.

"Yup," said Bernini.

They stopped at the door of Flora's new apartment building, where she had taken a short-term lease to get away from the Lorenzettis.

"You have my cell number." He leaned over and kissed her.

"And you have mine," she said with a big smile. "See you in Rome!"

ABOUT THE AUTHOR

Sarah Wisseman grew up in Massachusetts and Illinois and spent her junior year in college studying archaeology in Israel. This experience changed her life and persuaded her to earn a doctorate in Classical and Near Eastern archaeology. Now a retired archaeologist at the University of Illinois, Sarah enjoys killing off her favorite academics and museum staff in her Lisa Donahue archaeological mysteries. Two of her books (*Bound for Eternity* and *The Fall of Augustus*) are set in a fictional Boston museum and two are set in the Middle East (*The Dead Sea Codex* and *The House of the Sphinx*). The fifth novel, *The Bootlegger's Nephew* (2012), is a historical mystery with new characters set in Prohibition-era Illinois. Visit her at www.sarahwisseman .com.